Calarel

The Beginning Journey

Robert Gayhart

Published in the United States of America
ISBN 979-8-9920800-8-7 (SC)

For Book Rights Adaption and other Rights Permission.
Call us at toll-fee 601-608-7468.

Table of Contents

Chapter 1

Calarel woke up determined to change her life. For over a hundred twenty years, everything had been the same every day. She remembered when she and her father built her bed together when she was about thirty. She thought then it was too small at seven feet in length, and it still feels to be that way. Being a half breed, both races being tall. Half High Elf giving her keen senses and being virtually immortal, half Highmen being heavier boned, physically stronger and having traits from both races.

Once dressed in the same clothes she wore every day, Calarel grabbed her weapons belt, then left the house to do her daily practice.

This part of my life I will not change.

Finished, she sheathed her broadsword at four pounds and three feet in length, then wiped the sweat from her brow. She stood there and looked at the back of the house. She knew every board, every nail. She knew this house inside and out. Every board that squeaks when stepped on, every door that made noise when you opened or closed it. She knew how much wind must blow to make the walls creak. She could almost tell the temperature outside by the noises that the house made.

Inside her room, she hung her weapons belt and shield on the stand, then went to the kitchen to start making first meal. Tamara, her sister, came into the kitchen and started helping.

"Good morning, Calarel."

"Good morning, did you sleep well?"

"Yes, but you don't look like you did. What's wrong?"

"Nothing really, just bored I guess. How many eggs do you want?"

"Just one, you know that."

"Yeah I know." *The same old thing, day in and day out, it really is time for a change.*

Father came in and sat at the square table that he refinished last year.

"Good morning, favorite daughters."

Tamara, being the youngest, turned toward him. I saw the smile as she removed it from her face. She slapped her fist to her chest and bowed.

"Good morning to you, my favorite father." "You forgot to put your heels together, Tamara."

I turned to my father. "Good morning, Father." *This will be the last time we share first meal.*

Once done, I gathered the fresh eggs before going to pack my things. I put on my three-finger wide weapons belt which has the scabbard for my broad sword and a sheath for my dagger. Tying my coin pouch to my belt, I looked around my room at the many things I have collected over the years one last time. I did not know when I would see any of it again.

I walked through the kitchen and out the back door. Father sat at the grinding wheel in front of the barn with his back to the house. I walked over to him.

"Father."

He looked at me, then moved the blade of the axe away from the grinding wheel.

"Are you going somewhere, Calarel?"

He looked me over head to toe and back again. I wore light brown wool pants, pale green shirt, riding boots, and my leather chaps, I also wore the heavy leather vest I use for sword practice. Oiled and tanned many times, it is a little old and has a few marks in it. Beside me is my pack, filled with the things I need to travel. All I need is my horse and I am ready to go. I feel a heavy sadness but yet filled with excitement.

"Father, it is time I venture out on my own. I am ready to go and see what my life has waiting for me."

Before I could finish what I decided to say, he stopped me.

"Calarel, you have been the one child I have worried the least about over the years."

Usually a hard man to deal with, he seemed different today.

"I have been dreading this day for a long time. But I am happy it is here as well." His voice softened. "To me, this means you are no longer a child." His eyes started to well up with tears. "I wish your mother were here with me to see you off." He put his forefinger around the end of his thumb and rubbed his nose. "I think she would be proud of you. I am."

He got up from his seat.

"I think she would be more proud of you, raising the two of us alone." I had to clear my throat before continuing. "Tamera and I both love you for how you have provided for us. You have taught us both very well."

Father looked as if he might be upset with me. I could not leave him if he were upset.

"Thank you, I appreciate you feeling that way.

Take off your weapons belt."

He commanded as he started walking toward the stable doors. Father has the largest stables in the area, over twenty stalls to stable the horses we trained for the kingdom's army.

"But I need my weapons belt. Why would I take it off? You told me you always travel with your weapon belt on, even if only to hold your thumbs."

"Take it off, girl," he demanded. The look in his brown eyes told me he meant to be obeyed.

I unbuckled the belt so fast, I did not take time to think about why he was telling me to do so. I followed him into the barn. He headed for the work bench we used to repair bridles and harnesses or whatever tool became damaged or worn. He opened two of the upper cabinet doors and pulled something down wrapped in cloth.

He turned toward me. "May your ventures be good for you. I hope this will help to keep you safe so that when you are ready, you can come back and tell me about them."

He acted as if he was going to toss it at me. I reacted quickly. I dropped my weapons belt to the ground to grab it. Using my right hand, I grabbed hold of what felt round and solid like the hilt of a sword. My left hand slid a little as I grabbed the other end, flat, maybe two inches wide, and tapered down toward the end. I could tell it was sharp because of the pain in the palm of my left hand. He released it after a second or two, and I noticed he was looking at my hand. A small area of red formed on the object's wrappings.

"Now it has tasted your blood. Do not let it taste it again," he said, as I released my left hand to unwrap the gift.

As I pulled away the wrapping, I saw the blade. He bent down, picked up my weapons belt, and pulled the belt free from the loop of my scabbard.

"Father, this is your most valued blade. The one blade I have never seen you use."

As he turned to put my scabbard and sword on the work bench, he said, "That blade is over two hundred years old, it has seen the finish of two battles. It has saved some lives and taken a few. That is the blade of a warrior of the Kingdom."

"Yes. I know the story of this blade well. I can- not remember how many times I have heard it."

I ran my left hand down the blade so that the cut on my hand would leave blood along the blade to show I did remember the story. I cradled the blade in my left arm and released the wrap from the hilt. I gripped the hilt again with my right hand and turned the blade over. He had etched my name on the blade beneath his. The lineage of the blade was to continue with me. He held out the scabbard for this sword so I could sheath it. I did, but not all the way in.

My eyes began to burn. I fought it, but I was too late, the tears began to run down my cheeks.

He handed me the scabbard, then wiped the tears from my cheeks. I finished sheathing the blade onto the scabbard to symbolize that it was my blade now.

"So my little warrior girl is off to a tearful start." I reached to hug him tight.

He hugged me in return, saying, "I will miss you, Calarel, do try to write every once in a while." He hugged me longer than normal as if to gain control of his tears before releasing me. "Now, let me help saddle your horse."

He let go and spun toward the stalls. He walked right past my horse down to a stall that had a lesser warhorse named Blackie. Opened the stall gate and led Blackie out.

"You know this horse better than anyone. Besides, no one will buy him. He seems to give any- one who tries to ride him a hard time. So he is yours, he likes you."

"No, Father, you have already given me your prize sword. I will just take Thunder, he is a good horse."

"You'll take the horse that has papers with your name on them."

I am trying to leave, how can I argue with him? I would not win anyhow.

As I finished buckling on my weapons belt with its new scabbard and sword, he reached in to the same cabinet again and handed me the papers for Blackie. I never saw him put them there, but they did not look as if they had been there long.

Darn it, he sure is making it hard to leave. Maybe that is his plan. I took the papers, put them in my pack, and we saddled Blackie. I tied my bedroll and saddlebags behind the saddle and my pack on Blackie's back before we led him out of the barn.

I yelled out, "Tamara, are you going to say goodbye?"

She came running out the back door with a small pack slung over her shoulder.

"I'm going with you."

Almost in tears, her cheeks were rosy red as if she were about to cry.

I hooked the reins over the saddle horn and took off to catch her before she reached the stables. I have always been a faster runner. I slammed her against the wall of the stables, not vary hard of course.

Before Father got there, I told her, "No, you cannot go with me this time, you are still too young. Besides, I am the one to go find out how the world has changed from the stories Father has told us. I will be back, and then it will be you with your magic and me with my sword against evil. Just like we always talked about. You still have much to learn."

"That was one hell of a hug, Calarel, thought you two were going to knock down the whole barn."

Father pulled me back by my shoulder.

I stepped away. All I could think of to say was "Sorry, Father."

"You okay, Tamera?"

"Yes, Father, but she won't let me go with her."

"Well, I'm going to need you here with me for a while. You know, to get used to doing all the work that Miss Muscules"—using a name he called me sometimes—"there did, besides my work. And Mistress Blackwell will be here this afternoon to teach you more of the arts."

"Come on, give me a hug, so I can go to Cynar.

That is where I want to start." "Why Cynar?" Father asked.

"So she can see the big fort you told us about," Tamara spouted.

"No, you are wrong." Of course, she was right. "I want to check the announcement board, to see if I can find a job as a messenger or something like that. Come on, give me a hug, please?"

Tamara finally came over and gave me a hug. I wanted to cry, but held it back.

"Please help Father. I know he will need your help."

"I will," she replied as I wiped a tear from her cheek.

"Go on before we think you're not going. I have things to do, and if you're here, you are working too."

I knew Father hated long goodbyes.

I climbed onto the saddle and said "Move" to Blackie. A few paces away, I turned in the saddle to wave goodbye. Father waved and turned toward the grinding stone, then headed for the stable door instead. Tamera had plopped down where she stood. I turned back forward-facing to make sure Blackie stayed on the path.

At the road, I had my first choice south to Valeria or north to Cynar. I turned north. I looked back at the house; it looked lonely and cold.

"Not the house too," I spoke out loud.

No one answered. Blackie made no sound. I felt sad about leaving my family, but I was excited about what lay ahead on this journey.

Overhead, the sun hung midway to its highest point in the sky. I rode for a couple of hours before getting hungry. I slid my bow from its sheath and, while still in the saddle, strung it. Not an easy task, but Father always said, "Practice doing it, girl, never know when ya may need to."

He could string his bow at a run. I still could not do that.

A rabbit bolted across the road into the field. I pulled an arrow, nocked the end to the string, but could not see the rabbit anymore. I stopped Blackie and watched for a few minutes. I saw nothing, might as well move on.

After an hour, I returned the arrow to the quiver and unstrung my bow, then sheathed it before pulling my pack around to get something to eat.

"I have to make this last for four or five days," I said to Blackie.

Blackie and I wandered up the road for another four hours. I spied what looked like a good place to camp, so I stopped just off the road, not too far from it, but not to close either. I replaced the bridle with the hackamore which had a twenty-five-foot lead to let Blackie graze and move about a little, never knowing when dinner may pop up, I shouldered my bow and hung my quiver on my weapons belt. I scouted around a little and found rabbit tracks. By setting out a couple of snares, I hoped to catch at least one rabbit. Walking back to my camp, I heard voices, sounded like two males.

"Look at the size of that horse. He is probably a Warrior, or worse a Bounty Hunter."

"So what, that doesn't mean anything," the second voice responded. "We could still share the camp." I stopped behind a tree that offered good cover.

"We could tell him we want this place, and he has to move on, to find another."

I could not see who said that, but his companion, who I did have in my field of vision, was of a common mannish race. Maybe a head a shorter than I and not very muscular. I thought he was young to be out on his own.

"Are you crazy? He may have food and might be willing to share it."

I strung my bow and nocked an arrow just for show. It was time to show up at my camp.

"We could take his food and tell him to move on," said the one I could not see. The one I watched looked in the same direction when he spoke. That told me the location of the second one. Neither was close to my pack or bedroll. I pulled enough tension to hold the arrow in place and gripped my bow so as to be ready to pull before walking into view.

With the sun at my back, I said, "Good evening, gentlemen."

I held my bow at an angle easy for them to see.

The taller man was about to say something to his friend, a Halfling who stood almost four feet tall. He raised both his hands in slow motion to about shoulder height. The Halfling's hands shot into air above his head. He spoke first.

"We didn't take anything," his voice nervous and loud enough to be certain I heard him.

"Oh, shut up, Shorty. You would be dead if he thought we were taking his things."

"Stricklin, stop picking on me about my height, I'm telling ya for the last time."

"You are in my camp. Why?" I hope my words sounded stern.

The one called Stricklin spoke first. "We're traveling to Cynar and beyond, looking for historical places to study."

The Halfling wore a surprised look. "And you, Halfling? What is your story?" I turned my head to address him.

"You're an Elf, don't kill me. I'm not responsible for my birth. Damn, I knew we should have left sooner."

He shot his companion a nervous look.

I lowered my bow but held the arrow in place with my finger. "I am not going to kill you, unless you try to kill me."

When I moved, the Halfling made as if to bolt. "My name is Calarel. I am traveling to see what the world has to teach. You two talk loud enough to wake the dead. I am not a Bounty Hunter. I do not know if I would be any good at that or not. What are your names?"

I tried to sound tough.

Stricklin said, "This is my traveling companion, Abon, and I am Stricklin. Glad to meet you. Cala… rel?" He broke my name into two, as if it just hit him it was a feminine name.

Abon broke a smile. "She isn't a he. She's a she. You're a female."

"And that means what? That you can rob me after all?"

"Oh no, not that, Calarel," Abon said. "It means we will have a good meal tonight. Stricklin is a bad cook."

"Maybe so, but you eat my cooking well enough." He slapped Abon on the back of his shoulder. "So you have some food to share then? I will be glad to cook it up for us."

"Well, no," Abon drew out his words, "but you were out hunting, right?"

I was starting to like the little guy.

"Yes, but I found only tracks. Maybe with a little luck, I will catch a rabbit, and I can have a decent breakfast. And lunch if I get two."

"What about us?"

Stricklin broke in, "Ah, Calarel. If it's okay, could we travel with you at least as far as Cynar? You know there is safety in numbers."

Abon shook his head up and down vigorously. "Safety in numbers and you being alone, traveling with us would be safer."

"Well, I was not really looking for travel companions, but as you say, there is safety in numbers." I removed the arrow from the string and put it back into my quiver. "At least, most of the time, it is safer." As I drew closer, I watched Abon grow relaxed.

He sighed with relief, then started to smile.

"I thought you were big for being an Elf." Abon spread his arms to indicate my broad shoulders. "You're not that much Elf, are you? I've met a few Elf-mannish people before."

"He talks a lot when he is nervous," Stricklin broke in when Abon took a breath.

"I see that. Yes, Abon, I am Elven. My mother was High Elf, and my father is Highmen. I lean more toward the Highmen side of things, but carry a lot of the High Elf traits too."

"Well, I hope you don't have the prejudice that a lot of Elves carry around with them. It's really not that healthy."

"What would I be prejudiced about, Abon?" "Oh nothing, really. Just that a lot of Elves don't
    like Halflings, that's all."

"He didn't tell it all. He's a Tall fellow-Halfling," Stricklin said.

I unstrung the bow and slid it into the sheath, then started to clear a spot for a fire as we spoke.

"And he is afraid to tell me that because?"

"You weren't raised in an Elven town, were you?" "No, I was not, Abon. I was brought up by my father. My mother died giving birth to my sister. I was about fifteen. Besides, I can only think of a few
    people I do not like, but I do not hate anyone."

The puzzled look on Stricklin's face told me he was trying to figure out if he believed me or not. Abon looked more accepting.

"What are we going to eat?" Abon asked. "I don't know, let's see what we have."

Stricklin reached for their backpacks still on the horses. He approached the stones for a firepit I had set. They looked through both their packs and found trail rations; at least I didn't have to share my sausage and cheese and day-old bread. We ate and sat around the firepit, talking for the rest of the evening.

About ten hours after the top of the day, Abon lay down and promptly went to sleep.

I sat brushing out my hair and continued my talk with Stricklin. I found out they had been traveling for about a month. Stricklin lived in Bayward City by Farok Tesea, also known as the Forbidden Sea. Recalling the maps I'd studied, I knew Bayward City was a three-week travel from Valeria. They had done odd jobs to earn money or a stay for the night and then moved on the next day or two. Just out to see the world. Best I could tell, Stricklin was up with his history.

He finally lay down to sleep also. About four hours after sunset and just before lying down to sleep, I heard the sound of a rabbit visiting one of my snares. I went to get my prize. I retrieved my catch, a big rabbit hanging in the tree, and reset the snare. Back in camp with the rabbit cleaned and thankful to have a first meal, I too went to sleep.

An hour before dawn, I put on my armor and everything that I normally wore if I were going to a battle. Father and I did this every day. He told me with one of those tilted-head looks and one-sided smiles, "You never know when you may have to help protect the realm and King or maybe just yourself."

Just because I wasn't with him this morning didn't mean I shouldn't be prepared if I had to do the latter. I did my exercises and worked through the defensive stances, then the attack stances that Father taught.

When I finished, I went to check the snares. Much to my surprise, I had two more rabbits. Collecting my things for the snares, I went back to camp. I hung the rabbits in a tree to bleed.

I gathered some wood to build a fire and dropped it down by the pit before pulling my axe from my pack to chop it into smaller pieces. At the sound of my axe hitting the log, before the chopping sound faded, Abon was on his feet with a dagger in his hand ready to defend. Meanwhile, Stricklin barely man- aged to reach a sitting position in that length of time.

"Good morning, sleepyheads."

"What time is it?" Stricklin suppressed a yawn.

"It's morning." Abon looked around. "Why are you chopping wood so early?"

"First meal."

I struck the log again, driving the axe blade to the center point of the log. One more swing and the log broke into two pieces. I tossed the smaller piece toward the pit and started to chop another piece off the log.

"Why are you dressed like that?"

"She is a warrior, Abon. I told you that yester- day," Stricklin answered for me.

I swung the axe again. "It is a little chilly this morning, so I put on some warm clothes. Which one of you guys can start the fire?"

It took both of them to get the fire going. I pre- pared one rabbit for roasting and skinned the other two. I salted them and built a stand to dry them over the fire. The one I roasted finally cooked well enough to eat. I shared some of my bread so we could soak up the juices left on our plates. After putting out the fire and wrapping the two rabbits in one of my shirts, we packed for the move.

"We are getting a late start today. Half of the morning has passed us by already. Hope you two are in no hurry."

"No sense in being in a hurry. What will be, will be," Abon replied.

"Cynar will be there long after we have all died, I think," Stricklin finished, tying his bedroll to the back of his saddle

"One can only hope," I replied, as we all climbed onto our horses.

*****

We rode at a slow pace for Blackie most of the day; I had to rein him back sometimes because of the small horse Abon rode. At times, I would scout ahead just to let Blackie go at a more normal pace for him. I watched for food, either animal or plant. I did find some Arlan, which is good for helping to stop bleeding and speed the healing of cuts and wounds. And finding some radishes surprised me, usually not that easy find along the road.

Abon and Stricklin rode up to where I had paused. "What did you find, Calarel?"

I tossed a radish to Abon. "Have one."

"You can't eat that." Stricklin wrinkled his nose with distaste.

"It's a radish. I didn't know they grow wild out here. Only seen them in a garden. Wow, they're strong-tasting."

"Where do you think they got the first ones to start the garden, Stricklin?"

"I never thought about that."

"Keep going, I will catch up in a little bit," I said to them.

"Are you sure?" Stricklin looked a bit concerned.

"Yes, go ahead. That way, I can run Blackie a little. I want to get more of these radishes."

They moved on, and I pulled a few more radishes, leaving several, so perhaps the next time I came by, there might still be some. *If I keep this up, I'll have to get more saddlebags and more sacks to carry everything*, I told myself. Spotting some tuber plants as I was getting ready to mount up, I dug up a few of these as well.

"Okay, let's catch up to the others," I told Blackie as I got into the saddle. Blackie broke into a trot as soon as we headed down the road.

"Are you sure you do not want to go faster?" I asked him.

I tend to talk to my horse a lot. After a little bit, I spotted the others. When I caught up to them and reined in Blackie, I said, "You two would starve to death before we get to Cynar."

"No! We have our trail rations," Stricklin retorted. "And how many days will your trail rations last you? Three at most, I suspect, considering the amount of trail rations you had yesterday."

We moved further down the road at a slow walk. "Watching you two from behind, I noticed you do not watch the land about you."

"We watch the road. What more do you need to watch?"

"Watching the road is good, Abon. You would not want to run into a wagon or something. But what about the falcon that just dived into the field back there? Why did the vulture take flight from the old tree before we entered this patch of woods? Did the coyote bolt across the road because of us or some- thing else?"

Abon had a quizzical look on his face. "Did you really see all of that happen?"

"Yes, I saw all of that and more. You need to pay attention to more than just the road. A bear could spook your horse. If you are not ready for it, you could find yourself on your back in the middle of the road and your horse running for its life. While you are trying to catch your breath, you might find yourself as lunch for a hungry bear."

"That would never happen. I've never even heard of that happening before." Stricklin's face showed disbelief.

"Could happen if the bear was hungry enough.

Look to the left and a little behind us."

They both looked back at the bear that was standing on his hind legs watching us pass.

"By Phaon's name, how did you know that?" Abon turned back toward the road as if to spur his horse to a run.

"Relax. He has his dinner." I chuckled to myself. "How did you know that bear was there?" Stricklin asked.

"I heard it when a bone snapped as he pulled some meat from the carcass. Then I saw him." I glanced back in time to see the bear return to its meal. "Calarel, how long have you been traveling?"

Abon leaned forward to catch my eye.

"This is the second day of my first journey alone, without my father. He is a good teacher of the world, what I know of it anyway," I said. "I have been to Duintolea a few times and Sea Head once."

"Then you live close to here?" Stricklin asked. "Well, yes, I guess so. My home is in Valeria."

A few miles further, we found a good place to stop for the night. We set up camp and gathered wood for cooking. Firepit built, I went out to hunt, but didn't see anything. I started to set a couple of snares and then noticed a deer trail. I decided to get out here early in the morning, maybe get a small deer.

When I returned to the campsite, they had the fire started and were trying to build something to support a pot. I pulled a couple of the tubers and some radishes from my saddlebags, then peeled and cut them up. I also added some of the cut-up rabbit to the pot. Pouring in most of the water from my water skin, on the fire, the pot went.

Waiting for the food to cook, I sharpened my axe, ran the stone down my dagger once or twice. We sat and talked until the rabbit stew was done. We had a good meal, but more bread would have made it better.

Abon asked how old I was. I told him and I thought he'd fall over laughing.

"Why are you laughing so hard?" I asked.

Stricklin was starting to laugh too.

I couldn't help myself, even I began to laugh a little.

Finally, Abon managed to speak again. "I'm sorry I thought you said about one hundred and fifty years old. That just struck me funny."

"Why would that be funny?" I was still chuck- ling a little.

"Because at a hundred and fifty, you would be this old, dry, brown-skinned, boney thing with half your hair missing." He took a big breath. "And the picture of that just made me laugh."

"Dang, Abon, that wasn't nice," Stricklin said. "I am one hundred forty-eight, and in a year

and three and a half months, I'll be a hundred and fifty years into this life. I guess you didn't study much, did you? What race lives to be three hundred and fifty or more?"

Stricklin answered quickly, "Highmen!" "Right," I said. "What race is immortal?" I

asked, looking at Abon.

"Elf and ah something. But I can't think of it." "I am a mix of High Elf and Highmen. This would

mean that barring anything other than natural death, I could live over the three hundred and fifty years as a Highmen. I might make it to eight hundred years, if the Deities think that is best," I told them. "Just think, when I am considered a full adult by the High Elves, I will have lived two or three of your life times."

"Well, strike me dead if that isn't over two hundred years," Abon said.

Stricklin quickly replied, "Careful of what you ask for. There is that bear just down the road."

We all laughed. We talked for a while longer, and Abon was the first to sleep then Stricklin shortly after. I guess the smaller you are, the more sleep you need. I stayed awake until midnight.

I woke up, sat up quickly, listening to the sounds of the night. Silence. A light breeze moved leaves in the trees nearby. For at least three hundred feet around me, nothing moved. I thanked the deities for Elven sight. Beyond that, it was as dark to me as three feet in front of a common man. The faint light of the moon was all but hidden behind thick clouds. I dressed quietly, donned my armor, and put on my weapons belt. I laid my axe down on the tarp I used to cover my bedroll, just in case it rained. Then I pulled my bow from its sheath, strung it, and hung my quiver of arrows on my belt before slipping out of camp.

I found a good place to wait and watch. I listened and watched for over an hour, maybe two. The sky had started to lighten in the east. I nocked an arrow, but pulled only a little tension on the string. Hearing some movement toward my right, I moved slowly, turning my head to look. I started pulling more tension on the bowstring, I was almost fully drawn and only a little out of position when I saw them. One buck that would have fed Father, Tamera, and myself for a month. Father would have been proud if he could see me take this one down.

But I waited for a smaller one. I was in a good position. I released and the arrow flew true. No more than the feathers and a fist of the three-foot shaft stuck out of the side of the deer. The small herd bolted toward the woods. Most made it to the shelter of the trees except one, the one with the shaft of my arrow sticking out of its body from both sides.

I listened as everything became quiet again, only the leaves rustling in the breeze. I moved to my kill. Gutting it there, I dragged the rest back to camp, where I grabbed my rope and headed for the nearest tree.

Abon sat up and said, "Why must you get up so early?"

"Good, you are awake. You can help. Find a branch about three feet long and about three fingers thick. Good morning to you too."

He slowly got up and moved around getting dressed. I wasn't really watching, but I think he kicked Stricklin once or twice to wake him up too.

The first branch I tried to use broke, and I had to find another one to hang the deer from. It took two tries to get the rope over a higher and stronger branch. Abon came over with a good-sized branch. "Here ya go. Where did you get that?" And before I could answer, he asked, "What time did you get up?

The sun is hardly over the hills in the far distance."

I chuckled a little. "My father says I am making up for all the sleeping I did when I was little. He says I slept all the time, for about twenty years. Now I hardly sleep at all, maybe four hours a night. If Father were lucky, we would have food, until he started making food for me to eat before he woke in the morning."

I tied the branch to the hind legs spread the length of the branch. Then tied the end of the rope to the make a triangle shape.

"I sleep only about four hours a night. So I go hunt or mend or whatever needs doing. The little need for sleep is part of the Elven in me."

I started to pull the deer up off the ground.

Stricklin came over and began to help. "I could have used some more sleep."

"But she only sleeps four hours a night. It's no wonder she comes back to camp with something to eat."

"Yes. I guess I do." I chuckled.

"I have heard that is why most Elves are scholars and mages," Stricklin said.

"No, I think you're wrong about that. Most are scholars and mages because they live so long, not because they get up so early. It takes a long time to learn magic. I cannot, I do not have that ability."

As we gave the rope one last pull, it raised the deer two feet from the ground.

"There, that is good enough. My sister is learning magic. I hope she stays with it."

I tied the rope off to another tree branch. "Would that be good?" Abon asked.

"For some people, it is," Stricklin said disgustedly. "Yes. I think it would be good for my sister." Looking at Stricklin. "Why did you say it that way?"

"Haven't really met a good magic user." "Mistress Dawnly is a good magic user, she's a healer," Abon retorted.

"I wish my sister could learn healing," I said as I cut the skin around the ankles of the hind legs, then down the legs to the stomach area, before skinning at the ankles to loosen the skin. I asked Stricklin to help by pulling the skin down on one leg while I did the other. We stripped the legs and a little of the back before we had to raise the deer higher. We removed the skin pretty easy and didn't waste too much meat, to my surprise.

I don't think either of them had skinned more than a few rabbits before today. Abon stood around watching, looking like he was trying to memorize every move I made. After we finished, I asked if either one wanted the skin.

Abon said he would like it, to use as a cover at night.

"Okay, but you are doing most of the work," I told him, and he agreed.

We found some good straight branches and tied them together to make the frame. I think we used most of the cord Abon had to stretch the skin. I showed him how to clean it and let him do it. I salted the deer meat to help preserve it. As Abon cleaned the skin, I watched him do a pretty good job of it. I did a little touch up here and there. Then we let it dry. We would need to get it oiled soon.

We spent the day at that site. A few merchant wagons passed by and a family moving to Valeria. They had bought the old Hanson place in town. He was a tinker, someone who fixed just about anything, and she was a seamstress. He was going to open up the shop again. That would be good for the town. Don't know that she would do well there or not, but worth the try anyway.

We shared some of the meat with them, and they offered some coin for the meat. I told them that we didn't need it before the other two could open their mouths. That was pretty much the excitement for the day.

Night came; it was a nice night, not a cloud in the sky. They both went to sleep long before I did. I had to chase off a raccoon before I went to sleep.

I woke at my usual time, got dressed, and donned my armor before exercising and practicing. I was ready for the day ahead. When I checked on the deer hanging from the tree, I found it was drying well, but not quick enough. After the other two woke, we made some breakfast, then packed our things. We trimmed off the driest parts of the meat to tuck into convenient places in our packs so we could reach it while traveling.

I knew we couldn't take the whole thing without it going bad before we reached a smokehouse. So we cut some nice pieces to cook that night and maybe tomorrow. I pulled the rest of the deer carcass into the trees to the east and left it for the animals to eat.

We were moving again. We traveled for four or five hours before coming to the intersection with West Duintolea road.

"North or east?" Stricklin asked.

"I am headed north to Cynar. You are welcome to come along, if you like."

I never stopped or slowed.

They looked in both directions, as if looking for writing in the air farther down the road. I heard them say something to each other, but couldn't make out their whispers.

Then they hurried to catch up with me.

"We'll go to Cynar with you, but not sure how far after that," Abon said.

"Well, I am not sure if I well go past Cynar myself, but it would be nice to have company that far at least."

When the sun had moved to the top of mountains to the west and the forest had gotten rather thick with oaks and elms, I volunteered to scout ahead and find a place to camp. I was watching for a place when the hair on the back of my neck stood on end. I looked to the right in the trees just ahead of me.

An abandoned wagon, the back bow bent back at an angle, and the load gate down. The tarp torn, hung from the branch that had most likely broke the other two wagon bows. I stopped, looked, and listened before dismounting, nothing. As my foot touched the ground, I heard an arrow whizz past my head; it struck a tree by the wagon.

I threw my reins over the saddle horn so Blackie wouldn't step on them, slapped him on the hind- quarter, and yelled, "Move!"

I knew he wouldn't go far but hoped for farther than he went. I went into the trees, on the same side of the road the arrow came from. Only one arrow. If there were more than one archer there, I should have been hit by now. I pulled my backpack off and stayed low. Moving at a stealth, I looked around the tree I crouched beside, watching for any movement.

With a damaged wagon and someone shooting arrows at me, I said to myself, "Damn," then yelled, "Bandits, take cover!"

I heard the sound I will never forget, the sound of a man getting hit with an arrow. It is so much different than an animal. I thought I was going to get sick.

I heard an arrow coming toward me before it sliced my vest across my side. I felt some pain, but maybe it was only a nick. I knew the archer had to reload again. So I looked around the tree and saw him standing on a branch about seven feet above of the ground. I took off at a run toward him. Pulling my axe with my right hand from my left hip, I raised it up into the air. By the time I was right in front of him, he had the arrow nocked and pulled. It made for an awkward shot if he took it. I aimed my axe for his foot, but I was a little high. The blade hit his leg above the ankle, cutting the laces of his soft solo boot. I had to release the handle as it hung on the top of his foot. But the stout handle of my axe must have smashed the middle toe on his foot as I passed under- neath him. He yelled in agony. It took three steps for me to stop; I drew my sword as I spun around.

Trying to catch his breath from the fall, he grabbed for his foot. He sounded as if he were trying to moan and yell for help at the same time until my sword pierced his leather jerkin.

Then he froze, not even breathing. All he saw was the two-finger-wide steel blade pointed down from over his head.

"How many are there?" I said quietly and applied a little more pressure on his chest with my sword.

"Three of us out here," he replied just as softly as I did.

"Then there are more of you around?"

He surprised me by grabbing my sword's blade as if to prevent it from going any deeper into his armor as he kicked at me with his good foot. I pushed my sword through the center of his chest until it reached the ground. I saw no alternative.

He tried to yell, but it ended as a grunting moan instead. He kicked a couple of times and lay still. The last breath slowly released from his lungs.

I spun to the side and threw up. My stomach heaved everything out in one big hurl. I dropped to my knees, as my stomach heaved again.

I stood to retrieve my weapon. I pulled once, but all it did was raise his body. My hands shook at the thought of pulling him around. I put my foot on his shoulder to hold him down and yanked the blade from his chest. More blood oozed out of the wound. My stomach knotted up more.

I heard something behind me. *I am dead now,* I thought. My stomach heaved again. "No time to be sick," I told myself.

"You killed him, you bitch," someone yelled, as I leaped into a forward roll for added distance.

"Ooaww."

I heard the noise as I came to my feet, spun around, and took a defensive stance. Where I was kneeling just the moment before, a man fell face down. Abon stood two or three paces behind him, pulling another dagger out of his loose-fitting jerkin. There were two daggers in the man's back already.

Already, Abon was looking around, for what I had no idea. He motioned me down, then stepped up to the man with the daggers in his back. Abon pulled out his daggers and then slide sideways to use the tree as cover.

He said softly, "There is at least one more. Are you okay?"

He had a slight smile. I think he was hoping I was.

I nodded and moved closer to him. "What about Stricklin?"

"Dead, I think," he replied as he peeked around the tree. "Aha, looky there." He reached around the tree and pulled a shield toward us before sliding it to me. "Can you use it?"

"Yea, if I get the chance."

"He's coming." He put his finger over his lips to signal me to be quiet.

I could hear the third bandit whisper names, "Freeman?" He looked around. "Jacob?"

Abon took a stick from the ground. He motioned that he would throw it, and as soon as the guy turned that direction, we would attack. I nodded in agreement.

The stick sailed from his hand but went only four or five paces from where we crouched before hit- ting a branch five feet off the ground.

He halted and looked our direction. I could see him tense into a better defensive posture. It was then he noticed his dead friend who now had two bloody areas on his back. Before he realized it was an ambush and moved away, I had to make a move.

"Are you afraid of a woman?" I asked as I stepped out from behind the tree. I held the shield by one strap and my sword in a sloppy manner. I was hoping to lure him into false feelings. He appeared to be twenty-five in mannish years. That could mean he might know how to use his weapon.

He relaxed a little. "I'm going to have fun tonight," he said with a silly grin on his face. He stepped forward, and I copied him.

"I would say you have already had enough fun for one day, by the looks of that wagon." I put as much disgust in my voice as I could manage. "How many people did you guys kill?"

He stepped right, so did I. He glanced around real fast. He might have been able to see the other man lying by the tree, I wasn't sure.

"Where is your little buddy, the Halfling?" Taking another glance at the one with the wounds in his back. He stepped to the left and forward.

I followed suit, left and back. I lowered my arm a little as if the weight of the weapon was too heavy for me.

"He is around somewhere, unless you killed him too."

We danced around the small clearing, sizing each other. We had worked our way around to where we had almost traded places from when he first came into the area. He worked his wrist back and forth. I couldn't figure out if his wrist was hurt and he was trying to work out something else. He kept his distance just out of range. We stepped left again. He held his sword horizontal to the ground and reflected the sun into my eyes. The things Father had taught me flooded back. I stepped back into a defensive stance, braced for an impact to my side, and covered for a head strike.

He struck the bottom half of the shield with his sword with a loud clash of metal on wood. It jarred me hard. I saw him bring the sword back for another try at me. I moved forward and slightly to the left, trying to stab as if with a rapier. I gave him a small nick in his side. We exchanged blows several times before he stepped back to regain control of the situation.

"You're pretty good," he said as he took a stance Father had tried to teach me. I knew what was coming next. "But not good enough." He grunted as he began the next assault. His first strike was weak, as intended.

I blocked.

He started his spin, and at the same time, I turned to face the next blow which put my weapon arm toward him. If he carried through with the maneuver, he was a dead man. I blocked most of the blow, but the shield gave way, the bottom quarter breaking off. The strap of the shield twisted in my hand.

It took me by surprise when his blade slide across my leather jerkin just above the third button. I felt the blade on my skin beneath my clothes and winched instead of striking my opponent. I turned on him and used the shield to strike him, hoping to knock him off balance or something, anything.

I felt anger growing in me. *Anger will get you killed, girl,* I heard my father say in my mind.

I stepped back into an attacking posture. I did not pause for him to regain his momentum. I hit him. It was only a nick. But he noticed it, and I could see his anger growing. The more I evaded him, the angrier he became. He raced past me with a wild swing. I saw the reason for his move. The dagger fell to the ground before we settled facing one another

"You're next, Halfling," he called out loud enough for Abon to hear, who had worked his way around behind the man. But now, I was in his way.

The bandit came at me hard, all most knocked me down. The move unbalanced him as well. I saw the dagger come from behind the tree. So did the bandit, he tried to avoid being hit. With just a nick, he kept going toward Abon.

Abon switched the next dagger from one hand to the other so fast, it was almost a blur. He threw it. It spun two times through the air and hit the bandit in the shoulder with the hilt.

Abon moved to avoid the swing from the bandit but was struck in the upper part of his leg, sending him to the ground. The bandit's sword came up.

I was but a few steps behind the bandit. I stabbed my sword forward in hopes that I would be able to at least make him wrench in pain enough to miss the killing blow to Abon.

Abon rolled to the left hard. My blade hit the bandit in the back close to his side, maybe an inch of flesh. I ran into the back of him with the shield, pushing him off balance once again. As he moved forward, I yanked the blade out.

"Now you are lost," I called out.

He spun with a wild flat-bladed swing; I felt the breeze on my face from the tip of his sword. I swung in return, made contact with my target. I heard his collarbone snap from the blow. He spun around again with a wild swing; his left arm looked like a rag hanging from his shoulder. I blocked his swing with what was left of the shield.

The instinct to protect myself dictated that I swing again. I did and sliced into his neck. As he went to his knees, his lips moved, and his jaw worked. There was no sound other than gurgling noises. He knelt there on his knees for a second maybe and then fell over, blood gushing from his neck and shoulder. I wiped my sword clean and sheathed the blade, then hurried to Abon. He was bleeding profusely. I pulled my dagger and cut his pant leg open to check the wound.

"By Phaon, this hurts worse than my mother's switch," he said through clenched teeth.

I used part of his pant leg to help slow the bleeding. Once the bleeding slowed. "I need some Arlan to help stop the bleeding."

I went to get my axe from behind the tree, then dragged the closest dead person deeper into the trees.

The pain in my side made me want to stretch hard to the right while dragging his body.

I think Abon saw the pain in my face.

"Wait, check for valuables first," Abon called out. "I am no thief, Abon. I do not steal from the living, why would I steal from the dead?"

"They should pay for the healing we need. My horse has an arrow in her side. So you'll have to put her down and you need some new armor. Damn! You're bleeding."

"It is not bad," I told him as I dropped the dead man's feet. When I felt at my left side, blood oozed between my fingers. I stared at my hand.

"I did not think it was this bad."

I fumbled to untie my leather jerkin so I could examine the wound.

"That doesn't look good to me, Calarel. You better take care of yourself before you go wandering off looking for horses or anything else."

"Maybe you are right." I sounded a long whistle, hoping Blackie would come. "But I do not think this is a good place to camp for the night."

"Agreed!" He started to get up again. "Will you please lie still?"

I started looking for the archer's backpack. It wasn't near the tree where his shield was at.

"They must have a campsite somewhere else."
"What makes you say that?"

"No backpacks. No supplies. Two of them are only carrying water skins that are almost empty." I paused for a moment. "That means that there are probably more of them out here." I began cutting the dead man's shirt in to stripes, then stopped. "I need my backpack, stay still, will you?"

I headed back to the road where I dropped my backpack. I moved with caution, watching for movement as I approached the road. I found my backpack, picked it up, and stepped to the road's edge. I looked for the horses in both directions, but did not see them.

Once back with Abon, I then applied some of the Arlan that I had picked earlier to Abon's leg.

"I like this Arlan. It works wonders. It helps to stop the bleeding pretty good."

"I got the bleeding to stop. But you cannot move around for a while. Maybe a day or two, but we cannot stay here. That is for sure."

"I'm with you." He struggled to rise.

I pushed him back to the ground. "We do not have enough Arlan for you to keep your leg bleeding all the time. Lie still. I will build a litter and then find the horses."

I pulled my last clean undershirt from my pack to use as bandage. I used some of the Arlan and bandaged myself best I could.

"Where are your things?" I asked Abon. "Maybe five or six of your paces from the road

straight across from Stricklin."

He was beginning to sound tired.

I got up and laced my jerkin back up.

"This is going to restrict my movement now," I told him before moving south toward the direction he had come from.

"Look, I can find my things, if you help me!" Abon said.

"I can find it, Abon, you just lie there. Do not move around or your leg will start bleeding again. I will be back in a minute or two."

Tracking someone that was in a hurry is usually easy, but I found this place full of tracks, footprints, most of which had on riding boots. Some footprints were of children, two at least. The prints came from the road and headed deeper into the woods.

Shoed hoof prints, horses. Horses that stood, waiting for their next command. They used this spot to ambush travelers. If I was right, maybe eight horses. I kept going, looking for Abon's things.

I soon found them, then looked around to remember where they were. I found Stricklin, who was lying on the other side of the road. It didn't look like he struggled long. The arrow had a good angle to it, a killing shot that brought death fast.

I unsheathed my sword and then knelt to one knee. With the tip grounded, I held the hilt to my forehead.

"Tulkus, I pray to you. Take this man's soul and keep it sound and safe for the next life. And may those that took his life live a miserable life and suffer greatly. This I pray to you. May you be willing to grant it?"

I opened my eyes and looked at Stricklin's body. "If I can, I will avenge your needless death."

My heart ached more than my side with the loss of a friend I barely knew. I grabbed his arms and drug him into the woods. He was already starting to feel cold. I hid him behind a log with some foliage growing from it. I pulled his sword and laid it on his chest, but I took his backpack with me. I hope to come back tomorrow and bury him properly, but for now, I had things to do.

I looked up and down the road for the horses again. They would have gone out of the woods to the grass to graze. *Too far to go right now, I need to move Abon from that clearing.* On my way back to him, I picked up Abon's backpack.

When I got back to Abon, he was asleep. "Abon," I said softly. "We need to move from here."

"Not now."

"I think there are at least eight more bandits around, close by I think."

"Then we'll ride out of here."

"No horses. I did not see any of them. They could be miles back down the road or ahead of us." I paused a moment. "They would head for the nearest water. And we have not passed any. So they may be ahead of us."

I laid the packs down by Abon and started my search for some good saplings to use as a litter. After finding the right ones, I cut them down, and I made a litter using Stricklin's clothes from his backpack.

I helped Abon onto the litter. Using a rope to help, I dragged Abon to the road. I laid the litter down, then went back to cover the litter's trail. The two drag marks left by the litter would be a dead giveaway that whoever killed the three men was hurt as well and easy to track. With the tracks covered, I headed north toward Cynar, pulling Abon on the litter.

I still had to find a hiding place for the night and for the next day or two. We hadn't gone far, only about an hour, when I heard a horse whinny.

"Thank you, Tulkus," I whispered, looking to the sky. I moved off the road to the left, toward the sound of the horse.

The woods were thinner here, allowing me to pull the litter without too much trouble. My biggest problem was that it was uphill. My waist felt wet, but I had to find shelter to rest. I knew I was bleeding again and felt weak. The horses would be a big help when we moved on, if we did. I used the trees to pull myself and the litter to the top of the hill.

Chapter 2

When I did, I paused to look about. It was dark; night had fallen an hour earlier.

Light reflected on the branches of the trees. A faint light, not enough to be noticed from the road. It came from a small pond, maybe twelve feet across.

I could see two horses, one lying down and the other getting up. It must be Blackie. I headed down the hill toward the pond.

"You never looked so good to me before, Bla—" I cut myself off as I realized it was not Blackie.

The black horse shook its head, as if to say no. This horse was a good three hands taller than a lesser warhorse, making him seventeen hands high, with more defined muscle mass, and a much deeper black. He seemed prouder and more, more everything than Blackie was, smarter, maybe. I couldn't put my finger on it.

There were two well-worked saddles with high swells and high cantles up the bank from the water. Two saddle blankets, two sets of saddlebags, and a pair of hackamore. All paired up ready for use.

Before setting the litter down, I went down by the water and started back up the slope. Abon only groaned a little.

The horse that stood when I came over the ridge had drank from the pond, so I knew the water is good. I tasted a little of the water before filling one of the water skins lying with the rest of the riding gear. I drank some, then walked back up to Abon to give him a drink. He was too busy sleeping.

The horse moved closer to the saddles. He nudged one of the saddlebags three times.

"Would you like me to get something from the saddlebags for you?"

He scratched at the ground twice by the bags and moved his head up and down as if to say yes.

With a great effort and a lot of pain, I got up and moved around to where he stood. "You are a big horse. I think the biggest I have ever seen."

I bent to pick up the saddlebags and the horse nudged my side, the side where I was wounded.

"Ouch," I yelled and jerked away from him. The horse raised his head quickly. "Ooh, I am sorry I did not mean to startle you. But that hurt."

He gave me a look that seemed urgent and turn toward saddlebags again.

I stepped aside before trying to retrieve the saddlebags, watching him this time. The bags had too much weight to be empty. The bags closest to me were tied close. Apples, big green apples. I pulled one out of the bag and thought he would take my hand off trying to get the apple. So I gave it to him.

He took it to the other horse and dropped it in front of her.

I would swear on my mother's grave I heard a male voice say, "She needs." I looked around. With the light from the pond, I could see the whole area pretty good, even into the trees at the top of the ridge that completely surrounded the pond. *The pond must be fed by a spring underground.*

I noticed the other horse eat the apple. She started to get up, but the male whinnied at her, and she relaxed again.

"I hope your owner does not mind if I have an apple," I said aloud as I pulled another from the bag before tying the saddlebag closed.

"*No owner. Apple no.*"

It was the same male voice. But I could not pick the direction that it came from.

Father had a game of point to the sound. I could always point in the direction of a sound. I was the best at it. Even in town, we would stop, cover our eyes, he would pick a sound, spin one of us around. Tell us the sound we were to point to. At home, we were blindfolded. He would toss a rock or something, and we were to point to it. Later, it became pointing the tip of my sword at the sound. More advanced les- sons were try to hit him when he made a sound, with a practice sword of course. Maybe I lost more blood than I thought.

"Say more." I heard the voice was in my head. Not a booming voice, like the drunk in town said he heard.

"Okay, you are a mage on the other side of the ridge and you have cast some spell on me, I do not like it," I spoke loud enough to be heard from the other side of the ridge and in all directions. "Do you know healing? My friend is injured pretty badly."

"I am not mage, I am Scorch." I heard in my mind, again with no direction to choose from. I watched the horses. Maybe they would give me a clue to the origin of the voice. The mare was just resting on the ground. The stallion backed away from the other horse and turned to face me, just watching the only other thing moving.

I started to walk around the pond, hoping that I could catch a sound of movement or anything.

"Okay, Scorch, there is no need to hide," I spoke in a normal tone. Then I spoke quieter, "We only need to rest for the night." Then I whispered, "We will move on tomorrow morning."

"I do not hide. I stand in front of you, looking at you from across the pond. I have taken a blood bond with you, so we may communicate. It may be broken easily for now if you desire."

"You are speaking better real fast," I thought.

"Yes. As the bond grows stronger, the more I will learn from you." I heard in my mind.

"Okay, this is getting very strange. You need to come out now. And help me heal my friend."

"What is wrong with your friend?" I heard.

"He was hurt by some bandits down the road. He has lost a lot of blood. I hope he makes it through the night."

"Perhaps we can help. But explain a bandit to me." The voice never comes from anywhere. I only hear it in my mind.

"A bandit is a person who steals from other people and may kill the other person in the process of stealing. A bandit is a bad person. Now answer a question for me." I tried not to sound too demanding. "What is a blood bond? And how did you do it? No one has touched me. I would have known. I have not lost that much blood yet." Then I thought to myself, *I hope I have not anyway.*

"When you bent to get the saddlebags with the green apples, I bumped you with my nose where you are bleeding. The blood from your wound is sufficient to make a one-sided blood bond. The bonding that we now have is what you call magic. It lets me understand your words. In a day's time, I will feel your emotions and feelings. But it will be limited for a while. Unless we do a full bonding, then I will feel what you feel and you will feel what I feel. I am what you call a horse.

"We have been waiting for the right ones. You must be them. I did not feel hostility from you. If I had, you would have never found us. It has been a long lonely wait."

I'm really having a hard time with this. A test. That's it, some kind of a test. "If you are the horse, go to your saddle and nose the saddle horn."

That should do it, a horse would have no idea what a saddle horn was.

The horse turned and stepped over to the saddles and nosed the saddle horn.

"Pick up the hackamore by the reins."

The horse nosed the grass by the hackamore and brought his head up with the reins between his teeth.

"Are you satisfied now?" I heard in my head. "Okay, okay. How can you help heal my friend?" "I could take you to the Gray," I heard.

"I have never heard of that place. And Abon would not be able to stay in the saddle long enough to get there. Wherever the gray is?"

"Come saddle me. You will need all your strength to keep him with us," the horse told me.

Wracked with pain, I finished walking around the pond toward the horse.

"You are hurt bad. I hope you can keep yourself on my back without the saddle."

"I can. I am all right."

The horse gave me the hackamore from his mouth. *"Put it on me, and just lay across my back."*

I put the hackamore on the horse. And tried to get on, but he was too big. I was hurting too bad to jump up on his back. "Let me stand on the saddle, maybe then I can get on."

By the time the last of my words came out of my mouth, we were out in the dense woods. I was standing by a large tree trunk that had fallen some time ago.

"How did we get here?" I stumbled back and sat on the fallen tree truck.

"It is an ability of travel that Stormy and I have.
Now you should be able to get on my back."

I used the tree trunk to climb up on Scorch's back pretty easy.

Suddenly, we were in a place that was all gray, like being in a thick fog in the middle of the day. It was swirling, broiling, and flowing in every direction at once. It made me feel dizzy.

"Where are we?"

"In the Gray. We must come here once every time the bright star passes around."

"The sun, you mean the sun. You have to come here every day. I need to get down, before I fall off," I told him.

"No," his voice thundered in my head. *"I am sorry to be loud. I do not know how far it is to the bot- tom, if there is a bottom to this place."*

I didn't know how long we were there; it is hard to sense time without a reference.

"What are you standing on then? I tried to look, but it just made me really dizzy. I feel a little tingly too."

"Then we must go now," he said.

Suddenly, we were at the pond with Abon was still lying on the litter. The other horse stood beside him. She looked at us and moved away from Abon.

I slide off the horse's back, expecting my wounds to be painful but only felt a twinge of pain. Most of the pain was gone, just gone, and I felt refreshed.

"Stormy thinks he is near death. His breath is shallow," I heard in my head.

"Can you take us both to the gray place?"

"Yes. But you cannot be there long enough for him to heal complete. Maybe only half the time needed," I heard. "I do not know if I will ever get used to a voice in my head," I said as I went to where Abon lay.

I checked his breathing, and the horse called Stormy was right. Abon was close to death from losing so much blood. "I am glad you are light, little man," I said to him.

He did not answer, hardly moaned when I picked him up.

"How do I get to that log?"

"Turn around," the horse said.

I no more started to turn and I felt a hot breath on the back of my neck and then pressure on my shoulder. I found myself trying to catch my balance on the same log I had stood on before when I got on horse's back the first time. The horse let go of my jerkin after I got steady on the log. He didn't walk around the log, he was just there.

I still had Abon cradled in my arms. "How to do this? I could leap on your back, but that may hurt a bit."

"Put one foot on my back and leap the rest of the way on, sliding that foot down my side."

"I will try it." I worried about the outcome. I put my left foot on his back. *"I wish I were a carnival acrobat right now."* I pushed off the log, and landed hard on Scorch's back. He shifted slightly to adjust my balance on his back. In a blink of the eye, gray surrounded us. A swirling gray mist that was dry and warm. "Thank you. I guess I should tell you my name. I am Calarel."

"Glad to meet you, Calarel. I am Scorch." He made a noise that sounded like a laugh. *"Remember when you start to tingle, tell me. It will be time to go."*

"Okay. I will tell you."

"No one is to know of this place. I should not have brought you here so soon. The creators will not like that I have brought you here without being fully bonded."

"What do you mean by creators? Who are they, Scorch?"

"We, Stormy and I, were created by beings from another plain. They put us here fourteen days ago. Eight days ago, the saddles and other things appeared. The green apples would appear on the ground every morning as the sun came up. Now they appear in the saddlebags. We need one at least every other day, but daily would be best for us. The apples have a quality that we need to survive. But I do not think they would be any good for others to eat them."

Abon began to move around some, and I was tingling all over, not just the exposed flesh as before, but my legs and torso. Abon got lighter, not heavier. "I think it is time to go back now, Scorch." I hardly finished saying his name and we were back at the pond. I jiggled Abon as I spoke his name. He opened his eyes and looked up at me.

"I was having a dream. My mother was holding me."

"How does your leg feel?"

"It hurts a little, but not that bad." He looked around a little. "I see you found Blackie."

Realizing that we were on the back of a horse, he jerked. And I almost dropped him.

"You think you can stand on your leg now?" "I think so."

I lowered him as far as I could, but he still couldn't touch the ground. "You will have to drop from here." I gave him about a second to prepare and let go.

"Damn, woman. How long have I been sleeping?" "Not long."

"What's not long to you? A couple of weeks at least." He sounded a little angry. He rubbed his wounded leg. "My leg feels almost fully healed."

I looked for the moon to figure the time; I did not feel tired at all. "Wow, it is about one in the morning. So it is been about seven or eight hours since we were attacked."

He untied the bandage and wiped the damp blood from his wounded leg. "I know that cut was to the bone, if not into it! You told me you didn't know magic healing!"

"I do not. If you will be quiet for a minute or two, I could tell you what happened while you slept." I told him and then looked at Scorch. "I have one more question for you, Scorch."

"I will answer your question."

"Scorch? I thought your horse's name was Blackie?" "It is. But this is Scorch!" I said as if introducing him.

"What? Where did you find him?"

"What is your question?" Scorch asked while Abon still spoke.

"Hold on a second, one at a time. Scorch. Why were you put here instead of where you were"—I paused a little to think of the right word—"created?"

Again, they both started at the same time. I held up a finger to Abon to quiet him and listened to Scorch. *"Put here to help the…"*

Abon distracted me again. I turned toward him and said, "Be quiet a minute, will you." Turning back to Scorch, "I am sorry could you tell me that again?"

"We were put here to help the good fight the evil that is coming," Scorch said to me.

I thought he used the word destined the first time, but I wasn't sure.

"That is good enough for me. I will do the full bonding, if you wish."

"If you truly wish to do this. You must understand a few things first. After a full bonding, I would feel what you feel and hear what you hear. Even at great distances. For now, by the time you walked to the road, I would be gone from your mind. You would not be able to hear me. You would not know where I am. After a full bonding, you will know where I am even at the ocean toward the setting moon."

"That is over a hundred miles from here." "What's a hundred miles from here?"

"Quiet. I will get to you in a minute," I told Abon, a little harsher than I intended.

"Twice that distance and you could point to me. You could hear me as well."

"That is not bad," I told him.

"The bad part, as you put it, would be that if you die, I will die also. If I die, you too would die because of the bond. The loneliness of a broken bond would kill whoever survives. It would be a lonely death. Even with friends at your side. Your heart will break, and in a matter of weeks, you would die." He paused for a few moments.

I waited to find out more.

"Are you sure you want a full bonding?"

I turned to Abon. "I am sorry I was harsh with you. I did not really mean to be."

Picking up my backpack, I searched through one of the side pockets for some of the jerky and handed him a piece. "You will not believe what has happened. I will tell you all of it after you clean up and change your pants. I do not think we can get those repaired."

I turned back to Scorch. I thought about his offer and decided. "I will do the full bonding with you."

"What of your companion?" Scorch asked.

"I guess that is a choice he will have to make for himself." I looked over my shoulder at Abon. "How can I tell him any of this? He would never believe me anyway."

"Very well. I will bite my inner lip to make it bleed. You must get some of my blood and swallow it. The bonding will take a little time, but it will come. Once it is done, there is no turning back. Ever."

"Wait!" I said louder than I wanted. "How long is your life span? I could live eight hundred years or more. Most horses only live a useful life of about twenty-five years. This will not be a good bargain for me," I said sadly.

"I do not know. I will ask Stormy," Scorch replied. This whole conversation was happening in my head, the only sounds were those of a peaceful night and Abon washing himself at the pond. After a few minutes, Scorch said, "I have the answer. I will live as long as the person I am bonded to. If you live to the next age, so will I."

"Then bite your lip. I will bond with you."

He bit his lip, harder than he needed to. And when I pulled his lip to check, his blood flowed freely. I caught a drop or two and sucked the blood off my finger.

"Put on my saddle. I wish to show you something," Scorch said.

"Very well." I called out to Abon, "I need to go for a little ride. I will be back in a little bit. You can bathe clean in the pond."

"But you can't just leave me here."

"I do not want to watch you bathe. I will be back in about twenty minutes. Is that long enough?" "Ya, I guess so," he said as I put the saddle blanket and saddle on Scorch's back.

"Okay. Exhale so I can cinch up the girth strap."

He did, and I cinched up the girth strap, then I climbed on to the saddle. "Okay go."

Scorch started out at a slow walk. We twisted our way out of the woods. When we came to the road, I felt his muscles tighten and knew he was going to run. I found out Scorch was a good runner. Fast, smooth. But the more he ran, the faster he went. The trees began to blur into one big mass of brown at the bottom and green at the top. The sky was clear, then became cloudy and the mist of fog stung my face. The fog slowed him, but once we were out of it, his speed doubled, maybe tripled. Under a clear sky again, he slowed, taking much effort to slow to a trot. Ahead, there were lights. He slowed to a canter, then to a walk. About then, I realized the run had also affected me. I was breathing hard, as if just running myself.

I could see stone walls fifteen to twenty feet high, with watchtowers built into them. Large gates, big enough for two wagons to pass through side by side. As we approached the gate, Scorch began to high step, as if he were a trained horse of royalty.

"You're out late or up early" came a voice from the side of the gate. A guard in his armor, chain mail over his leather jerkin, stood there.

"Just out for a ride. What city is this?" I was hoping he would not say Cynar. But that was the next city on the Cynar road.

"Cynar, my lady. It is much too dangerous to be riding at night. Come inside where it is safe."

"No, thank you, I will be back later," I told him and reined Scorch around to head back.

"Before you say anything aloud to me, think it,"
Scorch told me.

"I am thinking too much right now."

"Yes, I know that. You need to learn to control your thoughts. Stormy wants to go to the gray, which might startle Abon, if she just disappears. And you did tell Abon you would be back."

"That was a three day ride in little more than quarter of an hour! How did you do that?"

I turned to look at Cynar one more time, and it just disappeared. I turned to face forward and the pond was right there.

"You just appeared there. How did you do that?" Abon asked.

I had never experienced anything like this before. It was exciting. My heart pounding at a furious rate.

"I think you need to know a few things. I did nothing, the horse did!" I told him as I dismounted from the saddle. "These horses are very special."

I put a hand on the horse's hindquarter. "Scorch, *I am guessing Stormy is the same as you?"*

"For the most part, yes. We were both created. Being as young as we are, it is hard to tell what other abilities we will learn."

I turned to Abon. "How is your leg looking?" "Looks like it will be completely healed in a few days. That in itself is unbelievable. You going to tell me what's going on?"

"The horses. They have powers."

Stormy disappeared suddenly, startling both of us. "They can communicate with us."

"You can't talk to a horse!" "You can these."

"Well, I take that back. You always talked to Blackie," he retaliated. "What makes these animals different?"

"It is through a bond. With the bond, you can understand their thoughts and they can understand yours," I told him everything. I told him about the ride to Cynar.

"You're lying. There is no way you could have gone to Cynar and back that fast."

"You do not have to believe me if you do not want to, but it is true."

"Stormy is willing to bond with Abon, but he sounds reluctant."

"I think you are right about that, Scorch."

"We could go for a ride. That would persuade him."

"Good idea," I said aloud. "Let us see if we can find our horses, Abon."

"Okay, I'm not tired anyway. I couldn't sleep if I wanted to."

"Yes, I know the feeling."

I headed for the saddle lying twenty feet away. Stormy appeared on the other side of her saddle, as if she knew what I was going to do. I saddled Stormy and prepared her for the ride.

"Okay, Abon, let us see if we can find the other horses."

When Abon walked over next to Stormy, I thought, *How in the world is he going to get on that big of a horse?*

Stormy folded to the ground. Abon jumped back, waiting for the horse to fall over.

"Tell him to get in the saddle."

"Mount up, Abon."

"Sure this will work?" he questioned as he climbed onto the saddle, grabbed the reins and saddle horn, then Stormy stood. It looked funny, but it worked.

I laughed as I mounted up on Scorch. "That works."

"How are we going to find horses in the middle of the night?"

"I figure they may have gone back down the road, back to that open spot would have grass to graze on."

"That sounds like good reasoning to me. But why would they not come here for the water?"

"This place is warded by the creators, so it would be safe for Stormy and I to stay. Wards misdirect creatures of all kinds to change direction and never know it was here," Scorch explained.

I relayed what Scorch said to Abon. He just looked at me a little funny and said, "Ooh."

I reined Scorch around to head toward the road, and we were there. Scorch and I with Abon on Stormy. Abon looked around so fast, I thought he would break his own neck. "How in the name of Phaon did you do that?"

"Do not look at me, Abon, I do not have a speck of magic in me, it is the horses. They can do things." I reined Scorch to the south to go look for Blackie and the other horses. "All right, let us go find Blackie and your horse too, Abon."

Both Stormy and Scorch started out at a walk. After about twenty paces, Stormy, head held high, nose pointed at the road ahead, started to prance. Abon was looking puzzled. She looked very regal, a knight's horse on a parade march through a town. She looked as if she had been trained for years. I remember them doing that from when I was younger.

"A very proud horse you are riding, Abon. How did you get her to do that so well?"

"I didn't! She just started doing it."

She went into a trot and passed us by. Scorch followed and stayed even with her. Pretty soon, we were at a dead run. Abon held on for dear life, and I was holding on too, but could not help laughing. I knew how fast they could go. Suddenly, the horses halted in the length of six feet from a fast run.

"Creatures near here. Riding creatures, you call horses," Scorch said as he started to move to the left off the road.

I looked hard and could not see anything other than the field we were in. *"Do you see them, Scorch?"*

"No, but I can sense the presence of two large creatures. Smaller than myself. At the edge of this area."

He whinnied, and I heard an answering call. It could have sounded like Blackie, maybe. I called out to Blackie, knowing he was too far for me to see.

"There is another there. Barely holding to life. I could not sense it before."

"Must be Abon's horse. He said his horse was shot with an arrow and might be dead," I thought. "I guess he was right." I realized I had spoken out loud.

"You guess who was right?" Abon asked.

"You are. Scorch sensed two horses as soon as we came into the clearing. That is why we left the road. Now he can sense your horse is almost dead."

I could now make out shadows ahead. It was two horses.

Blackie stood taller than the other, Stricklin's horse who stood on the other side of Blackie. Closer by, I could see a mound where there shouldn't be one. The area was rather flat, other than a few bushes and the grass.

"It is all right, Blackie, it is me," I said as I reined Scorch to a stop.

Blackie's eyes dilated as he watched me climb down. I talked to him just as I did any other time I went to him. Helps to keep him calm. I rubbed the bridge of his nose, as I always did.

"I bet you would love to have that bit out your mouth?"

Abon went to his horse. "She's hardly breathing. I hate to put her down."

"Take the riding bit out of her mouth if you can. At least make her last moments comfortable."

"I guess that would be nice. Are you always the thoughtful one?"

"I try, Abon, I try."

I got Blackie's hackamore from my saddlebags and replaced the bridle.

"Can you help me, Calarel?"

I went to help him and saw why he sounded so helpless. His horse should have passed from this life long before now. The arrow had broken off. She looked like she fell and got up more than once.

"Say your goodbyes, Abon, and let her go to the next life. She has suffered enough."

I pulled the reins out from under her and helped him get the bridle out of her mouth. She had bled from her mouth, most likely from biting the bit so hard.

I went over to Stricklin's horse. One of the reins was broken from being stepped on. I got the hack- amore from the saddlebags and replaced the bridle on him too. I hooked the leads to both Blackie and Stricklin's horse's hackamores. Abon's horse thrashed a little and then went silent. It grew quiet almost as if everything watched the horse's spirit leave to join the Deities.

"I hope he was not bonded to that horse. He looks as if he could die now as well. His eyes are emitting water down his face. Why does he do that?"

I knelt by Abon. "You all right?"

Tears in his eyes, he said, "Ya. I loved that horse.
She was good to me, and I was good to her."

He started to cry again, but held back his tears.

I reached and pulled him close. I held him while he sniffled and told him it was okay. He said he had raised and trained his horse, Sariff; he got her when he began his sixteenth year. The year he was considered a man.

"You are sad. Why? Because Abon has lost a friend?"
"Yes, Scorch. Because Abon has lost a companion of five years."

"Stormy is sad as well. She tasted his blood while you and I were in the Gray. She has yet to let him know that she has taken a blood bond with him. She wants to tell him now. I told her to wait, to let me ask you first." "I do not know if now would be a good time or not, Scorch. Ask her to wait for a little bit. I well ask him what he thinks of being bonded."

"She says she will wait."

"Abon," I said softly, "I told you Scorch and I are bonded. You overheard my half of the conversation I had with Scorch. I can hear him inside my head when he wants to talk to me. At first, it is a little unnerving to hear a voice in your head, but it is not so bad. They are both very smart. He says he will live as long as I do. When they bond to someone, they live as long as the person they are bonded to. Both horses are very smart."

"I think that he bonded to me too. I thought I could hear you crying. But it wasn't you."

Abon looked a little uneasy.

"I am not real sure, but I think they can only bond to one person at a time."

I looked at Stormy. Tears had begun to run down her face. Scorch must have told her what I said because she nodded as if saying yes.

"She does get emotional sometimes. And he may be sad enough for her to feel it through the small bond she has with him."

"Abon, you need to know something." I paused, gathering my thoughts. "Stormy, that is the name of the horse you are riding, made a one-sided bond with you while I was in the Gray. I think she did it so she could call us back, in case you were going to die. You will have to ask her to find out for sure. Try not to be upset with her. You can break the bond if you want. That is still an option, at this point."

"I am not sure that I want to be bonded."

He got up, knelt beside his dead horse, and tried to remove the saddlebags. We had to use another horse to drag the saddle out from under her. Stricklin's horse became a pack horse.

"Stormy won't leave me, will she?"

"I think you should ask her that, not me." I turned toward Scorch. *"Tell her to answer him now. She can break her silence."*

Once mounted, we started back towards the pond where we found Scorch and Stormy. Even before we reached the road, Abon startled in the saddle. "That just isn't right!"

"What is not right, Abon?"

"I can hear a female voice in my head. I'm sure it's the horse." He sounded excited.

"There are other horses nearby. About eight of them, and some of your kind as well," Scorch broke in.

"You mean men and horses? Are they headed this way?" I asked him.

"No, they are not moving, as far as I can tell. They are at the edge of what I can sense."

"Abon, there are others close by. We should take the horses back to that pond and find out if they are more of our friends from yesterday. Perhaps the family with that wagon needs help. I think we owe the bandits some payback."

"But we are only two, and you said there might be about eight of them, earlier."

"Scorch, how many people are there by the other horses?"

"I can feel seven, now that we are closer. They are to the west of us. Not far."

"Scorch says there are seven people there. I believe the family is there, that would be four at least. Two children and their father and mother. I hope they still live."

"Children? How do you know there are children?" he sounded shocked.

"I saw their little footprints where we were ambushed. I just hope they are not hurt!"

"Okay, I'm with you."

When we got to the pond, I hobbled Blackie and Stricklin's horse and drove stacks in the ground, so the horses could get to the water, but not to the trees. Abon and I unsaddled them and set our gear with the saddles.

I placed my sheathed bow under the fender of the saddle that was on Scorch. We climbed back on to Scorch and Stormy and headed in the direction where Scorch could sense others. He said he would show me later.

"Maybe later, we need to see to this first," I said out loud.

"Maybe later, what?"

"Sorry, talking to Scorch." The trees grew too thick to stay in the saddle. So I reined Scorch to a stop. "We need to find another way there. The trees are too thick."

Abon's voice sounded as if it was above me. But how could that be?

"Hold on."

Then Scorch and I were above the trees. I looked down and Scorch's hoofs barely touched the top of the tree's leaves. But it still felt like we were on the ground.

"Abon says you should look at the house in front of us instead of the countryside."

I quickly faced the front and saw a house, old and rundown with a barn in the same condition. A wisp of smoke coming from the chimney of the house meant someone was there. There were horses in the corral. And two wagons beside the barn. I hardly noticed that we stopped just within the edge of the trees.

"Someone is below us."

If anyone was below us even in daylight, they would never see us.

Abon reached out and touched my arm to get my attention. When I looked, he pointed down the tree line a little ways, then held up five fingers. Mouthing five minutes, he pointed at me, then down.

I nodded in agreement.

Stormy and Abon just disappeared.

I waited for five minutes to pass. *"Okay, Scorch, let us go down now."*

He ambled to the edge of the trees, then made a tight arch to face the tree we were above. A man, sound asleep, sat in a chair leaning against the tree trunk. His bow leaned against the tree, his sheathed sword leaned against his leg for quick use.

I started to dismount. I heard "Wait" and the saddle creaked from my weight being shifted. I froze, one foot in the stirrup, the other halfway across the arch of dismounting. I watched the man, but he never moved.

"Now." Scorch told me, and I finished my dismount.

My right foot hit the ground. A rock came flying from behind the tree. It curved toward us, I ducked to avoid being hit and Scorch stepped back. It continued to curve to the back side of the tree where it hit solid. Then I saw a rope wrapped the tree, and it crossed the man's shoulders.

He woke with a start and tried to pull away from the tree. The rope pulled tighter. He used his arms to move it off his shoulders. It slid to his neck. He started to choke and grabbed the rope that pressed against his neck. Then he looked straight at me.

I put my finger to my mouth to indicate quiet.

In a harsh voice, he said, "Yes, I will, you're choking me."

"With the back of your hand, knock your weapon away from you."

He reacted quickly, maybe even hurting him- self as his weapon slid soundlessly partway out of the scabbard when it hit the ground. I pulled the rope tied to my saddle.

"How many of you are there?" I asked as I stepped toward him, making a slip knot at one end as I approached.

"At least a dozen men. If you let me go, I'll give you a head start to get away!" he said the best he could with the rope wrapped around his neck.

I grabbed his hand to slide the loop of the slip knot over his wrist. Abon saw his strong resistance and pulled the rope tighter. The man's arm relaxed a bit, and I pulled the knot tight.

"Put your arm back, or I will." He did, with my help. "If you like to breathe, you do as I say, right?"

"Ya-ah" was all he was able to say as Abon pulled more on the rope.

I finished tying him to the tree and used a cloth he had to gag him. "Now once again, how many are there? I know you have two children in there and most likely their mother and maybe the father as well. That means, counting you of course, three. But I don't think we need to worry much about you. The rope across your neck will not slide down the tree, it is above a branch."

He looked relieved about that.

"But the rope holding your arms is below the branch. So the more you struggle, the lower your body can go, only to tighten the rope across your neck. So I would be still if I were you. You under- stand what I am saying?"

He nodded he understood.

"Good, not including the ones not here, how many of you are there?"

He said something that sounded like three. "You said three, right?"

He nodded.

"The other two asleep inside?" He nodded again.

"Good. We will be back. You be a good boy, do not kill yourself. Okay?"

I turned to walk toward the house because I couldn't look at him anymore. His eyes were watery and he had tears on his cheeks. But it was the people inside that worried me more.

"I just hope you did not hurt the children." As I passed Scorch, I grabbed the hackamore.

"Oh, don't grab me like that when you are angry."

Then the hackamore was yanked from my hand.

Scorch was right. I was angry, very angry. I had not realized how angry I was. I could rip that man's head off his shoulders, with the anger I felt. I took a deep breath to calm myself.

"I am sorry, Scorch, really I am." I reached up and laid my hand on the side of his face, then slid it from there to the base of his neck before giving him a strong hug. *"I guess we not only need to learn about each other but about ourselves as well."*

We started walking toward the house.

It was still very dark. We weScorch, whent along the side of the house toward the back. A faint light came from the window growing in strength, as if someone had lit a lantern. The window was low enough for me to peek inside. A woman, her cheek bruised, in a tattered dress stood there. She looked to be in good health otherwise. Picking up a pail and walked out of sight. I hurried to the back corner of the house. She was walking toward the well. When she started to lower the bucket into the well, I went to her. Watching the back door as I went.

In a whisper, I said, "I am here to help."

Startled, she let go of the bucket, and it hit the water hard.

"Damn you." she said as she turned to look at me. "Must all you thugs scare the life…" Her words halted when her eyes met mine.

"How many?" I ask.

She turned to the well and started cranking up the bucket. "Two inside and a third out here somewhere." "He is taken care of for now. Where do they sleep?"

"One by the front door and one by the kitchen door. He may be awake. I'm not sure."

A worried look crossed her face, and she glanced toward the back door.

"Make sure he is awake. Make some noise. Set the water bucket, so it falls if you bump the table. I do not care how, but get one of them to come outside alone. I will be waiting."

I turned and jogged back in to the dark shadows. *"Scorch, where are you? I need my bow."*

I no more got the last word out, then he was there facing opposite from where I left him putting my bow in reach. I pulled my bow from the sheath and pulled an arrow from the quiver. I heard the bucket hit the floor.

"Damn you, look what you have done," she said out loud.

I heard a man laugh. "Be quiet, woman, and clean this mess up!"

"Go get me some more water, please. That is the least you can do."

"Why should I? You dropped it, not me." They continued to argue as I strung my bow.

"You startled me and it fell. You did say you wanted biscuits this morning, did you not?"

"Okay, but it will be a few minutes, I need to go out."

Abon came to the corner of the house with daggers ready. I nocked the arrow to the string, and pulled some tension. From the darkened corner of the house, I watched for him to exit. He stepped out of the door and down the two steps on to the rock path with grass growing between the stones. Bow raised, my fingertips touched my cheek. I looked at the man's back. The arrow started to quiver. *Now or never*, I thought and I released. Holding my poise until impact was imminent. Upon impact, I dropped to my knees and threw up. *"Oh, forgive me, Tulkus, I just killed a man from behind."*

"You are only doing what needs to be done." I heard in my head. I realized it was Scorch.

I looked up to see Abon on the man's back. With the man's head pulled back by the hair in his left hand and pulling his dagger across the man's neck. The man's legs kicked only a few times. Abon got up and ran to the house's back wall and pressed his back against it. I looked to the door. No shadows in the light. I walked into the light from the door. I said to the woman inside, "Done. Go wake up the other. Tell him his friend fell out the door and is lying on the ground."

She hesitated. Just standing there looking at me. "Go." I moved away from the door. When I got to Abon, I told him, "I do not think I can shoot a man in the back again."

Scorch walked up to me. When I turned his direction, my quiver was in front of me.

"Take one" was all he said.

I pulled out one arrow, and he moved away.

After a few minutes, another man came out the door, big with wide shoulders and muscled arms. He wore his sword on his back. I drew back and my bow creaked audibly. He turned to look toward the sound and I released. The arrow flew straight. He tried to avoid being hit but was unsuccessful. Even as he leaped to the side, the arrow stuck out of his chest.

Abon was already in a run.

I yelled, "No!" as the man sat up. He broke the arrow a fist away from his chest.

"Is this yours?" he asked as Abon stopped well short of reaching the man, who was now getting to his feet. "You missed your target, little man. I can still live through this."

"That was mine," I said as he drew his sword. A nice bastard sword. As big as Father's or close enough. As hurt as he was, I hoped he would be lumbering that big sword.

I dropped my bow and drew my sword. *If I had a shield, he would not stand a chance,* I thought. Scorch walked to where I stood. The broken shield still hung from the saddle where I had left it. I pulled it off and Scorch moved off.

I slid my arm into the straps of the shield, which put the broken quarter to the top. I thought the man would laugh as he took one step back, trying to put me at a disadvantage with the light. He looked disappointed when I stepped into the light.

"Damn half breed," he muttered as he made his first move. I blocked it easily, watching him wince in pain when he moved. My defensive return swing hit him on his side. I drew back and stabbed him in the chest as he tried to wield his bastard sword around to strike again.

He stood there, looking at the sword sticking from his chest, two inches from the broken arrow. "I think you got it right this time."

I pulled my sword back as he dropped to his knees.

"I guess I did," I said as I stepped back. He reached out to grab me and fell on his face dead.

"You do well, Calarel. Perhaps you are the one I am to be with."

That wasn't what I was thinking, though.

I caught sight of the woman leave the doorway at a run. Using the man's shirt to wipe my blade clean, I headed for the door. The lantern was gone, but the light coming from the next room showed the way. I did not sheath my sword just in case it was needed.

"She has saved us, saved us all. These knots are too tight. Let me get a knife," I heard as I stepped into the doorway. She ran into me and threw her arms around me. Crying, she told me, "Thank you so much."

I moved forward, so Abon could get in past us. He cut the rope binding the man to the chair. He looked like he was going to fall over when the last rope was removed.

Abon told the children to bring the blankets and pillows for their father, and they did as he asked. "Go to your husband, he needs you. I will get the few herbs we have to help."

I felt as if I had done something wonderful. I guess I had.

"So this is what it feels like to be a hero," I thought to Scorch as I walked through the kitchen and out the back door. He was there waiting. "How fast can you—"

I cut my own sentence short. My foot was no more in the stirrup than we were at the pond.

"Your thoughts are faster than your words will ever be."

"Yes, I guess you are right. And you seem to be faster than my thoughts sometimes," I told him as I picked up my backpack. Looking over the other two horses, they appeared to be fine. I grabbed the saddle horn and started to pull myself up and the faint glow of the pond was gone. Any closer to the house's steps and I would have tripped over them.

As I stepped inside the kitchen, the woman was preparing food to eat.

"My name is Elayne, My husband's name is James, and the children are Ronald and Sara. I don't know how to thank you enough for saving us."

"My name is Calarel. Here are some herbs that may help speed your husband's recovery." I opened my backpack and pulled out the Arlan wrapped in a cloth.

She tended her husband and cooked us a good meal. I checked the livestock and found them all in good shape. Abon and I buried the dead men, not because they deserved it, but to prevent the stench from dead bodies coming and chasing us out. It was close to the midday meal when Abon went to get our other horses; when he came back, he told me the man tied to the tree had died. I felt bad because I had forgotten about him. After the midday meal, we drug his body into the woods and buried him and the other three. Then we gave Stricklin a proper burial.

Abon and I decided we would stay there for three more days. Just to be certain James recover. I went out to hunt and found a small deer, giving us enough food to last three or four days. James used parts from all three wagons to put together a good one for his family and belongings.

Abon and the children found the loot the thieves had stolen. He gave some to James for the inconveniences they had to endure, and I'm sure he kept some for himself, called it a finder's fee, I think.

Chapter 3

Six days later, we left, and three more days, we were riding into Cynar. Abon and I with our four horses followed by James in his wagon drawn by four horses along with the four tied behind drew many curious stares. As we rode past the four or five wooden shops per block, six blocks to the four span clearing to the twenty foot tall wall. Ten spans on both sides from the gate stood a thirty foot tall tower, twenty spans after that another thirty foot tall tower, the towers seemed to surround the city of Cynar.

At the gate large enough for two wagons to pass, we told the guards of the events. We told one guard how we acquired so many horses; he led us to the Constables Office. There we repeated the events as they happened. Of course, we did leave out the part about our new horses and the Gray. But other than that it was all truth, and nothing but truth.

We found an Inn that could take us all in. Elayne and James found a broker and moved in to a house a few days later. Abon and I found a few day labor jobs to earn some extra coin.

Everyone and everything was good in the world.

Cynar turned out to be a very big city. The market district went all the way around the castle in the middle of the city.

It is wide enough to drive a wagon on the top of it. It circles the city, except at the cliffs of the River Khind, which flows in to the Ulor Bay.

The bay is over half a league away from the docks of Cynar. At low tide, you could see the boats, or should I say ships waiting for the tide to make to the docks. The River Khind is wide and flows slowly, and I would say deep as well. The port was the busiest place in the city. I don't like going there much. The road down to the docks is steep and wide enough for the freight wagons to pass each other as they move back and forth between the warehouse district and docks.

Though Abon and I have been here only a little over a month, already people talk about us. Perhaps because of the company we keep or the deeds we have done. Cutpurses walk the streets. We have taken a few to the Constables already. The first one, a thin rail of a man, ran square into me. I stumbled out the door of a shop at the same time the thief grabbed someone's purse and started to run. Later, I received praise for catching a thief that had been running loose for some time.

Abon spotted the second thief; he pushed me into him as the thief made his break to get away. He returned his gaze to the front just in time to hit his face on the hilt of my sword hanging on my belt. I caught my balance and kept myself from crushing his chest under my big foot. The stolen purse flew from his hand as he grabbed my leg. Abon caught it and handed it back the lady from whom he stole it.

"Arrest him!" she demanded, pointing at the Halfling under my foot.

"We aren't Constables," Abon told her.

"You do well at serving the good of the people.

Bring him with you and follow me."

I picked him up, and he started thrashing about. "Do not make me tie you."

Abon produced some leather cord from his pocket. The woman led us to the nearest Constables office. We followed her inside, then stopped at the front desk.

"I am Lady Burtram. I want this man arrested for thievery." She pointed to the thief.

One of constables came to me and took him by the collar. I released the thief. "What is your part in this?"

"Abon and I caught him as he tried to get away with her purse."

The constable behind the desk started filling out a complaint form.

"Lady Burtram, Abon." He looked up from the paper to Abon. "What is your sir name, Abon?"

"Littlenight. Abon Littlenight, glad to help put a thief behind bars where he belongs."

"And your name, ma'am?" "Calarel Nessis."

"How can we contact you if we need to?" "At the Burtram Estate."

"Very well, Lady Burtram. Have a nice day." "Is there reward for turning in this criminal?" "I will check the files. It will take a few minutes."

Lady Burtram turned to face us. "Do you have employment?"

"No, ma'am. Not at this time, but we find odd jobs from time to time."

"Well, Calarel, was it? Abon?" She hardly paused enough for me to open my mouth to speak. "Consider yourselves employed."

The constable came back to the desk with a small pouch. As he sat back down in his chair, he reached across the desk and set the pouch down. "Six silver, Miss Burtram."

"That is Lady Burtram."

"Yes, ma'am. Have a pleasant day."

She took the reward from the table, then said, "Come along."

She dropped the small pouch of coin in my hand and headed for the door.

Abon spoke faster than I did, so I closed my mouth. "What kind of job do we have now. If I may ask?"

She stopped just short of the door. "Bodyguards." "I do not know anything about being a bodyguard." She stood in front of the door, as if waiting.

"You will learn."

"Abon, open the door for the lady."

He bounded to the front and opened the door. With the pouch in my pocket, I followed her out to the street, Abon right behind me. She led us to one of the richer parts of Cynar. I thought we looked out of place until I saw another lady who had a bodyguard with her. He was a large man in the shoulders, but his stomach said he was a lazy fat man. He did not look like he could run far if he had the need. His clothes were nice looking and clean. The woman wore a wide bottom dress that angled up to her slender waist, resembling a dinner bell used by a rich merchant. Abon tipped his hat to her. "Madam." And after a few more steps said, "Wow, she must be rich."

"Her family is rich. Not her. I see you both have a lot to learn."

"Yes, ma'am."

I dropped back a little more, for fear of stepping on her fancy wide dress.

We came to an intersection. Looking in both directions of the intersecting street, one side was obviously richer than the other. One side of the street had four houses to the block, very nice picket fences, some with archways at the gates. On the other side, each of the two houses per block had walls of stone and mortar with archways of stone. We turned down the street, and she stopped in front of the first gate in the stone archway.

I opened it for her and let Abon go in after her. I made sure the gate closed all the way. She left the stone walkway and headed to the side of the house. Two men sat at a table and both stood when they saw her. Together, they bowed to her at the same time.

"Mat, this is Calarel and Abon. They saved me from a horrible thug this afternoon. I may hire them as bodyguards if," she put too much emphasis on that if, "you think they can be trained."

"Yes, my lady. I'll see to it right away."

Mat was a common man; the top of his head maybe reached my chin. He was getting on in his years, over half his hair gone gray. His jacket had embroidery on the sleeves, and his pants tucked in high boots. The other man was a Highmen, much bigger build than Mat. He was little larger than me. I have not seen many Highmen here in Cynar. I am guessed him to be about middle aged, around one hundred eighty years at most. He wore a chain jerkin with no leather underneath except at the shoulders. A two-handed sword on his back and broadsword hung at his hip. He seemed at odds with the other man.

We watched as Lady Burtram continued to the house's back door.

Once she was out of hearing, Mat spoke, "Well, you saved her purse, I take it."

He looked both of us up and down. Abon nodded agreement.

"Good. Calarel?" he said, "Could you get us all another ale from that outbuilding over there?"

He grabbed his mug and drank down the last of it. The other man just picked up his mug and handed it to me.

"Okay" was less than what I wanted to say as I took the two mugs and headed for the outbuilding.

"So, Abon, you must have impressed her with some fancy sword work or something," the other man asked.

"Not me," was all I heard.

The outbuildings are barracks. Six beds with trunks at the foot end for belongings, a small table and chair to match each bed. Most had wash basins on them, some with paper and inkwells. A cask of ale stood on a large table by the front door. I set the two mugs down and grabbed two more, filled them all, then headed back out the door. I sat the mugs down and sat down before passing them out.

"Well, you're no barmaid," the second man said. "I have never tried to be. I am sure I would not do very well at that. A messenger, a guard for a merchant, but never a maid of any kind. I don't think I have the tolerance."

"My name is Hawk. Drink up, Calarel." He lifted his mug.

"Of course."

And I lifted mine. I only drank four swallows before he drank all of his. Tanned from the sun, the scar that ran from the right side of his forehead down across the bridge of his nose and halfway across his cheek disturbed me, but he seemed nice enough. We sat and talked for good part of the afternoon.

"Well, I guess now is a good time for a small test. Just to see what you know." Mat went to the barracks and brought out four practice swords. "That is if you're going to be bodyguards. But I don't really see you as a bodyguard." He looked at Abon with an amused expression. "You might be a messenger or that sort. But bodyguard? I have my doubts."

"He holds his own. He is like the surprise within the surprise," I told Mat. "We are kind of a team."

"Just practice. No need to try to kill each other. Hawk, you pair up with Calarel, I'll see what Abon is good at."

"Are you sure, Mat?" Hawk asked.

I took two swords from Mat when he passed them out and tossed one to Hawk. "Ready?" as I backed away from the table. I waited for one of those "Always keep an eye on an armed man slaps across the back lessons," but it didn't come. I backed five or six paces before I stopped and took a defensive stance.

Hawk stopped in a basic offense, and I changed my stance to a better suited one. "She knows what she's doing." He started with mild strikes, and the flow was easy for about five strikes. That is when I made my first offensive move.

"Good!" He increased the severity of his attack. I defended everything he tried. When I attacked, he would come at me stronger.

After about twenty minutes, Mat yelled, "Hold." That stopped both of us in mid-swing. We grounded the tips of our practice swords and scrubbed the sweat from our faces. "Is there any- thing left to those swords?"

"Damn, woman, you're pretty good with that.

Who taught you?"

"She practices every morning," Abon exclaimed. "My father taught me." Saying those words made me homesick. "I miss our workouts." I hoped that didn't sound as lonesome as it felt. "He was a soldier before I was born."

Hawk looked at me. "You are half Elf and I would say Highmen."

"Yes, my mother was High Elf and my father is Highmen. I lean more toward my Highmen side."

"What is your father's name?" "Locklin Nessis."

"Yes, I think I remember that name. It has been a long time since I last heard that name."

To meet someone that knew my father from before I was born is a surprise. I wonder if my father remembers Hawk.

Hawk and my father were here at the same time. Hawk works as a consultant for the military and part time trainer at the fort.

Abon and I moved into the barracks and trained very day. I had to go at Mat's slower pace. I did learn a few new moves and stances, but most I knew. According to Mat, I knew them well.

Over the next six months, Abon and I remained in the barracks with Mat and the others that sleep there. Since I was the only woman, we built a temporary wall so I would have my privacy. Some did not think I needed it until one night, I barely heard some- one say, "I'd knock first!" as the door swung open.

I had just dropped my night clothes down and in walked Samuel. He swung the door closed behind him. I told him to get out while reaching behind me to grab the water pitcher. But he kept coming. Once within my reach, I knocked the full pitcher against the side of his head so hard, water and pieces of the thick ceramic pitcher sailed across the room. Unfortunately for Samuel, I followed through with my swing. The handle left a nasty cut straight across his forehead and another across his chin under his lip. He spun onto my bed and just lay there. I thought I had killed him.

Mat came running and opened the door a little. "Calarel?" Trying to not see more than necessary, he peeked through the small opening. "Are you all right in there?"

"You okay? What's going on in there? Do you need me?" I heard in my head from Scorch.

"Yes, I am. But I may have killed him, the fool." I know I sounded worried. I was.

"I do not think there is enough room in here for you to pop in at the moment," I thought back to Scorch. I let Mat in along with Abon and two others.

They carried Samuel out after Mat assured me several times I didn't kill the man. Abon came back in, closing the door behind him. I plopped on the bed and tears ran down my cheeks. He pulled a small rag from my night stand and handed it to me.

I scrubbed my eyes dry.

"He might have hurt you. You had to either hit him or scream for us to get him away from you," Abon said. "You know that as truth. You are a woman, and I don't think that man has any respect in his bones. And he is worst when he has been drinking."

I smelled the drink on Samuel. "But does that give me the right to almost kill him?"

"Yes!" Abon started to say more but stopped when someone knocked on the door.

"May I come in?" a female voice asked.

"Yes, come in," I said. Abon grabbed my robe and handed it to me.

I stood to put it on and the High Lady Burtram came in. She cleared her throat as she entered.

Abon bowed, saying, "Good evening, High Lady Burtram. If you will allow, I will excuse myself." He straightened and edged his way to the door. "Sleep well, Calarel. Don't worry about the event. You did what was right."

Abon slid out the door faster than any grass snake I have ever seen.

I bowed deeper than necessary. "High Lady Burtram, I am honored by your presence. I am sorry for the mess. I keep my quarters clean under most circumstances."

I stood and started to use my robe to dry the only chair I had. She took hold of my arm before I could start wiping.

"Please sit down, Calarel." She sat on my wet bed and pulled me down to the bed with her. "Calarel, I am truly sorry something like this could happen within the grounds of this estate. I had no idea that you were sleeping in these quarters. I assumed you would be with the other females. When I heard you were attacked, I did not think it was in these quarters, until Sally stopped me and asked me to follow her. I will have your things moved for you. No need for you to worry about being attacked again."

I took a deep breath and interrupted her. "High Lady Burtram, I would rather stay here, with your permission, of course. I am more comfortable here. I have things in common with the men. Other than the obvious. That is why we created the wall."

She interrupted me, I let her of course. "My dear, you have nothing in common with these men. It is not safe in here for you."

"But I do have many things in common with these men. I was hired over six months ago as a bodyguard. That is what I am. A bodyguard. You yourself have entrusted your life to my skills. I have the trust of every man in these quarters, save one. I like my job. If reduced to a servant. I would have to leave my position."

"Oh my, I guess I did not make myself entirely understood, if I may finish what I am proposing. We might understand a little better."

"Yes, my lady, forgive me."

She turned to face me. "I think it would be better for you to sleep in the female quarters, but you would still be my bodyguard." She took my hand in hers and held it. "The talk done in these quarters is not really fit for a woman, unless they speak civil in your presence. I think you would rather converse with women rather than men. I have seen you chat- ting with a few of the maids. Besides, the gossip of this little incident could reach the streets. Neither you nor I would not like that much. I think it would be best."

"You almost make it sound like an order. If it is, I will try staying in the female quarters, but I would prefer to stay here. Do they have their own rooms in the female quarters? I have grown used to having my own room."

"No, they do not, I am sorry about that. It is also a barracks. If I must, then it is an order, if that is what it will take to get you to try staying there."

She stood up and smoothed the front of her dress and then tugged at its back. She noticed that the back of her dress was damp from sitting on my wet bed.

"Well, obviously you can't sleep here tonight on a wet bed. Gather some of your things for tonight at least. I will tell Margaret to expect you tonight," and she headed for the door.

I reached for the bell's cord and pulled it once.

It sounded on the other side of the door.

"High Lady Burtram in the house," Mat said loud enough so everyone could cover or whatever they needed to do before she walked out of my room. I listened for the scrambling noises to stop before I opened the door for her.

"I see you do have things worked out here. But I still insist on what we talked about," she said before leaving my room.

I stood in my doorway and watched her walk to the door leading into the yard. "It is not my fault the man cannot keep his head after he has drank too much."

My voice was louder than I intended. I turned back and closed the door harder than I should have, but it did not help my anger any. I undressed and put on the same clothes I had worn all day.

Someone knocked at my door. "Stay out, I am dressing," and continued. I packed clean clothes for the next day and personal items. I packed just enough to get me through the day and hoped I would not have to pack more. After donning my armor, I belted on my weapons belt, sheathed my sword, and hung my axe on my belt. With my backpack slung on my shoulder, I grabbed my shield. The blanket and the top sheet folded together and tucked them under my arm.

Remembering too late about the bell, I swung the door open. Thankfully, everyone was still dressed when I walked out. Abon jumped to his feet. Mat and two others were by the door, waiting for an invitation to come into the room.

"Are you leaving?" the three asked at the same time as I walked through. Abon hurried to grab his things.

"No, I am not leaving yet. But I have been ordered to sleep with the maids."

I walked past them. Abon stopped with a hand full, halfway from the foot locker to his backpack.

Mat followed me out the door. I saw him wave the others back. "Calarel, could you stop a moment, please."

I halted.

"I am sorry you to have to go stay with the maids. But maybe that is for the best. At least you will be with other women. You might fit in better there."

"I have no intention of fitting in there. I fit in where I was. Everything was good. We had every- thing worked out for the best of all of us."

I turned my back on him and stomped to the female quarters. I had to open the door with my leg as my hands were full. It slammed into the wall hard enough to make some noise. Two of the girls screamed and pulled their blankets to their chins.

Margaret, who was head mistress, stood and pointed to the door.

"OU—" she cut her word off so quickly, I thought she may have bitten her tongue doing it. "Oh, Calarel. It's you. We did not expect you so soon. Come in, come in. We have sheets and blanket for you, no need to bring more."

"I would like the bed in the corner. If it is available! I will help whoever needs to move, if that is necessary."

I walked the center of the room. It held twelve beds. The same as the men's quarters. But this was prettier, heavy curtains with sheers behind them. The beds that were not in use were nicely made and had soft-looking blankets. Pictures hung on the walls of family or nice scenery.

Margaret stood and said nothing.

Sally was lying in the bed I would have taken. She looked a little nervous. I laid my things down on the bed next to her.

"Good evening, Sally."

"Do you want to switch beds now, Calarel? I will if you want." Her words quivered.

I looked at her a moment and lost the edge of my temper. She looked as if she were ready to jump out the window if I commanded it. I looked over my shoulder at the rest of them. About half would have joined her, I think. It made me feel as if I were some kind of thug, the way I was acting.

"No, Sally, you do not need to switch beds or anything else. I do apologize for my behavior." I turned to face everyone else in the room and said, "Please forgive my rudeness. I apologize for being so harsh and…"

Mary said softly, "Being rude."

She slapped her hand over her mouth so fast it had to hurt a little, and her cheeks reddened a little.

"And yes, for being rude also," I finished.

Four of them gasped, as they never heard that word before. And the other five except Margaret chuckled. Margaret just smiled.

"Well, let's get you settled in, it is getting late.

And we do need to rise early."

I got myself settled in as Margaret called it rather quickly. I climbed in to the bed with my clothes on and started undressing.

"Surely you are not sleeping in your clothes," Sally said.

"No! Of course not. I am changing now." I dropped my pants to the floor from under the sheets.

"Are you saying no one has seen you undress, ever?" Her quiet laugh almost sounded childish.

"Other than my parents, when I was young and my sister, no one," I told her.

"There are no men in here. It is all right to dress and undress in the presence of other females, unless you have something to hide. How did you dress living in the men's quarters?" Sally asked.

Everyone else was quiet. Most lanterns were already dark.

"We built a wall and that was my room. If I needed to leave my room, I rang a bell so they would have time to cover or dress. I had a pot for the necessities, if needed."

"No wonder you were in a bad mood when you first came. I would have had a fit. They would have had to drag me out of there."

"I did like my privacy."

"If you two do not mind, the rest of us would like a little sleep," someone called out.

I had to slide out from under the sheets to turn the lantern's wick down, exposing half of my body. The sheets slid down from my shoulders to my waist. "Oh my!" Sally exclaimed a little louder than I liked.

"What is it?" Mary asked from across the room. "Calarel, you have some pretty defined muscles for a woman," Sally said.

In my hurry to slide back under the covers, I almost pulled the lantern off the wall, leaving it at a strange tilt.

"Oh stop. You're dreaming about that man at the market again," Mary said. "Go to sleep, Sally."

"My sister keeps telling me I am too tough to be female. If I ever fall in love, I would scare off the men." I made myself more comfortable in the bed. "I am what and who I am. I am a Fighter or Warrior, which ever you want to call me. A fighter cannot afford to be soft. My sister is soft looking like you are. But I have never been that way. I do not think I ever will be either."

"Well, now I know why you had your own room.

You look as strong as any of those men over there." "Good night, Sally," I said and turned over to the other side. *Maybe I am as strong as the men, but I like the way I am.*

I lay there for only a little while listening to the silence. Only one person had a soft snore. Not like in the men's quarters, where two snored softly and a third person snored loud enough to keep a forest awake all night. It was almost too quiet.

I awoke closer to two hours before sunrise. I got up, readied my clothes, and washed my face before the first person woke up. Not used to the noises of someone moving around so early. She only said, "Go back to sleep, it's too early." Then rolled over and went back to sleep.

Someone else called my name in a soft voice. I told them I was sorry.

I carried my things outside to finish dressing. I then donned my armor, buckled my weapons belt, and slung my cloak around me because the air was a little cool.

As I entered the sables, I heard Scorch. *"You seem to be in a better mood now."*

"Yes, I am. Thank you for noticing. I bet you would like an apple. And maybe go for a little ride too," I said out loud as I walked up to his stall. I opened the gate.

"You're changing your routine this morning. Why?"

"I just feel like going for a ride."

"We do that almost every morning after you exercise and practice. Why the change?" He sounded a little concerned. *"I can feel something of your emotions, it does not hurt as a wound does, and it is not an unhappy feeling, but sad nonetheless. What is the feeling?"*

"I just feel lonely. I miss my father and sister. I wish to see them. This will be a good test of your abilities, you have never been there before. I want to be there as quickly as possible."

I threw his blanket over him and led him out of the stall.

"Is there something wrong with your father or sister that gives you this feeling?"

I am sure my face showed puzzlement by the way he eyed me just before I grabbed his saddle.

"No. I do not think so. Let us hope not, but there could be." I lifted the saddle onto his back. "It is just that I miss them very much, that is all."

"And seeing them will make this feeling go away?"

"I am buckling. Yes, I think it will."

I heard a door open from the quarter's area at the back of the stables. Both Scorch and I looked that way. It was Jimmy the Stable Master. He held up a lantern trying to see who it was.

"Good morning to you, Jimmy," I said loud enough for him to hear.

"Miss Calarel? Are you going for a ride this early in the morning?"

"I did not mean to wake you. I am sorry. I will be back before nightfall, I think," I told him. "Go back to bed, it is still early." I started to slide the hackamore on Scorch. "You are such a good horse."

"Okay, are you sure you don't need anything?"

"Thank you. I am a good horse aren't I?"

"I am almost done. Thank you for asking, Jimmy."

He turned, went back in his quarters, and closed the door.

I finished buckling on the hackamore, led Scorch out of the stables, and looked around. But no one else was up yet. I climbed up onto the saddle.

"Okay, let us go."

He didn't move a muscle.

"I have no idea of where you want go to go. Picture the place in your mind."

I pictured the house I grew up in.

"Looks nice enough. But I need more than that to get there. It is like standing in the middle of a field and being told to find a blue rock. Expand the image to a bigger area."

"How about this?" I pictured the map hanging on the wall in the men's quarters. I focused on the dot that represented Valeria.

"That would be better if I was more familiar with the area. That must be farther south than I have been."

I pushed the image of the map back a little more to include Duintolea and the pond where we first met. "How about that?"

"Better."

We were standing in a field that had been plowed just a few days ago.

"Um, I think we might be in Johnson's field, maybe." I reined him to the south. "Close enough for a first try. You are good. I guess we can practice this some more. If I am right, we are only a little over half a mile from town. We go through town and are less than half a mile from home."

"A little more practice of you thinking of a place, and I'll put you within a few steps, if not closer."

We came to a wall grown over with vines. It was five feet in height. "Yep. This is Johnson's corn field. Down the road is Valeria. Let us go."

I felt him take a step, and we were on the road headed west. I let him set his own pace. It did not take long before we were in Valeria. The sun was still below the horizon. It seemed as if it was going to be good day.

Jeffery, a tall man, with rugged features who was the night constable stepped into the road that went straight through the town. He held up a hand to stop us.

"What is your hurry so early in the morning?" he called loud enough to be heard over the slight noise we made riding down the hard packed road.

We stopped. Then I edged Scorch closer. "Good morning, Jeffery. How have you been doing?"

"Calarel, is that really you? We heard you hired on with some big Lord in Cynar. What in the world are you doing here?"

That had to be the most Jeffery has ever said in one breath in his lifetime.

"Yes, it is really me, as you can see." Trying not to laugh. "I have come to visit Father."

"He didn't tell us you were coming."

I laughed a little. "He does not know that I am here either."

"I'd like to see his face when he sees you and this horse. He is what two or three hands bigger then Blackie?"

"Jeffery, with a memory like yours, you should be a banker or someone important like that."

He laughed a little. "I am. I'm the Night Constable. I can remember every bulletin of every thief that has been sent from Duintolea or Cynar. If I see 'em, then I can take 'em in for their crimes."

"Then I guess you do have an important job. Well, I will be on my way. Nice seeing you again, Jeffery. Have a good morning." I reined Scorch around him.

"You too, Calarel." I heard him say as I rode toward the road that goes north past Father's house. I turned up the road and rode another half a mile to the trail that led to Father's house.

Before we turned down the trail to the house, I told Scorch the dogs would most likely bark and make a fuss because they didn't know him. We rode to the house, and I even rode around it once just to make sure the dogs woke them up. I stopped by the back door, a little away from the house, but stayed in the saddle. The dogs' aggressive barking changed to a higher pitched bark because they were happy to see me. The roosters started crowing. I must have woke everything for miles.

Father stormed out of the house, wearing pants and a shirt, and with his sword in hand.

"What the heck is going on out here?"

The sun still low enough that the light did not touch my face.

"Not much. I just wanted to see you and Tamera."
"Calarel?"

Tamera, however, could see me as plain as I could see her as she came out the door.

I dismounted. My foot no more hit the ground, and she was hugging me from behind. I tried to turn and face her, but she was hugging me so tight, she turned with me.

"Hello, Tamera." I pried her arms from around my chest. "Hello, Father. I am so glad to see the two of you."

"You have been gone forever, it seems."

Tamera had tears running down her cheeks. I wiped them away and gave her another hug before Father came to us. I gave him a big hug.

"I take it the loneliness is cured." I heard in my head from Scorch.

"Yes, it is. Father, I would like you to meet Scorch."

"Scorch, try not to be too difficult, please?"

Father walked completely around Scorch, looking. Ran his hand from just behind the saddle to Scorch's hindquarter and halfway down the leg. Father grabbed the ankle and Scorch looked at me. I nodded agreement, and he picked up his leg.

"Nice," Father said. He let Scorch put his hoof back down. "Same bow, I see."

"Yes, the same one. I use it for hunting deer. I surprise the cooks some mornings."

He came around the front and examined Scorch's teeth and everything else.

"He must have cost you a fortune. I can't find a mark on him. No brand has touched him either. You know the dangers of that, girl."

"Yes, I do. But I do not think that is something I need to worry about. Speaking of horses." I stepped closer to Scorch and mounted up. "I will be right back in five minutes." I reined Scorch around. "Finish get- ting dressed." I urged Scorch to a run. "Can you now get us back here?"

"I can, now that I have been here. That would be no problem."

We turned toward the town at the end of the drive.

I looked back at the house. I couldn't see them, so Tamera couldn't see me. "Back to the stables in

Cynar, Scorch. I need to get something, and I guess I had better make sure they know I am coming back tonight."

Thankfully, no one was in the stables. I dismounted.

"I do wish you would give me a little warning."

"You said to come here. I did. What more warning do you need?" Scorch replied, almost sounding as if he were laughing.

"Guess I did. I will have to watch that. But do me a favor and do not do that around people who do not know your little tricks. Okay?"

"I will try to remember that."

If a horse knows how to laugh, he surely was laughing as I jogged across the side yard to the female quarters. I stopped before entering to slow my breathing a bit. I opened the door slowly and peered inside to see if anyone was awake yet. Most of them were.

"Ah good, Margaret, you're awake. I believe I am taking the day off today. I should be back before dinner. If not, I will be back shortly after. I need to move the rest of my things," I spoke as I walked towards where I had my few things, saddlebags in particular. I grabbed them, slung them over my shoulder, and headed back toward the door.

"I would hope you have nothing to do today,"

Margaret replied

"Nothing that I have been told of, Margaret. I do not believe that Lady Burtram is going out. We retrieved everything yesterday she wanted." I walked up to her. "She did not say that she needed me today, she does usually tell me the day before if she knows.

So today, I would most likely spend sitting in the court yard, waiting for nothing to happen."

"Very well. Have a good day. But remember to come back. She does seem to like you best for some reason."

"Yes, she does. I think it is because I am quiet," I told her, as I headed out the door.

As soon as the door was closed, I ran for the stables. Scorch came out of the stables before I got there. Once in the saddle, I spun him around and, not seeing anyone, said "Go" Then we were back on the path to Father's house.

"You were getting nervous, so I came out. Jimmy was just opening the door to his room when I turned the corner. I don't think he saw me leaving."

"I hope no one saw us leave like that."

I dismounted and took him to the area we tied horses that we showed, removed the saddle, put it on the saddle stand, and unhooked the reins.

"Could you pretend you are on a lead? Please?"

"I will pretend it is a long one. This grass is a little short," he replied while laughing again.

"I did not know horses could laugh," I thought as I turned to the house.

"Of course we can. And you owe me a good brushing. You haven't brushed me yet this morning."

"Yes, I will brush you real good tonight when we get back to Cynar," I spoke aloud walking back- ward toward the house.

When I turned, Father was standing halfway between me and the house.

"Oh please, tell me you did not hear that," I said, almost pleading.

"I heard. Come on in, so we can have first meal. You can tell us everything that is going on. I hope."

We walked inside to find Tamera mixing ingredients for first meal. I set my saddlebags on the table, opened one side, and pulled out a pouch. I shook it a little to make sure it was the right one.

"Here, Father, this is yours." "What is this for?"

"It is the money from the sale of Blackie. A friend arranged the sale for me. I sold him to a good man. Hawk trusts the man, so I figured Blackie would be in good hands."

The mention of Hawk's name sparked another conversation, and Father set the pouch aside. But he would come back to it later. It was like old times, bacon sizzling on the grill, flapjacks on the iron. We were all so busy talking that Father forgot to do his morning chores.

Around midmorning, a man knocked at the door inquiring about a plow horse. We sold him one Father had bought just two weeks earlier.

Close to lunch, people started coming to the house to welcome me back. They brought food to share. By the time the sun had passed the midpoint of its travel across the sky, most of the people that knew us were at the house. Even shy Jerrold, who used to want to court me. But I don't think he does anymore. He brought a very nice-looking young lady with him. I told them all about the great city of Cynar. Most had not been farther than halfway to Duintolea much less to Cynar. I told them of the people, their dress, customs, and anything else they wanted to know.

It was getting close to dinner when I told every- one I would have to leave soon.

"It is a long journey back to Cynar."

"Don't be foolish, girl, start in the morning," one person said.

"Yes, well, this foolish girl would like to spend a little time alone with her family. I am not trying to be rude, just visit with family. I do thank all of you for coming. It was great to see you all again. It will be dark soon, and I would hate to think you had to ride home in the dark because I did not have the sense to send you home before then."

They started saying their goodbyes and good nights and filtered out the door. Except Marley, he waited until everyone else was gone.

"Good night, Marley. It was nice seeing you again."

Marley was a man who was used to getting what he wanted. "I want to buy that horse out there." He always was straightforward. "The big black one."

"He is not for sale." Straight and to the point, I told him just as he would have.

"That has to be the best animal you have, Locklin. How much you want for him?" He completely ignored me and looked at Father.

"He's not mine, Marley," Father said. "That one belongs to Calarel."

We stared at one another until he broke the look, turned, and left. I was glad he did.

Tamera, Father, and I sat in the living room and talked for a while longer. The sun was its own height from touching the horizon when I started to leave.

"I really need to go. I hate to leave but I must." "I don't think you can make it to Cynar by morning even if your horse could teleport that many times in a night. Miss Connelly says it is very hard to do," Tamera told me.

"I told you that I am not sure it is really teleporting. But he can do it. Just remember not to tell anyone he can do it, whatever it is. I need to go."

As we walked toward the stables. I could see something lying on the ground by the fence.

"It is Marley," I said loudly as I walked toward the man lying on the ground.

"*Scorch, did you see what happened to the man lying on the ground?*"

"*Yes, I did. He got in the way of my hoofs.*"

"*I think you need to tell me a little more than that, Scorch.*"

"*He tried to take me from here. I know what a lead is for. His horse is around front. He was on his horse and tried hooking a lead to my hackamore. I bit his horse, and it ran to the front. As I walked away, something stung me on my hindquarters. That's when I kicked. Not my fault he was there.*"

"Sorry I should have watched him when he left. But I did not think he was that desperate to have you."

"Looks like he was going to try and steal Scorch," I said aloud.

"He surely wouldn't do that!" Father said in response.

"He must have. Look his lead is lying on the ground." I reached to pick it up.

"You sure it's his, Calarel?"

"One way to find out," I said as I dropped the lead in his lap. I reached down and shook his shoulder. He groaned a bit, so I shook him some more.

"Stand aside."

I stepped back and Father poured a bucket of water on Marley.

He woke up gasping for air and coughing. "Damn you horse. Wait until…"

He suddenly realized what happened and saw us standing around him.

"Marley, answer me truthfully. Did you try to take my horse? You know I know the truth already, so do not lie to me."

He started to stand, but couldn't, so eased himself back down. "I think my ribs are broken."

"You're lucky I haven't strung you up by your neck yet." Father stood with his fists clenched.

"Damn it, may the deities have pity on me. I just have to have that horse. He would save my ranch. I could get forty gold or better once I trained him to be a Warhorse." Marley sounded as if taking a breath caused pain.

"I hope you learn it is not worth the trouble of trying to steal. You have a good ranch, Marley. Work it the way you use to and you will do well. From what I saw before I left, you are beginning to become lazy."

Marley took another painful breath. "It's too late for that. I have gambled it away. I've gotten lazy as you say, and a fine horse like that would save me." "No, Marley, he would not save you or your ranch. Only you can do that. I have to go. I will not press charges, this time." I walked over to Scorch's saddle. "We need to go, Scorch."

And he came to me avoiding Marley.

"Are you sure, Calarel?" Father looked at me. "Yes, he will be sore for months as it is. I can

only hope he learns from this. If I find out different, then he and I will talk again. But he will not like it at all."

I saddled Scorch and, after I gave Father and Tamera a big hug, climbed into the saddle. After final goodbyes, I went down the drive. I looked back and the only one that could see was Tamera.

"Outside the city, in the meadow of flowers, we should not be seen just appearing out of nowhere." And we were there, a short distance from the road. Trotting toward the road, and then toward the city of Cynar. We strolled down the streets toward the Burtram Manor.

Someone rode up beside us, it was Hawk. "Where in the world have you been, girl?"

"Girl?" was all I said, as I rode on.

"Well, I heard what happened. Everybody is worried about you."

"I went to visit fam—" *That's too far,* I thought. "Friends. It helps to talk to friends that you are not living with. You know."

"No, not really. I live alone." He looked sad for a moment, a small moment at that. "No one lives out that way. Nothing for a mile or two."

"Well, I went for a ride. It is nice out that way. Almost reminds me of home."

It was the only thing I could think of that quick. "So how long have you been practicing magic?"

You would think the word *magic* left a bad taste in his mouth.

I chuckled a little. "I do not know any magic. My sister is studying magic, not me. I told you Miss Connelly says I do not have a speck in me, but yet Tamera does. She says that is the way it falls sometime." "Yes, I remember you telling everyone that. But explain how tracks start in the middle of a meadow," he asked.

"Ah, stepping from a large flat rock or something like that I guess. I have seen where deer tracks have done that. Or seem to disappear at a creek bed, but several paces up or down the stream you find them again," I said to him as if it were a game or something. "Not in this case. It was a meadow of green grass and small Pixiecups for a hundred spans all around where the tracks started," he replied.

"That doesn't sound right. There would have to be tracks somewhere leading to the start. That sounds like a puzzle worth looking into."

"That's what I'm trying to do. But you're not helping any. Let's hope others don't start checking into this puzzle you have presented to me. Someday I will find the answer, Calarel."

"Did you sense anyone close to where we popped in at, Scorch?"

"I didn't really pay attention. I thought we would be safe there."

"Well, I hope you do, Hawk," then I thought, You most likely will. That thought made me nervous. I wonder if he really did back track my trail. He sure sounded like he did. And his horse looked as if it had run hard.

"No one saw you leave this morning. Jimmy said he saw you very early this morning. You were saddling your horse. Then at daybreak, he saw what he thought was your horse leaving the stables by himself. He said your horse headed off the usual trail in to the grass."

We were in the warehouse district, not many people walking around, only those who were still working, carts or wheelbarrows and a few wagons, those last-minute deliveries.

Not much to watch for, but the crack of timber gave a small amount of warning. But not nearly enough, the gate of the wagon in front of us broke. The bottom cask big enough to hold fifty gallons of fluid hit the ground, the one that rested on top of that one hit the back of the wagon. Hawks horse reared. The second cask rolled from the wagon and hit the first, adding speed to it. Heading straight for Hawk and his horse, the other cask wobbled in my direction. "Look out!" Scorch knew what I meant. He swung his head into Hawk's horse. It felt as if the world shifted. The cask that would have broken both of Hawk's horse's legs rolled past Scorch and me by a mere foot.

Hawk gained control of his horse quickly.

A man behind us jumped out of the way just in time. His cart was hit by the barrel. His cart and goods were damaged. People came running to help. Some asked if we were okay.

"Yes, I think we got very lucky this time," I replied to them.

"Aye, ye did me, lady. I not be sure what I saw, but that did be luck sure as the sun float in the sky this day," the man replied as he started moving away to help the others.

"Let's move on!" Hawk said a little gruffly. He started away from the area. I followed. Not a word was said, except by Scorch.

"I guess I should not have done that." He sounded a little embarrassed. I know I felt that way, a little anyway.

"No, Scorch, you did what was needed. I'm glad you did. I guess I thought we could keep your abilities a secret forever. I'm not sure how I would do that, but I was trying."

We came to a house with a white picket fence. It didn't have a gate to close on the way to the stables around back behind the two -story house. It looked out of place with its fancy woodwork on the gables.

All painted white with blue trim around the windows and doors. The stables were painted the same. The chicken coop, the fence around the garden all white washed. We turned down between the picket fence and the stone wall that surrounded the neighboring house. A picket fence runs just this side of the stone wall, same on the other side of the front yard. It was all so out of place here. It belonged out beyond the walls of the city. Most homes were stone, only the framework of the roofs would have been wood, other than door and window frames. We rode to the stables. Before Hawk was all the way off his horse, a middle-aged man came out of the stables.

"Jamir, unsaddle Jasper and brush him down good for me. I guess that's all I have for you today. Have a good night," Hawk said to the dark-skinned man. He had a limp that gave him an odd stride to his walk. "If you have everything done, go ahead and enjoy tomorrow with your wife." He placed some- thing in the other man's hand.

Jamir never looked in his hand. Whatever Hawk put in it went straight into his pants pocket. I could have put both of my legs into one pant leg of those pants, had to be enough material to make two pair of pants out them.

"Aye, Master Hawk, I have but one thing to tend, I do it first thing sun rise. And then be gone for the day. If that be good for you, Master Hawk."

"That will be fine, Jamir," Hawk told him. "Calarel, come inside for an ale."

I hesitated a little but dismounted from the saddle. "No need to unsaddle him. I cannot stay long." I handed Jamir the reins to Scorch.

Jamir did the same slight bow to me as he did to Hawk. "Aye, me lady," and headed for the stables.

I turned and followed Hawk into the house.

The inside was just as plain as the outside, or would that be ornate, I couldn't make up my mind. There was a woman in the kitchen, the smell of food cooking was fairly strong, even though I wasn't the least bit hungry, my stomach rumbled anyway. I followed him into the front parlor. Two long benches with medium height backs, cushioned from one end to the other. One almost long enough for me to lie down and stretch out on. Both gilded nicely and a chair that Hawk sat in, they all matched together nicely. A matched pair of bookcases, one on each side of the front door. And a weapons rack, which was empty except for the sword and dagger he had just put there. I sat on the edge of one of the sofas.

The woman came in from the kitchen carrying one ale she handed to Hawk and one wine she handed to me.

"Will you be staying for dinner, ma'am?" she asked as she handed me the wine.

"Ah. No, I do not believe so. I need to get back soon," I told her. She almost looked relieved to hear that.

"Thank you, Mary. I'll eat in twenty minutes, if that is good?" he asked more than told.

"That will be good, Sir." She curtsied and left the room.

"Okay! How in the name of the deities did you do that at the incident at the barrels? No beating around the bush either," he demanded.

"You will not believe me." I tried to think of some elaborate story, but could not come up with anything. "I…I cannot tell you much. I do not know much either. But Scorch has some…" I paused, "abilities."

"What do you mean abilities?" he asked quickly. "You mean your horse can use magic."

"We, Scorch and I are bonded. I am not sure of how to explain it. But you have heard of twins that feel what the other feels or they both say the same thing at the same time mostly." He nodded slightly. "That is as close as I can come to what bonding is."

"You're telling me that your horse let you stick it with your dagger and suck its blood!" he said with a disgusted voice.

"On my life, NO!" I almost shouted back at him. "I'll tell you. But you must not tell others, please. Promise me. You will not tell a soul."

"Girl, I've been around a long time. I don't think you can tell me anything I haven't heard before," he said half-bragging. "I wouldn't tell anyone what is said to me in confidence."

"Then what I am about to tell is of utmost confidence."

His smile started to fade a little.

"Then I will tell no one." He sounded serious enough.

I told him how the three of us were attacked, myself, Abon, and Stricklin, who is no longer with us. I told of how we just happened on the pond where the horses were. How we became bonded. And why I agreed to bond to Scorch. How Scorch said there was a purpose to our meeting when we did. To start a friendship that we would both depend on before the purpose of our meeting started to unfold.

"What is that purpose? Do you know?" Hawk asked, breaking in on what I was saying.

"I don't really know for sure. But for now, I think it is to help those that need it. I mean to get prepared for that much, anyway."

"Well, with that said. I think I might know someone who could use your talents."

"Who would that be?"

"I found this a few weeks ago on one of the bulletin boards." He took a few sheets of paper from the small table that held his mug of ale. He thumbed through them and pulled one sheet out of the small stack in his hand. He started to hand it to me and stopped. "Honestly. Where were you today?" He held that paper out of my reach, waiting for an answer.

"Honestly, I don't think I should tell you that. But I was about one half mile north of Valeria, at my father's house. He says hello, by the way."

"For some reason," his eyebrows went up, as he nodded slightly, "I believe you. I don't know why, but I do." He handed me the paper. "You think about that a little bit. I think it could be something of what you are looking for. At least, you will not get bored there. You will here, sooner or later." He stood, at least as big as Father. Maybe a little bigger. "Well, my dinner should be about done by now."

He didn't give me a chance to look at the paper he handed to me. I stood and followed him to the door we came in. He opened it.

"You have a good night, Calarel. I don't need to know what you decide. I'll find out soon enough, either way. Think about it. Take your time in deciding, but not too long mind you," he said as he guided me out the door.

As I walked to the stables, *"I'm not real sure I understand what just happened in there, Calarel.* I hope you can explain it to me."

Scorch was still saddled and Jamir was nowhere to be seen.

I climbed up into the saddle and headed out to the street. *"I think I understand that he is one smart man. And he knows how to get the truth."*

We went back to Lord Burtram's estate. As I rode into the stables and was greeted by Jimmy. "Good evening, Calarel. Hope you had a good ride? You have been in high demand today. It would seem that you are a busy person. At least more than I thought you were."

"What do you mean, Jimmy? I know Hawk was looking for me."

I stopped preparing to unsaddle Scorch and looked at him, waiting for him to go on.

"Well, besides him, at least two others stopped to speak with you. One man, who said, you had helped him once. Said he was here to return the favor. A man with his wife, they wanted you to have something. They didn't leave the package. Both said they would return at a later time." He seemed to be relieved that he could tell me about the inquiries. "And Lord Burtram inquired about where you were as well as both the High Lady and Lady Burtram. Hawk was here two times. I can't count the number of times people peeked into the stables to see if your horse was here."

I reached to unbuckle the girth strap. "I told Margaret I would be gone until supper. I did not have anything to do today. I did not think I would be missed that much."

I pulled the saddle from Scorch's back. As I turned toward the saddle horses, I saw Lord Burtram coming into the sables. Jimmy bowed deeply, more than I thought need be, this was his domain.

"Good evening, Jimmy. Why is she unsaddling her own horse? Those are your duties, I believe. At least that is why you were hired, to tend the horses and other animals."

Jimmy stood straight. "Yes, my lord."

"I tend my own horse, Lord Burtram. I always have and always will. The more you tend to your horse, the more respect and alliance you and your horse have. My horse takes me where I want to go faster than I can walk. So I do as much for him as I can."

I did bow to him after I put the saddle down. It looked out of place with all the other saddles. Scorch's saddle had a high pommel and cantle both.

It was almost plain compared to some of the others that were there. I walked back over to Scorch to get the saddle blanket.

"Miss Calarel!" Lord Burtram said, demanding my attention. "Are you happy with your position here?" I reached the saddle blanket with one hand, not really looking, and searched for the middle while answering. "Yes, my lord, I believe I am happy." *For now anyway.*

"I find it hard for a person like you to be happy working for a lord, Miss Calarel," he said with a little bit of a concerned look on his face. I think he had to try for that look. Maybe even practiced it sometimes. He never shows too much expression, that I have seen. "I have a small task for you. Finish up here, have dinner, if there is anything left. Then you and Abon join me for an after dinner drink, if you don't mind." He tried to take the command sound out of it.

But it didn't work very well.

"Yes, my lord," both Jimmy and I said in unison. After Lord Burtram was far enough away not to hear, I told Jimmy to go ahead and get his dinner. I would be there in a few minutes. He did after a little hesitation. I brushed Scorch down quickly and told him I would be back to finish, well, do a better job of brushing him anyway and went to the dining hall.

When I walked in, both of the tables were half full. Most of the hired help were there. Only two others were missing.

"There you are!" exclaimed two people, Mat one of them.

"When you decide to disappear, you do a good job of it, don't you?" Margaret added.

"Yes, ma'am, I do." I smiled at her. "Only about a half a plate please. I am still fairly full from lunch." "Must have been a big party, where did you go for that?" Alicia emphasized the last part.

"Just to visit friends." She sat my plate down in front of me, the perfect excuse not to have to talk.

After I finished eating, I told Abon that Lord Burtram wanted to see us after dinner. He started to look a little nervous. Of course, everyone's goading didn't help any. I almost had to herd him into the main house. By the time we walked halfway across the kitchen area, one of the maids stood and said, "This way please," and led us through the dining room and down a hall to sliding doors, where she stopped. She slid open one door a little after knocking and being acknowledged. "Miss Calarel and Mister Abon are here to see you."

"Bring them in" was all we could hear from the other side of the door. She opened the doors wide enough for us to file through into the room.

Inside the office, Lord Burtram sat behind a large desk, nicely gilded. Only a few things on the desktop. A figurine of two people with arms around each other, it almost looked transparent. A stone pen set held sand for drying the ink on the paper and the ink bottle. Which he was just tapping the cork tightly in to. Hawk was sitting in one of the chairs to the side. Wearing the most formal clothes I have seen him in since I met the man. Most times, he sat relaxed, but now, he was rigid. Beside him sat a female High Elf if I ever saw one. She looked to be at least as tall as I am. She looked to be a very graceful person even sitting down in a chair. Lord Burtram stood after we came in and stopped beside the maid. She curtseyed and Abon and I bowed. She asked if that would be all. Hawk asked for another ale. The lord asked for one also. The lady only said, "No, thank you." Her voice was soft and flowing. The maid looked at the two of us, and we both said "No thank you" in unison.

"Calarel, Abon, you already know Hawk." Without giving us time to reply. "This is Miss Lotithil. Please have a seat."

He indicated two chairs across from Miss Lotithil and Hawk. The chairs were set to allow you to see the others without having to strain your neck, if someone were long winded.

"Thank you, my lord." I had to remove my weapons belt to sit in the chair. I laid it on the floor beside the chair as quietly as I could. "Sorry," I said when metal and buckles settled to the wood floor, and I tried not to make any more noise.

"Are you two happy working for me?" Lord Jeffery Burtram asked looking at me, then Abon.

"Oh yes, sir, my lord!" Abon said quickly.

"Yes, my lord. This is the best employment I have had," I told him.

"Glad to hear that. But I believe that you might be becoming a little bored with your present duties." "Calarel, how many different positions have you

held besides working for Jeffery?" Miss Lotithil asked.

"Three."

"And they were what?"

"Messenger or runner, all three times, my lady." I almost felt regretful. They weren't really jobs per se.

"How long did they last?"

"Only a day or two each, we did not know the city very well then. We had only been here a few days."

She cut me off with a motion of her hand. There was a knock at the door.

"Yes," Jeffery said loud enough to be heard, but no more than that. The door slid open far enough for the maid to come through with a tray. She passed out the drinks to Hawk and Jeffery. Which left two, which she handed to Abon and me.

I said, "Thank you," and so did Abon. She backed to the door, curtseyed, and closed the door.

Hawk spoke up for the first time. "I see why you like your jobs here, now. First real jobs away from home for both of you. And the two of you, there were three at one point, have had a taste of how cruel the world can be on your way here." I gave him a stern look. "You lost a friend to cutthroats, and you rescued a family from them. I know one of you have helped that family a few times since you have been here. You told the guards where to find the hideout. It's hard to believe that you left so much behind."

"What do you mean by that?" Abon asked. "The guards found fifteen gold, two horses, and

other things, that even I would have taken."

"It was not ours to take. We are not thieves or cutthroats," I replied angrily.

"That is good to know, Calarel. But there are times that taking from the dead will not hurt any- one," Jeffery said.

"Perhaps, if the need outweighs the want, you may be correct," Lady Lotithil said. "Are either of you inclined in the arts?"

Abon spoke up first, I closed my mouth. "I can draw pretty good, but only at times."

"I think she means the magical arts," I said softly. "No, neither of us is. My sister is studying."

"My guess is that both of you have at least experienced magic a little. Correct?" she asked. "Are you both good at what you have been trained for?" She looked at Abon eye to eye. "Gifted to do?"

"Calarel is quite talented in weaponry, knows how to use most weapons enough to survive if she has the need. She knows the weapons she has more than a lot of common men do. Most I have taught know less than she does by far. Abon hides his talent well," Hawk replied.

With a smirk on his face, Abon's comment sounded a little disappointed, "Thank you, I think." which was said softly. I don't think he really wanted to say anything.

"Why are you asking these types of questions?" I asked.

I was hoping Lady Lotithil would answer, but it was Jeffery who spoke first. "At times, Miss Lotithil has need of people she can trust that have certain abilities. Such as subterfuge"—he was looking at

Abon for that part and then to me—"fighters, magic users. And so on."

"This brings us to the point of my visit this evening. I am in need of two people that can deliver something for me. It is something of high value and of some importance in my cause. I would deliver it myself but do not have time for the trip," Miss Lotithil told us.

"But we were hired to be bodyguards for Lady Burtram. How can we work for her and you?" Abon asked.

"Your jobs will still be here when you return, Abon. As far as anyone will know, you are under my employment, even if you decide to do this task for Miss Lotithil. Understand!" Lord Burtram stated. He was the most animated I have ever seen him at that point.

"Yes, my lord," Abon and I chimed at the same time.

Miss Lotithil explained, "I do not foresee any problems with this exchange that you will do. But it would be best to keep a sharp eye. I do not com- pletely trust the woman you are to meet. Therefore, I have set a meeting of two others that will be present for the exchange, when you arrive at your destina- tion. You will send for the other two people that will witness the exchange. When they are present, you will send for Sara. Both items will be placed no closer than two feet of each other. They will be examined by the other two to make sure they are what they are supposed to be. I trust them. If they say it is the item that it is supposed to be, then you may take it Calarel. Then bring it back here."

"Are you sure you want it brought here and not your place of study?" Lord Burtram asked.

"At this point in time, I think it best for them to come here. If they are followed, it will be much easier for them to lose any followers in a large city. The two of you should think on this for a short time. If you could come back in twenty minutes to let me know your answer, I would appreciate it."

"Yes, my lady," I replied as I got up and grabbed my weapons belt. Abon followed right behind me. Once out in the hall and the doors were closed.

"Abon, go to Mat and find out what he knows of Miss Lotithil. I would like to know a little about her. She seems to hold too many of the cards. I will go see Margaret. We can meet at the back door in fifteen minutes."

"That's not much time," he said as we walked through the house. "We will not have time to find out much."

"I know it, but we need to try," I said as we went out the back door. "Fifteen minutes!"

We both headed to the places they might be this time of the night.

It took me five minutes to find Margaret; she said she did not know her. I was already at the back door when Abon came back to meet me. I looked around to see if anyone was there to hear or see us talk. No one was walking round in the court yard.

"Well, find out anything?"

"No one seems to know her. She didn't even ride a horse. Her and Hawk walked here," he said, a little disgusted at not finding anything out.

"Then I guess that means we go by gut feelings.

I trust her. What about you?" I asked

"If you do, so do I. But there is something about this I don't think I like. But I'm not sure of what it is," Abon replied as he opened the door.

When we entered the room once again Abon spoke first, "We have decided to take the job you offer." He paused long enough for Lord Burtram and Miss Lotithil to take a breath to begin speaking and continued, "As long as we may have our present job back when we return."

"I have already told you that your jobs would be waiting here for you, Abon," Lord Burtram replied.

"I would like to know what it is we will be carrying and what we are to bring back," I asked. "And how many people would know it's whereabouts now?"

Miss Lotithil leaned over the side of her chair and pulled a gilded leather satchel into her lap. She pulled a figurine carved from stone; it looked old. She set it on the arm of the chair delicately.

"This is what you will take to Sara in Spurrie. In return, you will receive one identical to this one. Only difference is the clear sphere is held in the right hand and one sphere that matches the color of the sky lays at her feet," she said, looking at the hand- tall figurine dressed in flowing robes. The figurine looked to be studying the sphere, as if seeing something in it. "Remember this. No man can touch it and live, same with the other."

Abon's breath caught, and I just had to ask, "Why is that?"

"It is the essence of the magic in them," she replied. "That is all you need to know for now. The other has the same traits as this one and a few others all to its own. I have need of those traits to continue my research." She pulled a small coin purse out of the satchel and tossed it Abon. "How much is in there?" she asked him.

"Six or seven, I would say, no more than seven if that." As he tossed it up in the air a little, it hit his hand again. "Six gold." His eyes betrayed his thoughts.

She tossed a second purse to him.

"Seven, eight." He tossed the second purse up as he did the first. "Five silver and three gold. I would say." As he weighed the purses as if a scale.

"Very good at weights and measure, Abon. That could be good to know in the future. May I have those back. Please. I will compensate you rooms and meals. Get receipts for them." She pulled another pouch from her dress pocket, opened it, and pulled out some coins. As Abon handed her the two coin purses, she handed the coins to Abon. "Two for you and two for Calarel. That should get you there and back, I believe."

Abon looked and said, "Silver! This would get us there and back at least a time or two. When do you want us to leave for this Spurrie place?"

"Tomorrow will be a good time, I believe. Remember, only a female can touch this or the other." She replied to Abon, "I don't foresee any problems unless Sara decides to become greedy."

"Does this Sara use magic?" I questioned.

"She does, but limited to utilitarian uses only, I believe. Both of these help her with that. The other has uses that she cannot use. That is why we are swapping, and I am also giving her a little incentive to do the trade."

She wrapped the figurine back up and placed it in the satchel, then pulled yet another coin purse from the satchel.

"You will give her this when you have the other figurine safely in your hands. But not before then." She gave me a rather stern look, and then continued, "After the dealings are done, give Tomas and Jerral two gold each. And make sure you thank them for me, please."

"Of course, my lady, we will do this task as you ask. I think the two of us should begin preparing for the journey. We will leave right after first meal tomorrow," I said as I stood.

"You will need to come see me before you can leave. I will keep the satchel in my safe until then. And I have a request of you also. I will tell you of it in the morning. Until morning, I bid you a good night," Lord Burtram retorted.

Abon and I both bowed and left the room after telling everyone good night.

"Well, the pay is damn good," Abon said after we had exited the house. He handed me two silver. "I hope this is as easy as she makes it sound," he said laughingly.

"I would not count on that, Abon," I told him as we crossed the court yard. "But we could hope for the best."

Chapter 4

We went to our quarters. I began to prepare for the trip. I was asked by at least two people where I was going or if I had quit my job. I told them I was to run a message for Lord Burtram. And we would be back in about two weeks. That sounded odd to them, but he is a lord, so no one pressed for more. After I had most everything packed, I went to the stables to check Scorch's gear.

I checked the gear for Stormy as well. Everything was ready. I brushed Scorch and told him of the journey. He said he was ready to travel. He was feeling weary of doing nothing. He said Stormy was too. I went to bed around my normal time.

I awoke at my usual time, about an hour before sunrise. Everyone else in the female quarters was still sleeping soundly. I dressed and donned my armor. Buckled on my weapons belt and headed outside to the practice area. And started my exercises.

"*Good morning, Calarel. How was your night?*" I heard in my head.

"*Good morning, Scorch. I slept well, thank you. How was your night?*"

"*It was good. I think I should tell you that the Elf you call Lotithil came out here last night.*"

"*What is wrong with that? Maybe she likes horses,*" I thought and stopped my exercises. I was beginning to feel a little nervous. "*Did she do anything wrong?*"

"*Well, not really. She does have abilities of the mind.*"

"*What do you mean the abilities of the mind?*" "*She was inside my mind, like you are. But it did not last. Was there in the deep parts that you cannot touch as I cannot touch you there."*

"How much does she know?"

"I am sure she knows more than I do about myself and as much as I know about you. I don't know that any of that knowledge will hurt us or perhaps help her. But both she and the one called Hawk know we can, she called it teleport. Stormy was afraid it might change our abilities somehow, so she left. The elf told me that our secrets were safe with her. Said she would not tell a soul. I believe her."

"I would have come to stop it, if you would have called me."

"Yes, I know you would have. But it was done before you could have arrived. And no damage is done."

"But it does mean someone else knows of your abilities. I am not sure I like that." I started doing my morning routine again.

"I agree with you, but what is done is done. Have a good work out. I'll see you in a little while."

I finished my work out. Went to the stables to give Scorch his apple, like any other morning. Brushed him down, checked his tack, and cleaned the saddle blanket. I waxed Scorch's saddle, saddle- bags, hackamore, and reins.

"Oh, stop it!" I told myself out loud, just as Abon came into the stables.

"Stop what?" he asked as Jimmy came out of his quarters at the back of the stables.

"Good morning to you both. About time for breakfast, I think."

"Yes, I agree. I need to stop worrying about the tack and go eat some breakfast." I followed Jimmy to the mess hall. Abon joined us of course. We had a good breakfast and lingered there for a while.

"I hope this is a good time to meet with Lord Burtram" I finally said.

Abon only nodded and headed toward the office we met in last night. When we got there, the doors were closed as always. I knocked and waited for an answer.

I was about to knock again.

"You're a little early, I think," Lord Burtram said from behind us.

"Yes, we maybe, but it is a long road, my lord."

"Good answer, Calarel. I do hope that Miss Lotithil does not steal you from my employ," he said

almost regretfully.

Abon turned toward him. "I don't think you have to worry about that, my lord."

"Good! Then let's get you two started on the road, shall we."

He opened the door and gestured for us to go in ahead of him. He went to a picture on the wall and pulled one side of it away from the wall to reveal a safe made of metal. Heavy hinges riveted to the front door. A strong looking lock held it closed. He used a key to unlock it and pulled the satchel out of it. He closed the safe and sat down behind his desk. He started to stick his hand into the satchel.

"Stop!" I said a little louder then I really wanted to. Abon said "Don't" almost as loud.

Lord Burtram froze with his hand half into the satchel. Then removed it slowly.

"Yes. You're right. I had forgotten about that little part of it." He relaxed. "Well, I guess that you should remove the contents to make sure it is all there, Calarel."

"Is there a reason it would not be?"

"Let's just say, this is done for peace of mind. Yours and mine." "Okay."

I laid the satchel down in front of me and removed the figurine, unwrapped it and stood it on the table, pulled out the three coin purses. We checked each, the two black ones had two gold each and one brown one to give to Sara, and it had a small piece of paper and two gold. And a note that she did not mention last night, I left that in the satchel. I would check that later.

"That is all that is in here. Just as she said there would be," and started putting everything back the way it was.

"Good." He opened the top drawer of his desk and handed me a letter that had a wax seal with his signet in the wax. "While you are in Spurrie, could you deliver this to Lord Tharon? He is the Governor of Spurrie."

"Of course, my lord." Abon almost hit his head on the table as he bowed.

"Two tasks in one trip, we will see it is done as soon as possible, my Lord."

"Good. You may even tend to this before the other. Depending upon what time you arrive, of course," Lord Bertram suggested. "Well, I will not keep you any longer. You have a long journey. Five to six days depending on the weather and how fast you travel. May the deities keep watch over you."

"Thank you, my lord, may they watch over this house while we are gone and keep it safe."

I bowed, then turned to leave, Abon followed suit and we both walked out of the room. We gathered our things, and we saddled our horses. I think almost everyone came out to say goodbye to us as we lead our horses out of the stables.

"We'll be back in about two weeks," we told them. We climbed into the saddles and started to leave. Sally was standing outside the gate. "Calarel,

will you walk with me just a little bit please?" "Abon, meet me at James and Elaine's house

please. I will be there shortly." I dismounted and began walking with Sally.

"Okay. See you there in a little bit." He rode on. "What's the matter, Sally? I will be back in about two weeks."

"I know that. But I had a dream of sorts. Not really a dream, but kind of one."

I was a little confused, but said, "I have dreams like that, they feel real in a way. But they are just dreams."

"Right! But most of the time, the dreams that I have like the one last night." She looked around to see if anyone was nearby, then continued, "They come true."

"Okay, what happens in your dream?" I looked around also.

"You are unconscious in a cell, like a cell in a dungeon. A female says, 'Good, now we have both, that will make him happy. One more and the conjuring circle can be completed.' That's all I could hear in the dream."

"Can you see what? What the woman is talking about?"

"Yes. They looked like little dolls or something, each holding a little ball in opposite hands. At least something close to that."

I hope the expression on my face did not change.

I think I may need to work on that.

"I will keep a sharp eye for any dolls. I do not think we need to worry about it. You will have to tell me more about these dreams you have. Maybe you might want to keep these dreams to yourself. I will tell you about anything I see like that when I get back."

"I wouldn't tell a soul that it did not affect, but it affects you. That's the only reason I even said any- thing about it. Please be careful, Calarel."

"I will. I will see you in about two weeks." I stopped to climb back into the saddle.

She said my name and I turned to face her and she gave me hug. I hugged her back.

"Go back and get to work, Sally, before they miss you." I turned and mounted up onto the saddle. "I will be back I promise." I reined Scorch to go.

As I arrived at James and Elaine's house, Abon was just dismounting. James was walking to the gate at the front of the yard. "Mount back up, Abon. We need to go."

"But you only just got here, Calarel. Please come in, the children would love to see you both," James said, almost demanding.

"I would love to, but we have work to do. I only wanted to let you know we would be gone for a couple of weeks," I told him as Abon climbed back up into the saddle and settled in to it.

"Where are you two going?"

"We are headed to Spurrie to deliver a message for Lord Bertram."

"A long ride, I hope I get used to the saddle again." James laughed a little. "You will, have a safe trip.

The deities watch over you. And hurry back. We will have a grand dinner when you get back."

Abon turned in the saddle to look back. "Sounds good to me."

We started our journey and rode out of town. About a mile or so away, I told Abon what Sally had told me. At least, I wasn't the only one who had to work on holding their expression from showing. He looked more nervous than I felt.

We rode until almost nightfall. We found a good place to stop for the night. We set up camp. I tended the horses and our gear. Abon set up the tents. And I started a fire, mostly for light and little else.

I checked with Scorch to find out if anyone or anything was near that he could tell, one of his abilities. He sensed nothing near. I opened that satchel and pulled out the letters, the one from Miss Lotithil, sealed with wax. The one from Lord Bertram, sealed with wax. And the third, "To the Carrier," written on it.

"Where did you get that from?" "It was in there this morning."

"But you didn't show it to Lord Bertram when you showed everything else."

"No, I didn't. It is addressed to us not him." I unfolded it and started to read it aloud. "'To the Carrier,' that would be you and me. 'So far, you have done well. I did not know your name when I wrote this. But you know who I am and I know you. I will meet you before you reach Spurrie. We will need to talk more about what you have been hired to do.'"

"That is interesting, kind of," Abon said in the silence that followed.

"That makes me wonder what she is up to. At this point." I took a deep breath and let it out again before continuing, "It would seem that we have been woven into a web. Are we the flies or the spiders?"

"I don't know. But I don't think I'm going to like it either way."

We had our dinner, sat around doing much of nothing. I read from the book I was reading from Lord Burtram's library that I had borrowed *Tales of a Navigator*. "Can you imagine ships floating on the clouds? I find that hard to believe."

"It's only a book, Calarel. That could never happen. I'm going to sleep," he said in the middle of a yawn.

It was a peaceful night. Morning came. I was up and had done my exercises. I gave Scorch his apple and brushed him before Abon woke up. I think Stormy woke him up wanting her apple too.

We had some breakfast, packed up, and were on the road again. It was nice to be out of the big city. I like it much better out in the country. We rode all day. Abon spotted a good place to camp, so we did. In the morning, we were traveling again. About two hours after the sun had reached its highest point in the sky, Scorch stopped cold in his tracks. So did Stormy.

"Is something wrong?"

"Why did you stop like that?" Abon said, looking at the back of Stormy's head, then at me. Then back again.

"There was a magic used by the creators. I have only felt it that one time, when we were brought here," Scorch told me. *"It was strong, almost as if right in front of me. There is someone ahead of us."*

I looked as far as I could see and couldn't see anything. Abon was looking ahead of us as well. "I do not see anything. But be ready for anything. Keep moving." As we started out again, I pulled my bow and a string to string my bow.

Abon watched me. "Never happen." Shaking his head in disbelieve, than stopped as the bow creaked and the string snapped into place. "Well, I've never seen that done before."

Ahead of us was a person standing in the road. I grabbed an arrow from the quiver and set it to the string and pulled only enough tension to keep the arrow in place with one finger of my left hand, while I eased my sword with my right.

"If they prepare to cast again, let me know so I can stick an arrow in them first," I told Scorch.

"It is a woman standing on the road. Miss Lotithil, I bet," I said to Abon.

"Could be, I guess. You can see farther than I can." "Yes, it is her," I said as I reseated my sword and then put the arrow back into the quiver. I am sure she saw the arrow go back into the quiver, a little before we stopped in front of her.

"Good afternoon, Calarel, Abon. Travel going well, I hope."

We both gave her a small bow, more like a nod from our horses. "Yes, Miss Lotithil, it has been."

"I hope he did not see the note I left for you." "Not when I was present. I do not believe he did. When he pulled the satchel out of his safe, he was going to show us that everything was there until we reminded him of the figurine. He pulled his hand out empty. So I showed everything that was in there except for your note." Abon nodded in agreement.

"Good. I had hoped you would not let him know it was there. Why don't you two dismount and walk with me?" she asked.

We dismounted. I laid the reins across the saddle, so they would not fall and trip up Scorch. Abon did the same. We walked up beside her.

"I asked both of you if you know of magic. You both said you did. That will be tested shortly. I also discovered that your horses are very special." I started to say something about that, but she forestalled me. "I know they can understand what I say through you two, or at the least Scorch can. So please do as I ask." "We will try our best. Please do not try to use magic on my horse again. Too many people are starting to wonder about him already."

I didn't really mean to sound as stern as I did.

But I meant what I said.

"I have no reason to use magic on your horses, now that I know about them. I know more about them, then you will ever know and maybe more then they themselves. I am going to create a gate. It will open further down the road, about an hour ride, for a normal horse. I want your horses to travel at a nor- mal pace. Do not let them port to you. Their tracks are important."

"*Scorch, do you and Stormy understand what she wants you to do?*"

"*Yes, we understand. But I for one don't want to be away from you in the way she would like,*" he replied.

"*If I need you, you will be able to get to us fast enough, that, I am sure of. And I guess your tracks may be of some importance.* She seems to be a fairly smart person," I told him.

Miss Lotithil turned around, did a few motions with her arms, and said a few things in a language I did not understand. I turned to watch.

"The magic of the creators," I heard in my head.

"She is strong with it too."

"What type of magic is that?" I asked.

As a small bluish-colored dot formed about five feet above the middle of the road, she moved her arms as if to spread it. It became a line of bluish light. The light became thicker and divided making a long rectangle. You could see through it and passed it at the same time. The road beyond us curved to the right. The road through the light curved to the left. I could see the road an hour ahead of where we stood. The opening grew until it was ten feet across and ten feet tall. A large square outlined by a bluish light.

"It is Arcane magic. The most useful and the hardest to learn. Follow me please. Do not touch the light or you might not survive." She started walking through the opening.

We followed as closely as we could. I looked at the line of light as we walked through, it was hair thin. I was hardly able to see it until I was on the other side. Then it was the same width as before, about a finger thick. It started to shrink. It flattened to a line. Then shrank into the dot again and was gone.

"I can still sense you, Scorch, but you seem far away. It makes me feel a little uncomfortable. Begin walking down the road. No short cuts, mind you," I thought to him. Then I said, "That has got to be the strangest feeling I have ever felt."

"I agree with that," Abon said quietly.

"Must be the greatest distance you have had from your friends since you have been together. This is only about a mile. You should be able to feel them in Duintolea if we were there. Let's get down to business." She walked off the road to a spot along a stone wall and took a seat on the wall. I followed her to the wall but remained standing. "Let me see the satchel please."

I hesitated a little, thinking about the letter from Lord Bertram. I handed it to her anyway, then crossed my arms.

She opened it and pulled out the two sealed letters and the letter to us. "You will not need this any longer," and put her letter to us in her pocket. "This you will still need to give this one to Sara. She will be surprised that you showed up." She put it back into the satchel. "Now, to find out if what I believe is true." She looked as if concentrating. Then murmured something and the wax seal fell from the paper into her other hand. She opened the letter and began reading. "I had hoped I would be wrong. They do work together. That is unfortunate."

"What is wrong with working together? I always found that to be a good thing," Abon stated.

"As you and I would think of working together for the betterment of the living beings on this world, there are those who think the opposite. We work for a peaceful existence in the light. But there are those who would foolishly rather have the evil and dark- ness rule."

I uncrossed my arms. "Are you saying that Lord Bertram is working to make the world an evil place? I never thought of him as a bad person. How could you say that?"

"Read this and see what you think. Remember, you do not know what the powers of the two figurines are. Nor do you have any idea of what they represent."

She handed the letter to me.

I opened the letter and began reading aloud.

Lord Tharon, allow me to introduce myself as we have yet to meet in person. I believe that will be remedied soon. I am Lord Bertram of Bertram Estates in Cynar. I send this with hope that you see the urgency of our actions. The woman that stands before you is Calarel. The Halfling is Abon. They carry and guard the Angelica of the Light figurine, which can only be touched by a female. They are to meet a woman there in Spurrie by the name of Sara Doltman. In Sara's possession should be the Angelica of the Dawn. The two figurines will be tested to make sure each is the true item. Have Calarel watched, two people will test the items. If Calarel makes the trade, the items are real. If so, have Sara arrested after the meeting. That will give you one of them. The other will be brought back to me by Calarel. If the trade does not take place, Sara will surely have the other in her possession, hidden somewhere. You will need to find it. What happens to Sara after her arrest is of no concern. Her usefulness will have ended.

Signed and Sealed
Lord Bertram of Bertram Estates

"Does he mean to have this Sara killed or something?"

"I guess that is up to the interpretation that Lord Tharon puts to what he reads. But my guess is yes. If Lord Bertram has the two of these figurines and the third of the set comes into his possession, then they can be used to summon demons of the night."

"What do you mean demons? How can you summon demons?" Abon's voice quivered.

"The third figurine is called Angelica of the Night. That figurine holds no small orbs in its hands, but touches the other two when placed correctly. The three together produce the power to summon a demon once a day while they are together. And after every ten days, the demons that are summoned are half again as strong as the previous. But that is more than you need to know at this time."

"And we would have helped in this. Not know- ing what we were doing. But that leaves Angelica Dark, or whatever its name is, with someone else that may or may not know what they have. Where is that one at?"

"The Angelica of the Dark figurine is safe where no mannish race can get to it," she replied confidently. "Does it need to be a mannish race to make it work?" I questioned.

"No. Anyone. Even beasts could activate the summoning. But they would need the intelligence to place the figurines correctly. The magic is within the figurines. That is why you will continue with the trade as if you know nothing of that I have told you. Of course, you will not deliver that letter."

She put her hand out as if asking me to give it to her.

I handed it to her. She murmured something and threw the paper into the air toward the road. It burst into flames and was consumed long before the ashes hit the ground. I stepped back away from the ashes as they drifted toward me on the light breeze. I stood there looking down at the ashes. After a moment, I asked, "What will happen when Lord Tharon does not come to Cynar with the figurine Lord Bertram is expecting him to have? He will know then that we did not give the letter to him. What will he do to us? Have us killed?"

"I do not think he will be around long after you return with an imitation of what he needs," she said.

Abon cut into the conversation almost before she finished speaking.

"So you're saying he intends to steal the figurine that we are getting for you. How does he plan to do that?"

"That I do not know! Perhaps he intends to intercept you on the way back. He may wait until you return and try to buy it from me, although unlikely." "So we are to make this trade for you. Overt this Sara woman from being harmed and getting attacked ourselves. Most likely on our way back to Cynar. I do not think I want any part of this anymore!" I started to step toward the road.

"Wait! Before you call your horse to you, listen to what I have to say." She paused, waiting to see if our horses appeared. "If that was what I planned, I would not have met you here today. On your way back, spend the night at the Red Feather Inn that is in Rime. There is where I will meet you. You will tell the innkeeper who you are. Tell him you are to meet me. In the morning, we will have breakfast together. Do not leave until I have talked with you." She looked at the both of us. "Can you follow this easy enough?"

"Yes," Abon said, and I only nodded agreement. "Good!" she stood from sitting on the wall. "Then I will see you in seven or eight days. Have a

good journey."

She took two steps away from the wall, murmured something, and vanished.

"Dang it. Where did she go?" Abon asked.

At the same time, I heard in my head. *"I felt magic. Is everything okay?"*

"I do not know, Abon."

"Yes, Scorch, everything is fine."

"I have no idea."

"Yes. Stormy. I wish she wouldn't do that." "This is getting a little strange." I looked at

Abon. "What do you think?"

I looked back down the road hoping Scorch would come into view soon. Wondering how much longer before our two horses would arrive.

"We are just around the bend. She is a very powerful being. With the ability to use Arcane magic, why would she want you to do such an easy task? She should be able to Gate to Spurrie, get the item, and Gate back in an hour, maybe less."

"Why did I not think of that?"

"Why didn't you think of what, Calarel?"

I turned to face him. "She uses arcane magic. She could gate to Spurrie. Trade or take the other figurine she wants and be back in her house in an hour or less."

"I hadn't thought of that either."

Scorch and Stormy came around the bend in the road. I never thought I would be so glad to see a horse, as I was to see Scorch.

When they came to where we were, we mounted up and rode to the town of Lugard. We arrived in time for dinner. Maybe thirty or so people lived in the town. We had passed some farms with all types of crops, from beans to squash. Cattle, sheep, pigs, and goats all close to the town.

The town was on the road that we have traveled for the past two days, it went straight through the town. There were only a few buildings on the main road. One had a sign hanging out above the street that read the Wayward Pine Inn.

"There is the Wayward Pine Inn, Abon. We can stay the night on a bed."

"Sounds good to me."

As we rode up to the inn and started to dismount, a young boy came running around the corner. "Are you gentlemen going to stay the night? If so, I—" His cheeks turned a little red when I stepped toward the porch and became more visible to him. "Oops, I'm sorry, my lady. I didn't mean anything wrong."

I laughed a little, mostly because he was so red. "No harm done. What is your name?"

"Paul."

"I think we need to go inside and see if there are any rooms available first."

"We have rooms available. You could even get a private room if you want."

"How would you know that?"

"Cause my father is the owner, err, innkeeper," he said the last part as if just remembering it.

"Well, in that case, I guess you can help me, in a minute." I untied Abon's bedroll and saddlebags and handed them to him "Get us private rooms, Abon. They seem to be available. And see about baths too."

Abon looked at Paul.

"Yes we have two of them. You can have baths too. And we have a library too."

"You are a wealth of knowledge, aren't you?" Paul looked at him. "I hope so."

I handed Stormy's reins to Paul. "You take Stormy and I will take Scorch. Lead on, Paul."

He stepped down from the porch and almost stumbled. "Wow, these are big horses. I bet they are close to sixteen hands. Most are only fourteen or fif- teen hands."

"You are pretty close, Paul. Stormy is fifteen and Scorch is sixteen hands. You know your horses," I told him as we walked between the buildings toward the back and the stables.

"What breed are they? I don't think I have ever seen horses like them before."

"Ah, they are Greater Warhorses. These two are from across the oceans somewhere."

I could not think of anything else.

"You have been across the oceans? You must be ri— wealthy. Wealthy, I mean."

"No, I have never been across the oceans."

The stables were larger than I expected. Twelve stalls, all good sized, big enough for the horses to be able to turn around in. A work bench by the front, tools for repairing leather goods. Gardening tools stood in corner behind the door. A small flatbed wagon backed in at the back of the stables and a rather nice-looking carriage in front of that.

Paul took Stormy to the second stall. "You can use the first stall for your horse if you like, my lady." "Thank you, Paul. Call me Calarel. I am no lady by far." I walked Scorch into the stall. I took off the hackamore and hung it on the front of the stall. "I will tend our horses, Paul. The saddles are very heavy."

He must have been standing on something. He was tall enough the grip the saddle and strained to left it, but couldn't get it high enough to pull it off.

"Ya, these are heavy," he said, easing the saddle back down on to Stormy's back. "Maybe I'll get some fresh feed."

He took off running toward the back of the stables.

I finished unsaddling Stormy and took off her hackamore. Then I finished unsaddling Scorch. I still hadn't seen Paul. I walked to the back of the stables. I heard sniffling behind the door of the storage room. I opened the door and said, "Paul, are you okay?"

He wiped his eyes on his sleeve and said, "Yes, my lady, I'm fine. I caught my finger in the door."

"Let me see." He reluctantly put his hand back for me to look at, nothing wrong with his hand or fingers. "Did you feel ashamed of yourself because you could not unsaddle Stormy?"

"Yes, my lady. I am sorry I couldn't do it for you. I wanted to help you, that's my job. My da says I have to do it." He was trying to hold back the tears.

I sat down on a bale of hay and turned him to face me. "Paul, there will be times that you cannot do everything you want. It is not anything to be this sad about, there were times when I could not do everything my father wanted me to do. Like putting a saddle on a horse. My father sells horses. I learned how to train horses, it is not that easy."

"But Da will get mad at me when you tell him I couldn't unsaddle your horse."

"Why would I tell him that?"

"People always tell him when I do not do something the way they think I should."

"Well, not everyone is the same. I even said the saddles were heavy, right?"

"Yes, my lady. You did say that."

"Come on. Let us see what kind of brushes you have. I will show you the kind Scorch likes best." I got up.

We walked out of the storage area, and he led the way to where he kept the grooming supplies. He had two good brushes, I pointed to the one that was like the one I had.

"This is like mine. He seems to like it. Brush them both real good for me. Make sure they both have plenty of water and feed. I will check back later to see how well you did. Okay."

"Yes, my—" he stopped himself, then continued, "Yes, Calarel. Thank you for being nice."

"You are welcome, Paul," I said to him as I carried my backpack, bedroll, and saddlebags out of the stables.

I walked into the inn through the back door. Stairs lead up to my left, a hallway ahead of me lead to the common room. Ten feet from the door was another door, through the open door, I could see a large kitchen. Two women were busy at work cooking and cleaning. Must be the cleanest kitchen I have ever seen. I walked into the common room. It was larger than you would think by the looks of the building from the outside. A long bar almost the length of the room on one side of the room, two long tables extended from the front wall, left of the door. Nine smaller tables all arranged in neat rows of three. There were three semi-private dining areas along the wall across from the bar. Abon was sitting at a table drinking an ale by himself. There were a few other people in the inn, eating and drinking, some laughing, and talking. I walked over to Abon and sat down at the table with Abon.

"Well, did you get the rooms?"

"Ya, I got the rooms. Yours is the first room on the right, I'm in the room next to yours. I was talking to the innkeeper. He claims the next inn is in Spurrie. Says there is not another place along the way there." A musician came in after we had eaten. She played a harp and a flute and sang some songs. Some of them I knew, but most were different than what I knew. She had a nice voice for the songs and played the instruments very well. The service from Elayne was very good also. She did not keep our mugs full. It did not seem as if the innkeeper or the maids rushed about filling mugs unless that is what you wanted. I guess to keep you from getting drunk and causing trouble. I was thankful. Abon headed up to his room almost about the time I normally would.

After a good night's sleep, I over slept a little myself. I went out back and did my exercise and worked out with the sword. I finished my work out. Then went to the stables and gave Scorch his apple and brushed him down. He told me the young man did a very good job of brushing him and Stormy the evening before.

"Good, I will be sure to give him a little extra tip when we leave."

I went inside and woke up Abon. I gathered my things and went down to the common room. Abon came down shortly after I took a seat at one of the tables. We ate a good first meal. The serving maid commented about how early we were up. I told her, "It is a long road to Spurrie."

Next thing we knew, she brings us out a bundle wrapped in cloth, saying, "Here are a couple of sandwiches of roast lamb. Make sure you eat them before the day is out."

We thanked her, I left a tip on the table. I paid our tab to the innkeeper and asked him to give a tip to Elayne and Paul. I went out to the stables and began to saddle our horses. Paul helped as much as he could. "If you come back this way, please stop here. I like your horses. I did not know Greater Warhorses were nice."

"Okay, Paul, we will try to do that if we can. Oh, I just remembered something," I said to him and pulled a bronze piece out of my coin purse and handed it to him. "Shh, this is between you and me. Okay!"

His face lit up, and the smile he got on his face, I thought it was going to go to the back of his head. About the time I had Stormy saddled up, Scorch was already to go. Abon came out with his things.

"Just in time," I told him.

I lashed his things to the back of his saddle. We walked the horses out to the road. Mounted up and headed down the road to the east.

The next two days were good traveling. We rode into the town called Rime. We found the Red Feather Inn. It looked like a good place to stay for the night. "Welcome to the Red Feather Inn. My name is Junior and I'll be taking care of your horses will you stay with us."

"I guess that means there are rooms available." "Yes, sir. Just go inside and my father, Fred Al-Vere,

will help you with rooms, baths, and of course, meals." I dismounted and untied Abon's belongings from the saddle. Abon went inside with his things to get rooms for us. I handed Stormy's reins to Junior and led Scorch around to the stables. Junior and I talked while we tended to the horses. He agreed to brush both horses, and we agreed on the fee for the services. I took my things inside through the back door of the inn. Down the hall to the common room and found Abon sitting at the tables in the corner. "Good evening, we have ham or mutton. Both come with corn and beans. We include a half loaf of bread."

"Abon, which are you going to have? I think I will try the mutton."

"Then I'll have the ham and could I get an ale with that too?"

"An ale sounds good, I would like one as well." "Yes, ma'am, I'll have your meals out as soon as I can."

The meals were good and the beds soft com- pared to the ground. In the morning, we had first meal, paid for the rooms, baths, and stabling. And on the road again.

The weather stayed warm, with occasional clouds. On the third day, about midday, the winds shifted and blew from the north. The clouds started to become thick and gray. The temperature started to drop and became cooler, almost cold. You could almost smell the rain.

"Let's step it up a little, might beat the rain to Spurrie, if we're lucky," Abon suggested.

Scorch looked to the north and perked his ears. *"Thunder."*

"I think I agree with you. We need to step it up a bit," I said.

Before too long, we were at a run. We could see the wall of rain racing us to the town.

"I can see the town, but I think we will get wet," I hollered loudly to be heard.

Trees along the road blurred for just a second, Scorch and Stormy slowed to a trot. The town was much closer.

We had enough time to get to the stables. Abon went across the road to the inn to get rooms and see if the two that were to check the figurines were there. I tended the horses.

"These have got to be the worst stables I have ever seen," I told Scorch. I found some fresh water for Stormy and Scorch and replaced the feed that was in the stalls with some that at least looked fresher. Two people worked at the other end of the stables. The stables were long enough to have at least three wagons with the teams hitched to them. One wagon had no horses hitched up. The other did. I broke one of the saddle horses when I slung Stormy's saddle onto it and had to use a different one.

"Sorry about the saddle horse," I hollered out to the men working at taking things from one wagon and putting it in the other. One man only waved acknowledgment. I gathered my things and headed across the road to the inn.

Inside the inn looked much better than the stables. Floors of hardwood were clean, the few tables that were empty were clean. Six men at one of the larger tables with benches all had the same emblem on their vest or coat. I stopped at their table.

"Do all your employ and wagons have the emblem on them?" I asked no one in particular.

"Ya! Why you askin'?" one man in a vest questioned. "It would seem to me that you have a lot of people for one wagon." I paused for a second in thought. "But if the other wagon is not yours, then why would those two men be taking things from your wagon?"

I thought they were going to knock me over in the rush to get out the door.

One man stayed seated. "I do hope you are not some prankster, lady. I don't think they will take lightly to a joke like this."

He looked as if he was ready to try and stop me if I ran.

I adjusted my things on my shoulders. "If I am wrong, then I offer my sincerest apologies. But I find it odd that one of your wagons has a crest and the other not. If you will excuse me, I wish to unburden myself." I walked toward where Abon sat.

As I came closer to Abon, he nodded toward two gentlemen sitting at a booth along the far wall. Two children stood at the end of the table, both laughing at whatever was going on at the table. A man stood back a pace or so behind them. Intent on watching as well, a woman sat at a table not far away with a toddler, trying to tend to the child and watch the other things going on in the common room. I took a seat at the table Abon was at.

"Which room is mine?" I asked Abon.

"You have the second door to the left. I'm in the next room. This is a rest stop for the freight companies, mainly. Is what Martha said. And some are trying to work some mine a little ways up the road." "I'm going to guess that those two," I looked in

the direction of the two at the booth still entertaining the children, "are the ones we are to meet."

"I believe they are. They have not asked about anyone. Martha says they arrived midafternoon.

They didn't get rooms or anything. Just asked for some snacks and Mead Tea," Abon said.

"Then only one way to find out," I said to him as I got up. There were mostly families and a few other people in the room. No one looked to be a thief, but I took the satchel with me anyway. I walked over to the booth where the two men in robes were sitting. They both looked to be concentrating on the little figures walking around on the table top. The figures were no more than a hand tall, one male and one female. The men were talking for the little figures. The children laughed at whatever the man said that was playing the female part as I leaned against the end of the portion of the booth. He looked up that me.

"Good evening, ma'am." His figure flickered out of existence and back again.

"Continue. Please," I said with a smile.

"No. You can stop. Our dinner is coming now. Come along, John, Mary. I am sure that they would like to eat as well as anyone else."

The one little figure waved goodbye to the children and vanished.

Sighs of disbelief as the father herded them to their table.

"The female figure reminded me of some- thing I have seen before," I said to the man that was talking for the female illusion on the table that was no longer there.

"Really!" the other man declared.

"Yes! The dress is about the same, but she held her right arm out and in her hand she had a small ball of glass," I told him.

The older of the two slid to the end of the seat.

I stepped back. He got up from the seat.

"My name is Tomas and this is Garal." Garal nodded, and Tomas sat down beside him. I took the seat Tomas had. "May we see this figurine you are talking about?"

"I was told that a woman named Sara Doltan would be here as well," I told him.

"She is." He reached behind him and tapped on the wall. And a woman stood from the seat of the next booth from the other side of the wall.

I stood up. "If you do not mind?" I motioned her to sit to the inside. "My sword is a little trouble when sitting on a bench," I explained.

"I understand. But I would never wear one myself," she replied.

"Well, Sara Lotithil, let us get this done," I said. Just to see where it would take me as I sat down again. "I am not Miss Lotithil, nor would I try to pretend to be her," she said as she started to try and push me out.

"It is okay, Miss Doltan. I just want to be sure we are the right people," I told her sternly. "If you have the item, please place it on the table."

She reached down in front of the seat and pulled up the figurine, still wrapped in a cloth tied with a cord.

Garal reached out to the figurine. "Let us see what we have here."

I drew a breath with a gasp. "No."

The word came out of my mouth faster and louder then I wanted by far. Sara's mouth was open in amazement. Garal continued to pick up the figurine. He untied the cord and pulled the figurine from the cloth and sat it down on the table toward the wall. Sara was stunned, her hands gripped the table's edge, and her fingertips were white. Her eyes closed. I thought she would leave impressions of her fingers in the wood.

"How…You couldn't. How did you?" Sara sat there, staring amazed.

It had to be a fake and Sara never knew. "I have seen enough to know not to waste any more of your time. Thank you. Have a pleasant night." I started to get up.

"Wait," Garal said. His voice was different. Not so masculine.

"We are truly sorry. We were only playing a joke. This is Geraldine, my wife," Tomas said softly, trying not to laugh.

Garal or Geraldine pulled the hood of her cloak up to unhide her face. I watched as the man face just evaporated to a woman's face. Mid-thirties, smooth, soft-looking face. Nothing compared to what it was. "I am sorry. We just had to see your faces when a man touched the figurines."

"You have no idea what really happens, do you?" Sara exclaimed in a harsh tone. "I have had the unfortunate experience of seeing it. It is a terror that will haunt you for the rest of your life." She was shaken by the image in her mind. "Let's be done with this, can we."

"Yes, we should," I commented. "Is it Angelica of the Dawn?"

Tomas looked at the figurine for a moment or two. Then seemed to relax just a little, hardly even noticed it myself. But his face gave it away. Geraldine watched his face intently. He gave a slight nod.

"Yes, it is Angelica of the Dawn," she said sadly. "And which do you have, Calarel?"

I pulled the figurine out of the satchel and placed it on the table. I kept my hand on it a moment. They both looked a little nervous for a second. Geraldine let an audible sigh of relief escape her lips. As I removed the cloth that covered the figurine, I looked around to see if anyone was paying much attention to us. *Nothing to worry about,* I thought.

Tomas relaxed again. The same small nod as before, and Geraldine watching him again, as before. "This is the Angelica of the Light figurine. As we were told it would be."

Sara slid the other figurine toward me. The small spheres began to cast a small amount of colored light at a distance of one foot from each other. At a little more than a hand's distance from each other, Sara pulled the figurine back to her. As the Angelica of the Light began to move towards the other by itself, as I said, "Too close."

"I didn't know they would do that!" Sara said.

I looked at Geraldine and then Tomas who shook his head as if reading my mind. Geraldine started to say something, but closed her mouth. She looked more nervous than Tomas.

"I was told no closer than two feet apart," I told them. "I was not given a reason, and I do not want one either." I slid Angelica of the Light closer to Geraldine. "Hand me that one now!" I told Sara. She did without hesitation. I wrapped it up and put it into the satchel. Geraldine slid the Angelica of the Dawn figurine toward Sara. She wrapped it in the cloth she had and retied the cord.

I pulled the coin purses for Tomas and Geraldine out and gave them each one and thanked them.

Tomas opened his and looked inside. "Ah, is there a note in yours, Garal?"

She opened hers and pulled out a small piece of paper with something written on it. She read it. "If you will excuse us, I think we should earn our keep for the night."

They both left the booth. She went to a table to one side of the room and he went upstairs.

I pulled the last coin purse out of the satchel and gave it to Sara. I thanked her and started to get up and leave myself. She grabbed my arm to keep me from leaving. "Wait a moment. Please?"

"Okay." I settled back down on the bench.

She opened the coin purse. Looked at the coin- age and then pulled out a small note. She read it. "Do you know the purpose of these figurines?"

"Only what I have been told."

"I know that Angelica of the Light can be used to foretell the winds. The weather is more accurate, I guess. And Angelica of the Dawn can be used to foretell the future."

"That I was not told. Only that a man's touch would bring death to him."

"Well, that part is also true. But there is a third figurine. I hope to find it someday," she paused, trying to read my face. I don't think I showed any emotion. "So that I can destroy it."

"I wish you luck. I hope you do not call misfortune to yourself in the process." I started to get up, and she caught my arm again.

"Do you want to know why you were hired to do this exchange?"

"I was hired to do a job that I am only half done with. The pay is good, and it gets me out of Cynar for two weeks. That is all I need to know."

"I take it that you must be paid very well or honest enough not to snoop where you shouldn't." She looked a little surprised as the words came out of her mouth.

"I would like to think it is both." I looked at her sharply.

She pulled a second piece of paper out of the coin purse. Unfolded it and laid it on the table in front of me. A certificate for fifty gold, signed by Miss Aravea Lotithil. "She wants to buy it back. Do you know what can be done if all three Angelicas are put with each other?"

"I would rather not say if it is true."

"The summoning is true. It is an evil thing that comes."

"She told me she has the ability to keep them safe. I was also to deliver a message to someone else in this town. And that person was to take the figurine you now have from you after tonight. That message was burned by Miss Lotithil. But she did have me read it before she did. It came from a person of some influence. I would have delivered the message without knowledge of its content, if not for Miss Lotithil. I trust her."

"I pray I am making the right decision." She put the certificate back in the coin purse and handed me the figurine of Angelica of the Dawn. "Please be careful with both of them in your possession. I do not know what happens if the two of those come together. Please be careful."

"I will. You have a good life. With that much, I think I would go someplace and start my own horse ranch. At least that is what I would do. I wouldn't stay here anyway."

I got up and went back to where Abon was sit- ting. He had a good seat for watching the two that were entertaining the other people in the common room with their illusions.

One of the men from the freight wagons came over to our table and sat down.

"Ma'am. Sir." He nodded to each of us. "I would like to thank you."

I broke in on what he was going to say. "No need. I was not sure if what I saw was enough to war- rant saying anything."

"I'm glad you did. You helped put a ring of thieves behind bars where they belong. My name is James. If you're ever in Duintolea, go see Gath Bashere. He owns the Northeast Freight Company, and I'm sure he will give reward for the help in saving a rather large sum of freight tonight."

"I do not know when or if I will be in Duintolea anytime soon. But who knows? I will keep that in mind."

The serving maid came to our table with two plates covered in food and two ales and set them down in front of us. "You joining them, James? I thought that you were all leaving."

"Just had something to take care of out at the stables. We're here for the night."

"All right, you're usual?"

"Ya. And, Christine." She stopped and looked at him. "Put their tab on mine." then he looked at me. "I'm sure Gath wouldn't mind. But you pay for your own drinks." He chuckled a little and slapped the table lightly, as if a bargain had been struck after long debating and got up and went to the table where his friends were.

We ate our dinner and had another ale. We went upstairs to our rooms. We put one figurine in the bottom of Abon's backpack, and I carried the other in the satchel. Abon was a little nervous about having the figurine in his backpack.

"At least no one will know that we have both of them with us this way," I told him.

After a good night's rest, I was out behind the inn practicing my styles with the sword, when one of the men from the freight company came out.

"Mind if I join you?"

"It is okay with me, just going through practice forms."

"Good. Anyone using forms are hard to find."

We practiced for an hour, giving me an extra quarter hour. I did not mind. He was interesting, tall, and had a ruggedly handsome look to him. I taught him a few moves with the sword he claimed he did not know. And I learned a deviation of a form I knew. He called the move "Cutting the Thistles." During your swing, you did a lunge and pulled back toward the end of the swing. Very close to "Slicing the Barley." After we stopped, we walked out to the stables. I brushed Scorch and Stormy. He was impressed with our horses. I told him they were from the other side of the ocean somewhere. I think he was trying to make advances toward friendship beyond just friends. But I always brought the conversation back to horses or weaponry, or anything else. *I am just not sure I want to be tied to anyone yet,* I thought. I had brushed both horses and checked their blankets and the tack by that time I knew all about him. Down to how many pickets were on the gate where he lived in Duintolea. I finally had to tell Scorch I would give him his apple a little later. We went back to the inn. Abon was already awake and waiting for me for a change. Of course, the other men that were with the freight company were awake and eating when we came in.

"I hope we meet again, Calarel. I enjoyed your company," he said as we crossed the common room toward our respective tables.

"Yes, that would be nice if we did. It was nice meeting you, Wil."

I went to the table Abon was at and the serving maid came to our table. We ordered our breakfast, ate, and packed our things.

When I went to pay for our stay, Martha, the innkeeper, said that it was already paid. I was not about to argue with her. We went out to the stables. I saddled Scorch first as usual. Before I could finish, Wil was saddling Stormy for me.

"I can't believe you ride this big of a horse, Abon. This saddle looks to be built for this horse and you." I looked at Wil. "Yes, my father said these were going to be the last saddles he would ever make." I turned to put the hackamore on Scorch.

I had not thought about the saddles in a long time other than regular maintenance. Abon should slide all over the place in his saddle. Come to think of it, I thought I had just grown use to the saddle I used. It was a very comfortable saddle.

"That's too bad. If he can make a saddle to fit horse and rider, he is a very talented craftsman. There ya go, Abon, ready to ride?"

"Yes, thank you for your help. We appreciate it, Wil."

"Let's go, Wil," one of his companions called out.

"I'll be right there." He looked at Abon. "You watch out for her." Then he looked at me. "You be careful in your travels."

I had to bite the inside of my lip not to laugh. "We will. You do the same," I told him as I climbed on to the saddle. Stormy bent down for Abon to get into the saddle and stood up again. And we were headed back toward Cynar.

Three days travel, we arrived at the Red Feather Inn in Rime in time for the supper meal.

"You're back!"

"Yes, we are, Junior. How are you?" I asked as I dismounted.

"I'm doing good, Calarel." He reached for the reins as Abon dismounted. "I'll take Stormy if you like, sir."

"What? You remember my horse's name, but not mine?"

"Truth or can I lie?" Junior hesitated only a moment. "I am sorry, but you never told me your name. She told me her name and the horse's names. I remember names pretty good."

"Well, I can fix that. My name is Abon."

"I'll remember now Abon. Hope you had pleas- ant travels. I'll tend to your horse for you. We have private rooms available if you like. We have baths so you can clean up too. Maybe your clothes need cleaning. We can take care of that too."

"That sounds like a good idea. I'll have an ale first I think. See you inside." And he headed straight for the back door.

"Are there many guests today, Junior?" I asked as we walked into the stables.

"Just two that I know of, but it is early yet. I'll undo the girth strap for you and get some feed."

"Thank you, Junior." And I started to unsaddle Scorch. When Junior and I finished with the horses, I went inside to the common room.

There was a couple sitting at a table by the front. A group of three armed and armored men sit- ting at another table. I went and sat down at the table with Abon.

"You get the rooms already?"

"Ya, I got the rooms. Ordered us a couple of ales. Then they came in."

"Hey, half-a-man, you have her trained enough to fight for ya?" one man called out.

They started the bad jokes and name calling almost as soon as they sat down.

"I am glad ignorant people like him do not stay around too long. The world would not be a safer place to live with them," I said loud enough to be heard.

One of the men, about 5 foot 8 inches tall, wearing leather armor, stood up quickly. "You have a smart mouth for a woman."

A small bell sounded from behind the bar. The innkeeper held up a cudgel. "I think it is time for you gentlemen to leave now. I run a respectable inn, and I'll not have you in here causing problems."

The man standing pulled his weapon. "You have what I want, woman. I'll have it one way or the other." The other two got up and spread out, trying circle us.

"I think you are trying to think for yourself, ignorant man. You are not to take what I have until I am almost home I bet. But I could be wrong. I guess the man who hired you did not tell you too much, at least not enough," I said to him as I stood. Grabbed the satchel and put it on the table. Reached inside and pulled out the figurine. Unwrapped it and sat it on the table next to us. "There you go. That is the thing you want. I will not die for a man who tries to stab me in the back." I stepped back beside our table.

The innkeeper was coming around from behind the bar. "You men had better leave now!"

The one doing all the talking stepped closer to the table that I placed the figurine on and stretched to grab the figurine.

"Greed kills," I said loud enough for him to hear. He looked up at me just as he gripped the fig- urine. We heard the smallest part of the start of his scream, as he looked like little sparkles of shimmering light. Then the sparkles turned to black ashes and fell from the air as if a shadow cast from the sun at the zenith upon the man's back. The room was silent.

No one breathed or moved a muscle.

"What is wrong?" I heard in my head.

"Nothing, Scorch, just startled at the truth of what I have been told."

It was a long second, the door to the inn opened. Two guards entered. They held the door for a man, his wife, and two children.

The other two men looked at me.

"It's yours, you keep it," one said, as I picked it up and blew the dust from the base. They picked up their things and headed for the door.

The innkeeper was still just standing there, with his cudgel in hand. Scrutinizing the ash that was lying on the table, chair, and the floor where the man had been.

The guards walked over to the innkeeper. "Fred, you all right?" one of them asked the innkeeper who was just staring at the dust. "Fred."

Fred shook himself. "I can't believe. Yes. No. What? Everything is fine." He glanced around real quickly. "Everything is fine, the trouble makers just left."

The other guard came to our table and asked, "Everything all right, ma'am?" He gave a slight nod. "Sir?" Another slight nod toward Abon.

"Yes, sir, everything is fine now. The innkeeper seems to run a nice quiet place here. Chased those would be trouble makers off before they could get themselves into any troubles. Right, Abon."

"Yes, he handled that very well. Better than most I would say."

"That's good to know. Have a pleasant stay here in Rime." He nodded again to us, turned, and went back to where the other guard and Fred stood. Fred had pulled himself back together. The guards bid him a good night and headed for the door.

Fred headed back behind the counter. Once there, he looked at us. I tapped the side of Abon's mug and held up two fingers. Fred nodded. The younger waitress came from the kitchen. Fred stopped her and pointed at the table next to us. She nodded acceptance of her task. And went to the table the family had just sat down at a moment ago.

Fred brought three mugs and sat down. Slid one to Abon and then one to me. "Okay. Explain what just happened to me."

I spoke softly. "More than what I was expecting. At least she is not mopping up blood from the floor." "What do you mean more than you expected?" "Fred, I am not sure I can tell you much. It is an item of power. We are just messengers doing our job." "What happened to that man?"

"You know as much as I do. You saw the same thing happen as I did."

Fred took a long drink from his mug. "There aren't any more after that thing, are there?"

"We do not think so."

"Damn, I don't like this, Calarel. I have one of those in my backpack!"

"Do not worry. You are safe. Just do not grab it."
"What are you doing with that thing?"

"We were hired to purchase this one for someone."
"Ya, Miss Lotithil is to meet us here in the morning."

"Yes. Well we were paid well to get it and keep it as private as we could. We knew that there might be a little trouble. But we did not think it would happen this far from where we are going," I told Fred. "We will be back on the road as soon as she meets with us."

Some more people came into the inn.

"I had better get back to work. I guess," Fred said as he stood up from the chair. "If you need any- thing, ask!" and went back behind the bar.

It was getting close to dinner time. More people came in. One half elf came in, went to the bar, and talked with Fred. Fred got a little animated, waving his arms as if something big was going on. They both looked in our direction. And she left. Nothing much else happened for the rest of the evening. The evening meal was very good. I walked about the town afterward. About the same size as Valeria, seems to be a nice little town. I went back to the inn and had another ale and went to bed.

I woke up around my usual early morning hour. I cleaned up a little, dressed, and donned my armor and weapons. And quietly went down the back stairs and out the back door. I was glad the yard in the back was a good size. There was a wagon that was not there the night before. I practiced my forms and did my exercises. Went inside the stables to check on Scorch and give him his apple. And went back inside the inn and woke up Abon. Not many people in the common room when I arrived and sat at a table. I picked one that I could watch both the front door and back hall.

"Good morning, Calarel," said the waitress. "Ready for some breakfast?"

"Not yet. Thank you. What is your name?" I asked.

"Verin. I'll be your waitress this morning. When you're ready let me know."

"Thank you, Verin, could I get a glass of water for now?"

"Of course." She headed for the kitchen.

A few people came in and sat at tables. Fred or Verin took their orders for food. Abon finally strolled down stairs and joined me. A finely dressed woman came in. With the light coming in through the door behind her, she looked like a lord's wife. She looked around and then headed to our table. Once away from the door, I could tell it was Aravea. When she arrived at our table, both Abon and I stood. Abon stepped around the table to pull out a chair for Miss Lotithil.

"Good morning, Miss Lotithil."

She took a seat there and thanked Abon. And we all sat down.

"Good morning, Calarel. I hear you may have had a little trouble yesterday."

"It was no trouble. Just a foolish man who will not be a bother to anyone again. I did not really believe you about a man dying if he touched one of your figurines. I do now, however."

"Yes. So I hear. That was rather foolish of you to test that." She took a breath, and I cut in on her scolding she was about to give.

"I chose the way I did to avoid other people get- ting hurt. Fred was already coming around the bar with his cudgel. I am sure he would not have been the only one hurt. Only moments later, two guards held the doors open for a family with small children. The fight would have still been taking place. I am glad I made my choice the way I did."

"Good morning, Miss Lotithil," Fred said, walking up to the table. Fred bowed as if to royalty. "I do hope your travels were safe. I can have a room made ready for you in short order if you wish."

"Thank you, Fred. Arise." He stood back up. "I think we would like a private dining room this morning."

"Of course, Miss Lotithil. Right this way."

He stepped behind her chair, held it for her as any gentlemen would. After she stood, he led us to a private dining room, a room large enough for ten people to dine. There was a fireplace, though not large, but it would be enough to heat the room more than enough. Two service stands. All the wood paneling polished. Not a speck of dust anywhere. A painting of Duintolea with the river that divided around and went through the city. "Verin will be here in a moment to get your orders and a pitcher of cool water for you."

"Thank you, Fred," Miss Lotithil said as she seated herself at the chair he held for her. Then he bowed himself out of the room. After the door closed. "I wish you wouldn't have done that." She looked at the door. "What you have done is add yet another soul to the mill that can be used against us."

"What do you mean by that?"

"I have been waiting for you for some time now. At least it seems to be you that I have been waiting for. A person wanting to make the world a better place to live. Not afraid to use what is available to use, when it is needed. And cares more for those around them, than for themselves, from what I know of you so far. You are that person." Aravea had an expressionless look to her. I could not read anything else into what she said. I tried.

"And if she is this person, then what?"

"She will have many challenges in her future. And I will try to be a guide. There will be things I cannot be involved in and things I must. I will try to offer direction."

"I already do what you are talking about. I assist the authorities when I can, if I can."

"Yes, but you are just scratching around the rim of the problem. You need to start looking below the sur- face.

Reaching for the roots of the problem." Someone knocked at the door. "Enter," she commanded.

The door opened, and Verin stepped in and closed the door behind her. "Good morning, Miss Lotithil. I haven't seen you in a while. Would you like a traditional Elven first meal this morning?"

"Yes, it has been a while, hasn't it? I'll have a light first meal this morning. Some bread and fresh preserves and whatever they want as well."

"Yes, ma'am. I just made some blackberry preserves yesterday. Or we have some boysenberry from a few weeks ago. It is still very fresh tasting. Or a peach jam that is just up from Duintolea."

"I'll try your blackberry. Thank you, Verin." Her smile looked honest.

Verin looked at me. "And what about you, Calarel? Bread and preserves also."

"No. I will have three flapjacks, some ham or sausage, and two eggs, and a glass of cool milk."

"Which would you prefer sausage or ham? We have both."

"Good. Then I will have both."

She looked at me for a moment, then to Abon. "And how about you, sir? What will you have for first meal?"

"I'll just have two eggs and some ham. A glass of milk sounds good too." Abon looked at me. "I have no idea where she puts all that."

"We'll see if she finishes it all. I'll get this for you right away." She quickly left the room and closed the door.

"Calarel, did Sara say or perhaps give you anything?" Aravea asked.

I looked at her only for a moment. *What barrel am I going to clean now?* I thought. "Yes, she gave me back the Angelica of the Dawn and told me to be safe. She also told me that what you said about the three being put together was true. She wants nothing to do with it."

"Good. Could you go get the Angelica of the Light for me please? Maybe by the time you get back, first meal will be here. Abon, I have a question for you." I heard her say as I left the room.

I went up to my room and grabbed the satchel. I pulled the few things I had put in there out and laid them on the bed. Then I went to Abon's room and removed the figurine from his backpack.

"Abon? Are you sure you can stand with Calarel? Stand by her when things get hard or bad in her life?" Miss Lotithil asked.

"What do you mean? Are you asking if I will stay with her? If that is what you are asking me, the answer is yes. She is my friend, she has saved my life at least once. We make a good team. We work well together." Abon rubbed his forehead. "What is it you really want to know?"

"You are basically a thief, and I just don't see you working well with Calarel. I just want to make sure you will not leave her in a bind. You will have to be able to back her up."

"Of course, I would and always will and I am no thief." Abon almost came out of his chair.

§§§

I headed back downstairs. As I knocked on the door, Verin stepped up beside me with the tray of food. I heard Aravea say, "Enter," and I opened the door for Verin to enter and followed her in.

"Just in time. I am starving."

Miss Lotithil looked to be relaxed. Abon however looked to be mad enough to spit fire if he could. "Everything okay?" Looking at Abon first, then

Miss Lotithil, and back to Abon. "Sure, everything is good."

Abon sounded a little upset. I guess I will have to find out later.

The food was good. And Verin must have some way of telling how long it takes people to eat. I no more finished eating, wiping my mouth and hands. I folded the cloth napkin and laid it on the plate. And she knocked on the door.

"Enter," Aravea called out to the door.

The door opened, and Verin came in. "Miss Lotithil, Constable Garret has asked to see Calarel. Should I send him in?" She began stacking the plates on one of the serving carts.

"Yes. Please ask him to join us. Is someone with him by chance?" Aravea asked.

"Yes, ma'am, there is a man with him and Claira Tarnel. She looks a little nervous, if you ask me," she said as she finished cleaning the table. "I'll send them in."

"Thank you," Aravea replied.

Verin wheeled the cart to the door, opened it, and said, "Come in please, Miss Lotithil and Calarel will see you now!"

The Constable had light leather armor that had the red cord that ran down the seam of the arm. That marked him as the highest ranking Guardsmen in the town and wore the standard issue sword at his waist. Maybe a little over middle-aged, stern-faced, and looked knowledgeable. The other man was one of the three from the day before. He looked to be wear- ing someone else's shirt. Claira Tarnel at first looked fairly nervous, wishing she could be someplace else, until she saw Aravea sitting in the room. The relief on her face spoke friendship, trust, and knowing that whatever the trouble, it was all but over.

"There are the thieves!" he demanded as he pointed at me.

I stood up and said, "I remem—"

Aravea interrupted, "Excuse me. But what is it that she has taken from you?"

"They stole a family heirloom that has been in my family for three generations."

"And what does it look like exactly? I mean, is there anything that makes it different from another like it? An inscription or something of that nature."

Aravea's face showed no emotion of any kind since they first came through the door.

"Well, it's a figurine of my great-grandmother in a flowing gown with her arm out stretched like this." He held his left arm out and up a little.

"Can you show me the object in question, please?" the constable asked.

"We can. And will in a moment. There is nothing inscribed on the bottom or anywhere else? Perhaps the color of the figurine. Is it painted? Does it hold anything perhaps in her left hand? I would think that if it has been in your family for so long, you could be a little more descriptive than what you have given so far." "I've told you what it looks like. What more do you need?"

"Miss Lotithil. Do you know anything about this I should know?" The Constable put his hand on the hilt of his sword.

"Yes, I believe I do. Mrs. Tarnel, why are you here?" "She is here to verify that it is what I say it is," the man spoke before she could get a word out.

"I'm sorry, Sir. But Mrs. Tarnel could not tell you what it is. She has the ability to heal and foresee what might happen to others when she concentrates. Although we are working on other abilities when she has time to make the journey to my home. Now I would like Mrs. Tarnel to answer my question," Aravea told him, then looked back to Mrs. Tarnel.

Mrs. Tarnel stepped away from the man to curtsy to Aravea. "Of course, Miss Lotithil." She straightened. "I am here." She looked at the man a little concerned. "I am here because." The constable slowly inched toward the door. "Because he came to my house early this morn and asked if I could heal his friend."

He tried to get to the door, but the constable was already in the way. He froze, he didn't move. He could have pushed the constable off balance with luck and maybe made his way out the door if he were quick enough. I couldn't imagine standing in that way without losing my balance.

"Hey, what is this? I can't move." I could tell he was trying to move by the sound of his voice. "I'm stuck. Let me go."

"Silence," Aravea commanded. "Please con- tinue, Mrs. Tarnel."

"Well." She sounded more in control of her voice. It was now matter of fact, with no hesitation. "Once inside, his friend needed no help. They over- powered my husband and tied him up. The fight woke my son. They said they would kill my son if I did not help them. I had no idea what I was to do until I was at the constable's office."

"Mrs. Tarnel, I have known you a long time. Please tell me you are telling me a story," the constable said.

"Only the truth, Thomas," she replied. "But if we don't return, I fear the other man may hurt my son or my husband."

"I doubt that Mrs. Tarnel that would add a great deal to his problems he already has," Thomas said, trying to comfort her. "I'll take care of that in just a moment." He pulled hand irons from one of the pouches on his belt, and he locked one side to one wrist. "I'll have no trouble from you, sir. Right?"

"No, not from me," he said. "Okay, release him, Miss Lotithil."

She released him, and the constable had him on the floor, I thought he would come up with a bloody face, but he didn't. The constable put the other side of the hand irons to his other wrist and helped him up.

"Now, that you have him secured. Perhaps Calarel can watch him while you tend to the other man. That would also give us time to learn why he is after this figurine and who he works for," Aravea said to the Constable.

"Very well," he replied, eyeing me as I stood up, "She looks as if she could handle him easily enough." Nodding as if accepting me for someone who could be a guard. "I'll get a few more men and see to the other. I'll be back as quickly as I can," he exclaimed as he turned to the door.

I moved to stand a little behind the thief.

Miss Tarnel said, "I am glad you were here, Miss Lotithil."

In the half hour that the Constable was gone, we learned that the three were hired to retrieve the figurine from us. They were hired by a shady man in Cynar. He most likely worked for someone under Lord Bertram. The thief gave a name of Martin Thanual. Someone else we would have to watch out for most likely.

Mr. and Mrs. Tarnel and son were united unharmed; other than a few bruises on Mr. Tarnel, they were fine. The two thieves were put in jail until the Lord Samuel was available for the trial.

We gave Aravea both of the figurines, and she gave us a note explaining she took possession of the figurine we were to bring back.

*****

The next two days of travel were nice. A little windy and cloudy, but it was nice. When we came to the small town of Lugard, we headed straight for the Wayward Pine. We rode back to the stables, and Paul came out to meet us.

"Hello. Glad you are here again."

*****

And we headed back to Cynar. On the second day, we joined in with a family from Haalkitain, which is in the Rhakhaan realm. They seemed friendly enough. They do have some different customs than what Abon and I are used to.

We did have a little problem midmorning the next day. A few bandits tried to give us a bad time. But between the four adults and a lucky shot with his bow from their ten-year-old son. It was handled before any of us were hurt.

I did find out that they were hired by the same man, Martin Thanual. I think I might have to find out a little more about him. We brought two of the six with us to Cynar.

One of the guards at the gate to the city was one of the guards at the other gate the first time I arrived. His name is John, a big square-shouldered man.

"You find another family to rescue, Calarel?" he asked as we passed through the gate.

"In around about way." I nodded to him. "I guess you could say that. Meet me at the tavern tonight, John."

"Okay, I want to hear about this rescue too," he called out.

Two of the other guards started laughing; I knew they would give him a hard time. Once inside the walls of the city, we stopped at the first intersection in front of a constable's office.

Before I could dismount, Hawk was coming out the door.

"Calarel! How was the journey?" he asked, then eyed the two sitting in their saddles with hands tied behind their backs. "I need two guards out front. Now!" he called back over his shoulder as he continued to walk toward us. "I guess you have had a little trouble."

"Just a little, the others are about a half day's ride up the road. I left a marker of four stones as a base with two stones stacked. So they can be found easily. Their things are on the horses, behind the wagon," I told him.

"Does anyone need a healer?" he asked, looking at everyone.

"I'm okay, thanks to Calarel and Abon. We wish to file complaints against these men for attempting to kill and thievery. Assault against a beast of burden. And ah, well anything else you can think of. I am Mazba Benwe," he gestured toward his wagon, "and that is my life partner Juzlin and my son Jeremy." He gave Hawk a bow. "She is a fine Warrior of the realm, Sir. I'm glad they stuck with us at our slow pace. If all your warriors are trained as well as she, I know why we are at peace between the realms."

"Thank you, Master Benwe. She has taken to the sword better than some men I know. But she does not work for the realm, although I would like it if she did."

"Yes. Thank you for the compliment." I looked at Hawk. "Where they are from, if you help protect the citizens. You work for or as part of the realm."

"Oohh," as if realization came with understanding.

One of the three guards that came to Hawk's call said, "Excuse me, Sir. But this horse has the brand of the Bertram house on it."

"Yes, and so does one of the others tied at the back of the wagon," I told the guard.

Hawk nodded to the guard. And the guard nodded back.

"I'm going to take them to the inn and help them get settled in," I said to Hawk.

Mazba climbed back onto the wagon, and we led them to the inn that Abon and I stayed at. It is a nice inn, peaceful and quiet. After getting them settled and their horses looked after. Hurin is a very good stable master. I think he can heal animals with magic, but I couldn't say for sure.

Abon and I rode back over to the constable's office and to see about the horses that belonged to Lord Bertram. We took two horses to the stables of the estate.

Jimmy was surprised to see us so soon. "You must have pushed your horses hard to make that trip so fast. Can't tell by the looking at your horses. Did you have a good trip?"

"Yes, for the most part, it was a good trip." I paused as I dismounted. "Are you missing some horses, Jimmy?" I asked as I handed him the leads. Then I led Scorch into the stall.

"Where did you find these two?" "About a half a day ride east of here."

"How long have they been gone?" Abon slung his saddlebags over his shoulder

"Tonight would have made the third. I still haven't figured out how they got out."

"Thieves. Horse thieves might be a better description," Abon responded.

"Is it okay if Jimmy unsaddles and brushes you down tonight? I need to go see Lord Bertram."

"Yes, but just this once. Don't make it a habit."

"I would not think of it," I said aloud as I grabbed my saddlebags. "Jimmy, would you mind tending to Scorch just this once?"

"Not at all, Calarel. That is my job, you know." Both Abon and I headed inside to see Lord Bertram. It was dinner time so everyone was easy to find. We entered the dining area from the rear door. There were no guests, so I proceeded to where he sat at the head of the half-empty table. I bowed sharply. "My lord. A letter from Miss Lotithil." I pulled it out of my saddlebags and handed it to him. "Were you able to attend to both tasks?"

"Yes, my lord. He did not give a return message.

He looked at it. Smiled and said thank you."

"We did not expect you until tomorrow. You made good time."

"We had good travel both ways," Abon spoke up. "Good. Get something to eat and clean up after the long journey. We can talk of it tomorrow." He looked a little disappointed with what he was reading. "Thank you, my lord. Good night, Lord Bertram, High Lady Bertram, Lady Bertram. Enjoy your meals."

We bowed our way back out of the dining area.

Just as the door was closing behind us, I heard the paper being torn and wadded into a ball.

"Damn it," Lord Bertram said through clenched teeth.

We didn't stop until we were outside the mess hall. "I do not think he liked the letter from Miss Lotithil much."

"I think you're right, Calarel."

We were welcomed back by everyone. We told a light version of our travels. After we finished eating, while drinking an ale. It was starting to get dark. I told everybody I was going to see a friend and left to meet John at the tavern.

It is really a nice tavern. Usually quiet, some- times they have some performer to entertain patrons. Tonight was one of those nights. A young-looking middle-aged woman playing her harp. She played well, as long as she didn't sing. She recited some poetry she wrote five weeks ago. I had heard it already at least twice. I saw John shortly after walking in and over to the bar.

I sat at an empty stool, and Frank, the bartender, came over to me with an ale.

"How are you, Calarel? How was the trip to Spurrie?"

"I am good, Frank. I cannot keep a secret from you. How is business?"

"Pretty good. It keeps getting better too. Yes, sir, two ale coming up," he said to another customer. "Well, back at it. Good to see you back, Calarel," he said as he grabbed two more mugs and went to fill them.

I looked back toward where John was sitting. Two of his friends were getting up to leave. They all looked to be guards, even out of uniform. John waved for me to come join him. I did, he introduced me to Steve. He is a few years older than John, his face has seen better days, two scars on the left side of his face. Short hair on the sides and long on the top, tied with a leather cord at the back.

We talked for a little while before I said anything about the real purpose of my being at the Tavern tonight.

"What do you two know about Martin Thanual?"
"Well. Time to go, I think." John started to getup from his seat.

"Just a minute, John. Not so fast. I will buy the next round."

"That's not a good subject there, Calarel." "Right, John."

"That's kind of a deadly subject actually. Unless you're thinking of becoming a thug or something like that? But from what I hear about you, I have my doubts."

"No! I am not going to turn into a thug. Stop one. Yes. What can you tell me?"

"In truth, not too much." John looked around again. As if looking to see if anyone was trying to listen in on the conversation. "He is a small-time merchant. Nothing big. And his prices are a little high." He lowered his voice more. I was already leaning on the table. Now I was having to lean a little closer to hear him. "He might, mind you this is only hear say, be one of the biggest ring leader of the biggest thieves' guilds here in town. But no proof of that."

"Well, you have proof of that or something close to that now. The two thugs, as you called them, that I brought in this afternoon and two more in Rime. They are sitting in a cell there. With charges of kid- napping and assault against them, I do not think they will be getting out soon. I would hope that a man who hires someone to do his dirty work is as guilty as the men he hires."

"That all sounds good for now. But getting them to point a finger while still alive is another story."

"We need to find out. I have had to deal with his thugs twice now. Here and in Rime."

"What happened here?"

I think Steve was going to ask the same thing, he closed his mouth.

"Well, not here in town, about a half a day's ride from town, when they attacked us this morning. Abon and I found out they worked for this Martin guy. The same guy the two in Rime said they worked for, as if his name would save them or something."

"It could be possible." Steve looked around again. "If the connection is high enough. There could be corruption in high places, which might be able to get them out. Not that I'm saying there is. But possible."

"If there is? I have put four of his men in the ground and four in cells. I think I have made my first real enemy." I hoped I did not sound as nervous as I just started to feel.

"I can tell you two of the three cutpurses you've turned in have gotten out for this or that reason."

John kept his voice low and looked around. "I'm not sure why or who. It might be best if you watched your back from now on."

"Let me ask you something? Why do you think you were attacked twice? There has to be a reason," Steve asked, starting to lean closer.

The serving maid came to the table. I ordered another round of ales.

While she was getting our ales, I told them, "We were doing a job for Lord Bertram. We carried some- thing of value to Spurrie and something else back."

"Who all knew what you were doing?" John asked.

"No one other than those that needed. I do not think High Lady Bertram even knew or knows for that matter."

The serving maid came with our ales. "That will be six tin, Calarel."

"Make it eight, because I would like one too, Serena." Hawk came around the table and sat beside me. "I thought I would find you here. What do you think of that job posting I gave you?"

I forgot all about that. It was still in my back- pack, somewhere. "I am still thinking about it. I have not decided yet."

"Okay." A slight nod. "Let me help you decide a little faster. The two you brought in with you today. The two out of six."

"What about them?" John and Steve looked at him as intently as I did.

"They are free already."

"What? What do you mean free? Benwe pressed charges against them, how can they be out already?" I said a little louder than I wanted to.

"It would seem that you got help in returning stolen horses from Mister Benwe and took the law into your own hands, killing four of the eight people that were traveling to Lugard this morning," Hawk told us.

I guess he could tell I was getting a little upset.

Well, okay, downright furious.

"We'll walk you home after you cool down a little. One is outside watching the door now." Hawk grabbed my arm forcibly before I could move. "That would be taking the law into your own hands, and you know it. And he would have fifty witnesses to it."

"I cannot believe this."

"I guess you were right, you have made an enemy today," John said.

"And a bad one at that." Steve just had to add that little tidbit.

"Rumor travels fast in that circle. And you two will have a transfer to Duintolea waiting for you in the morning," Hawk said with a false laugh.

"What in the world for?" John sounded shocked at the news of that.

"It's only temporary, just until we get this under control." Hawk took a swig from his ale. "I'm sending you there for some training at the castle. And a well-deserved break. Be in my office first thing in the morning."

"But I've never even been there before. I have a house here. I just can't leave everything," Steve retorted. "I need you and a few others alive. And this is

the best way I can think of to keep you that way. Two squads headed out for training. Steve, you'll be in charge. Word will be sent when I need you to return." Hawk turned to me. "You done with that ale yet?"

"Sure, I'm done." I then downed the rest. "We'll walk you home." He finished off his. "I think you may have drank too much tonight." He winked at me.

I guess I can play like I have.

"I have not!" I said it a little louder than talking normal as I got up from the chair. I held the table and slid it a little bit toward me and pushed my chair into the one behind me.

"Hey careful!" the man in that chair said. "Oops," I said, smiling. "Maybe I have had more than I thought. Sorry I am going home now."

Hawk grabbed ahold of my arm to keep me from possibly tripping over the chair.

"How many did you have, Calarel?" John stood. "I do not know. Only a couple. I think. I do not remember."

A few people were looking now.

"I do not feel so good. Are we going to the other tavern now?"

"I don't think so. It seems you've had enough already." Steve stood with his ale, finished it, and set it on the table.

"Okay, cute one. Take me home," I said as they led me out the door. I swayed this way and that. Started to go the wrong way twice.

After a few blocks, I looked back behind us to make sure no one was following us. "If I take this job? How will I know when to come back when Martin is on the bench before the Magistrate?" I stopped acting like a fool drunk.

I did not want to let go of Hawk's arm. I could feel the strength of his arm. It reminded me of being with father walking home from the chapel when I was younger. Me on one side and my sister Tamara on the other side.

"You'll hear about it. Don't worry about that," Hawk said as he pulled his arm free. "I would leave before sun up, you and Abon both. I don't want you two to be involved in what is going to happen, any- more then I want John and Steve or the other men I'm sending to Duintolea."

"If it's going to be that bad, maybe we should be here to help," Steve almost whispered the other side of me.

"It may be as long as two weeks before it happens. And in that time, a lot of things could happen. I would not want to lose any of my friends in this tactical move to rid the city of some troublesome trash. But Calarel has pushed a few more buttons than needed to be pushed already." Hawk looked at me. "And from what I know of you so far, you'll be pushing more before it's over."

"I can stop pushing. If need be," I told him as sternly as I could.

He laughed. "It's too late now. You're in over your pretty little head. You need to disappear for a while." I had not noticed, but we were coming up to the gate at the Bertram Estates. "I've taken the liberty to put a few guards around here." He stopped and turned to John and Steve.

"You two wait here. I'll be right back." And then started walking again.

"I will see you guys tomorrow. Have a good night," I said to them both.

"Good night, Calarel. Sleep well," John said on top of whatever Steve said. I am sure it was about the same. But he kept his voice lower than John.

"Calarel! You and Abon need to disappear in the night. I have set guards so that there would be no denying that you just left in the middle of the night. Don't let anyone know about it either. Don't leave a trace that you were ever here," Hawk explained. "Leave nothing you own behind! Go get some sleep. My suggestion would be to check on that job posting I gave you. Have a good night, Calarel."

"Okay, I get the message. I hope you sleep well." And I turned to walk through the gate.

At the table by the barracks sat Abon, Mat, and few others. I headed for the stables. Just before I went inside, I yelled out, "Abon, could you bring me an ale? If you do not mind. I need to talk with you anyway!" "Sure, let me get you one." He got up and started to head for the barracks. Jimmy got up and followed Abon with three mugs in his hand.

Once inside, I turned the lamp up a little, not for me but Abon.

I was brushing down Scorch when Abon finally came into the stables. "Anyone else coming?"

"No. I looked just before I came in. Everybody else was still at the table. Why?"

He handed me the mug of ale.

"I have been informed that we have stepped on some toes. And action has to be taken to stop it."

"Ya, I know," he said as he rubbed his cheek. He had a pretty good bruise there. "I was talking to someone a little while ago. He told me I was dead men, and he named you too."

"You okay?" I asked, but did not give him time to say anything. "We should leave early in the morn- ing. I have been told that it would be a good idea not to be here when it starts."

"I'm okay. Guards have followed me round all evening. I slipped away from them for a few minutes. That's when I found out about us being wanted by Thanual. Wanted dead mostly. I guess we are costing him too much."

"Plus his mob is turning the truth around on us. Did you know we attacked his men out on the road?"

"What? That's crazy." He almost spilt his ale. "Yes, I know. So we just disappear in the night.

We should get some sleep. I have no idea what tomorrow will bring. But we will find out," I told him as I put up the brush.

We went out to the table. Only Mat and Jimmy were still out there. We sat and talked for a little bit.

Jimmy headed for the stables. Mat and Abon for the barracks, I went in to the female barracks. Almost everyone was asleep. I took off my weapons belt and armor. I was as quiet as I could be. I laid down on the bed for an hour, waiting for everyone else to go to sleep. I started to pack my things.

"Calarel," I barely heard her. I looked at her. Sally was awake. I moved over to the side of her bed. "You're packing. Are you leaving?" she whispered.

"I'm just straightening things out. Go back to sleep," I whispered back.

"I had a dream that woke me up."

"It was just a dream. Go back to sleep."

"It was more. I have never seen you as you were in my dream," she said. It is dark, but I would say she shook with fear just for a moment.

"What way was that?"

"I saw you in a rage. A killing rage. It scared me awake," Sally said in a whisper. "And you are packing!" "I am only cleaning up things after my trip to Spurrie. In a killing rage? I would never do anything like that. In a rage, you lose thought. And if you are fighting, you have to have your wits about you. Go back to sleep. I am almost done straightening up my things, and then I am going to sleep. I will see you in the morning."

I went back to the trunk at the end of the bed and finished packing. I hate lying, but this time I had to. I undressed and went to bed, and asleep.

I woke up around my usual time.

"Good morning, Scorch. Have Stormy wake up Abon. It is time to go."

"Okay, he is wake."

I got dressed and carried my backpack and saddlebags to the door. Went back and got my armor and weapons belt and shield. Opened the door and set everything outside. Once out there, I donned my armor. Put on my backpack, hung my shield on my arm. And picked up my bow. Hang my quiver on the hilt of my sword. Grabbed my saddlebags and went to the back of the barracks.

The long way to the stables, but in the shadows. I froze for a second when I saw something moving in the dark. It was Abon. He waved at me to come on, as he headed toward the stables. He seemed to fade in and out of view, close to it anyway. But to a common man, you might have only caught a glimpse him here and then there. I have seen him sneak around before, but never this good.

When we arrived at the stables, he motioned me to wait. He ducked inside. After a few minutes, he motioned me to follow. Inside was dark even for me. I wanted to open at least one door to let in some light. But Abon suggested not to. I gave Scorch his apple, which he was thankful for. I saddled Stormy first and lashed everything down for the trip. I found our tents in the storage bin.

"Someone is coming," Scorch told me. I dropped to sit on my heels. I heard the sally door open, then close. I sat there a moment, listening.

"Where are they, Scorch?"

"Just outside the door."

I finished with Abon's horse and went to start on Scorch.

"He is walking away now," Scorch reported or at least it seemed that way. I finished saddling him and tied everything down. Abon was already sitting in the saddle. I bent to pick up my bow.

"Someone is coming," I heard in my head.

I stood up and grabbed his mane. *"Five miles south on the road. Go!"* I was standing in the middle of the road still holding Scorch's mane in one hand and my bow in the other.

"Thank you, Scorch," I said in a normal tone of voice. Abon and Stormy appeared beside us.

"Damn, that was close. I wish you would tell me when you're going to do that." Abon exhaled.

I started walking around to the other side, so I could put my bow under the saddle fender. "Sorry, this was the first thing I thought of. No time to explain. I hope you have everything."

"Ya, I do. I hope you do!" he replied.

I pulled my backpack off my back and opened it to find the job posting that Hawk gave me. I turned to Abon and said, "We will go toward Duintolea.

If you want, we can go down the road a little piece and let you sleep a little more."

"No, that's okay. Let's just get away from Cynar," Abon replied.

Chapter 5

We traveled until the sun was making long shadows from the east. It was going to be a beautiful day.

"Horses ahead. Four of them," Scorch told me. I could not see them yet. Must be in the shadows of the trees. I shook my shoulder so my shield would slide down my arm.

"Stormy says there are horses coming this way.

Can you see them yet?"

I looked again up the road. There were two or three horses with riders headed toward us. "Ya. Hard to tell, a couple of horses headed this way."

I kept watching them as we approached each other. They were wearing dust cloaks. The four riders fell in line to pass. Abon fell in behind me.

"Good morning, ma'am, sir," the first one said as he rode by.

"Good morning. Have a safe journey." "And you as well," said the third rider.

We just kept riding. The fourth rider could have been no more than three or four paces past Abon. I heard something hit something else.

"Abon is hurt," Scorch shouted. It rang in my head.

"Give me enough room to draw my sword and start to charge!" I felt the shift of ten more paces. We were facing the four men. They looked startled. Abon and Stormy were gone, already in the gray. Only the tip of my sword still in the scabbard, and I am over half-way to them. I felt Scorch tense more than what he already was. My shield is in

position to defend at least one attack. Another gallop of the charge, my sword was almost in position for the first attack.

Scorch snorted. The man on my left almost fell off his horse from the blast of air that startled his horse and him. The first man on my right, his cloak blew back as if in a heavy wind. He closed his eyes. He was the first to die as my sword ripped from my hand. The tip of my sword sticking out of his back.

The second horse on the right reared up as the first rider fell off the back of his horse; he missed me with his swing. The second man on the left stood fast, perhaps trained better than the others. He made his attack, I blocked it with my shield. I was already pulling my axe from my weapons belt.

"Back to the same place and start again."

From to the same spot as before, my axe halfway out. The charge was started again. The hilt of my sword was sticking up from the first man's chest. I could reach down and grab it, but then there would be no time for offense or defense. I had to use the axe. I used my knees to guild Scorch; I am glad we practiced this a lot. Headed straight down the middle until the very last second and went down the left side of two left in the saddle. The one who was hit the hardest by Scorch's little trick was standing. Scorch was about to trample him. He yelled and leaped for the bushes at the side of the road.

The big guy with the sword had little time to position himself. I used my shield to block his swing. At the same time swung my axe down toward his elbow to cripple him. I saw the blade of my axe slice through the sleeve of his leather jerkin. I felt it hit something solid, like bone. At the same time his sword hit my shield, it nicked my arm as I rode past him. Almost losing my grip on the axe, pulling his arm in the same direction I was traveling.

His sword hit the ground, not having the muscles intact to hold it any longer. He kneed his horse to move and started away. The other man still in his saddle was almost in position to throw his dagger.

"Fifty paces down the road, Scorch, I need some time!" I was looking back to where the battle was from about fifty paces away. Not enough time to pull my bow and string it. But enough to check my arm. At least I could still use it.

He watched me for moment. Then turned his attention to his friend, who was just getting him- self out of the bushes. I heeled Scorch to move. He did. *"Faster."* At charging speed, I could hardly hear his hoofs hitting the ground. The man on the horse looked at us heading straight for him. He threw his knife side armed. I blocked it with my shield. It stuck there, a little more than the tip sticking through the wood of my shield, but still enough to cut my arm.

He was fast. Just before I got to him, he had another knife in his hand. I swung my axe toward his rib cage, he used his arm to try and deflect the blow. Only problem with that was that the weight of the axe and speed of the swing and Scorch drove the blade through his arm and became lodged in his chest. I lost grip of that too. I heard him hit the ground hard.

"Damn it, I lost grip of my axe."

Scorch came to a halt. I felt him tense as before. Then came the snort. It was unnatural. Enough force to blow the man just getting out of the bushes back into them. A little harder than when he had jumped into them the first time. I pulled my feet from the stirrups. Swung my leg over and pushed off the saddle. I picked up the other man's sword from the ground.

Only two murders left, soon to be only one. I walked over to bushes where he flew into them. He was just climbing out of them. Just as the swing of the sword was about to hit him, he tried to deflect the blade of the sword, but he missed. Which left his side open, the blade slide neatly between his ribs, until it stopped about halfway to his spine.

I held the hilt still even though he wanted to fall. I just held him there.

"I don't want to die," he said as he grabbed the blade with both hands. Tears rolled down his face and blended with the blood from the scratches from the bushes.

I felt my insides become tight. I felt the inside of my head tighten as well. I could feel emotion leaving me. It seemed to just flow out of me. "You tried to kill me. Kill me for money most likely. So you are going to die right here. And I am going to watch you until you do."

"I…I didn't want…"

He gasped for more air. Wrenched in pain again.

Every breath was pain. I could see it. "Too."

His hands fell from the blade. Both hands bleeding from gripping the blade so hard.

He started to fall over. I yanked the blade free. The rage I thought I would never be in left me. I heard something hit the ground. The emotion I felt from Scorch physically hurt. I spun around expecting another attack, but Abon was lying on the ground.

"*Calarel, help him,*" Scorch pleaded.

I dropped the sword and dropped down on my knees to check him. A knife sticking out of the middle of his back. Placed so neatly you would think they did it while Abon was sleeping.

"He is not breathing."

I tried to feel his heartbeat. I checked all the places I have felt a heartbeat before. His neck, his wrist, I tried to listen at his chest. Nothing. "I am sorry, Stormy, but he is dead. There is nothing I can do."

I have heard a horse scream before. But what she did never came from any horse I ever heard. She reared up, screamed again, and came down on her front legs so hard, I could feel it in the ground. A burst of flame shot from her nostrils, it looked like it did at least. The two bodies lying in the road caught fire, almost white-hot flames. She knelt down beside Abon. I stepped back. I could not help but want to pick him up and put him on her back, over the saddle. I started to, but the look she gave me made me stop. I could not stop the tears that started to run down my face. I tried to stop the tears so hard my head hurt.

"I loved him too, Stormy. Tell her I said that Scorch. You tell her."

I heard Scorch as he replied he did. Even the thought of what he was saying was shaky as if he was crying to.

"Something or someone is coming. I can barely feel it. We only have a few minutes before they can see us," I heard Scorch say.

"Then we need to go. It may be more of them," I said to the horses. "I will put Abon on your back, Stormy, and we can take him somewhere and bury him properly." I pulled the dagger from his back. As gently as I could, then picked him up and laid him over the saddle. "Tell Stormy to go ten miles east and wait for us. I want to find the last killer of this group." I grabbed my sword, it was still hot from Stormy's fire breath. I sheathed it anyway. My axe no longer had a handle, so I left it.

"She will wait as you ask," Scorch replied.

Did I ask? I do not remember, I must have. I picked up the sword and the dagger and slid them behind my belt. I put my foot in the stirrup and grabbed the pommel. As I pulled myself up to sit in the saddle.

"Let us move."

I was no more seated in the saddle, and there was the other man's horse. It looked about a half a legion from where we were. His horse snorted at us defiantly. Scorch snorted back, and it lowered its head submissively. I saw the man's blood on the saddle and on the horse. He was bleeding badly. I climbed down, pulled his sword, and started tracking him, using the trail of blood. Twenty paces into the forest, not very dense, but plenty of cover if you needed it. I found him sitting against a tree.

"So here you are!"

"Come to finish me?" he said.

"No. You look like you are already finished. I do not think you will live long enough to get healed." I just stood there watching him bleeding to death. "I was just wondering how much you were going to get paid to kill me and my friend."

"I guess as much as you have on you," he replied. "So you are telling me you're just thieves. You

are not paid by Thanual to kill us." I could feel the heat on my cheeks again.

"No! Who is this Thanual person?"

I started to laugh. I was laughing at him. "You are just a bunch of stupid thieves. That is funny." I dropped his sword and pulled his friend's dagger from my belt. I was on him so fast, that I trapped his arm across his body still holding the other. "Now, I am going to kill you. Just because you are a thief and you killed my friend." I slit his throat from one side to the other. Without guilt, I unbuckled the man's weapons belt and removed his spare sword. I needed the scabbard for his other sword. I took his coin purse. I checked him for anything else. That might be useful, but did not find anything.

I slid the baldric of the scabbard to the hand and half over my head to carry it. I wiped the blade clean and sheathed it. The broadsword would not fit into my scabbard. So I had to change that as well. I walked back to Scorch. Even though he had moved down the road a little, I walked straight to him. The other horse stood close by.

"Are the others still coming this way?" I asked Scorch.

"They have stopped where we were at before," he replied.

"Good." I checked the things that were tied to the saddle of the other horse. I took off the saddle and the bridle.

I threw them into the woods. "You are free of that bastard. Now be on your way, horse," and slapped it on the hindquarters. It bolted away. I climbed back in to my saddle.

"Let us go to Stormy, so we can take care of Abon."

Next thing I knew, we were in the gray. "Why are we here?"

"You need to heal a little!"

"I will heal fine. I need to tend to Abon!"

"I am starting to argue with my own horse. This is crazy," I thought.

"When you stop bleeding, I'll take you back. Besides, you need some time to let the anger go!" Scorch told me.

I tried to make him go back but to no avail, a horse with a strong will, just what I needed. Maybe it could be a good thing. I do not know.

After about twenty minutes, I started to feel tingly all over. I told him, and we were back on the ground and beside Stormy and Abon.

I climbed down and removed most of my gear. I pulled Abon from the saddle and laid him on the ground. The ground was hard and a lot of rocks showed through the grass. I would have to build a pyre.

I worked hard for over half the day or what was left of it. I only removed what was not going to be needed in the afterlife, his coin, and I started to take the food he carried. But do you use food in the after- life? I am not sure, so I left it in his backpack. I put him on top of the pyre. I placed his short sword on his chest as Father had told me was done. I never really saw him use it. I placed all of his belongings on the pyre with him. I started a fire where I would camp for the night. I made a torch and lit it, then set the dry grass I had placed so that the pyre would start aflame all the way around. I tossed the torch in at the middle to ignite the grass and kindling there as well.

I stood there waiting until Abon himself was aflame. I pulled my sword from my scabbard. Grounded the tip and knelt on one knee.

"Tulkus, I plead to you. Please see Abon to the arms of his Deity. I know he is not your follower, but he is a good and trusted friend to us both. Let him know that I have avenged his thoughtless death to all those involved. I thank you for the strength to bring that justice to them. Let him know he can live in the afterlife without hate to anyone. I am your humble servant. May the light shine on you and Abon."

I knelt there for some time. The sun was only half its height above the ground, when Scorch said something.

"Sorry. I did not hear you. What is the matter?" I said as I stood. Rather stiffly.

"Are you okay?"

"Just stiff from being in one position for so long, I guess. What was it that you said a moment ago?"

"Something is coming."

"What is it?"

"I can't really tell. They are big enough to be animal, but I can sense the intelligence of man as well."

"How big? A dog or bigger?"

"Big enough to be a man on a horse. But it is not. I have never sensed anything like this before. Nor has Stormy" He turned a little to the right.

"Where are they?"

"They are coming from the direction the smoke is traveling, to the right side of it."

I moved to the right side of the pyre, which was still burning good. A high flame that burned hot. I had to stand a little away from the blaze. I could feel the heat. It seemed to match the heat of the sun at the hottest part of the day.

I watched while three people on horseback approached. The closer they got, the more I could tell what Scorch was talking about. But they were just characters in stories. Half-man and half-horse. I had to shake my head and rubbed my eyes. Centaurs do exist. I stood there with my sword grounded and watched them as they moved closer.

"Those are Centaurs, Scorch. They are half- man and half-horse. I think there are different kinds of Centaur. But these are the first I have ever seen."

"Are they good or bad to people? That is something I cannot tell."

"That would depend on what book you read. I am going to say they are good to people, for now. We will find out. They have spotted us."

The group of four gathered closer to each other. The oldest one used his spear to point us out to the others. Like a father teaching his children how to hunt. It looked as if he were giving strict instructions. They formed a line behind him as they moved closer.

When he was in speaking distance, a good four or five paces away, he stopped. He said something in a language I did not understand.

I was still standing with my feet shoulder width apart. The tip of my sword grounded.

"I am sorry, I do not understand you. My name is Calarel."

"You speak with the new tongue. Forgive me.

Why do you burn the woods?"

The younger ones behind him started talking behind him. He said something I did not under- stand. They became silent.

"I used only the dead wood and grass to send my friend to the afterlife. I did not know you were near."

"Then we wait in peace. You attend your friend's parting in peace. We will talk again."

With that being said, he turned to the others and issued what sounded like commands. He walked away a good thirty paces and stopped. The other three took up positions forming a box centered on the funeral pyre. I walked back to where I was in front of the pyre and watched it burn for another hour and a half. Only half the sun was visible above the horizon. I began gathering my things. The others circled back around to where the eldest was waiting.

Then the eldest came to where I was.

"I am called Chrav. I am chief of my clan. I invite you to join in the evening meal," he told me more than asked.

"Are you sure that would be wise? I have read in books that mannish races and Centaurs have many problems at times."

I could almost place the upper torso as a Highmen if it were not on the front shoulders of an almost lesser warhorse. Short by a hand by definition, maybe. All most the right muscular tone for a warhorse too. But the torso of a man threw every- thing off.

"We know of the mannish races. You are not pure."

I chuckled just a little. I do not think he saw the humor I felt.

"The one called Zebron, we know him. He lives not far from here. We take his horses back that get away into the woods. He ranges the horses. They need that. Come, the meal will be ready before we arrive."

I have heard that name before or maybe read it.

"Scorch, will Stormy let me put the lead on her?"

"She will follow us. She is sad and will not leave my side for a while. She says."

"Very well, Chrav. I will accompany you to your camp to eat the evening meal." I climbed into the saddle. At least we were about the same height now that I was in the saddle.

We traveled until there was but a small sliver of the sun showing above the horizon. There were guards posted around the little village. I heard the signals before we got to close. We went under a dense canopy of trees. And after a hundred paces or so, I could see tall huts with straw roofs. Most of the huts had gardens either at the side or behind them. There must have been close to fifty Centaurs in Chrav's clan. Ranging in age of perhaps ten days to fifty years. But then again, I do not know how long they live. Some of them gathered ahead of us. And the talk, more like questions, began when we were close enough.

Chrav put a stop to it quickly. "In the presence of our guest, we will speak in the common mannish tongue!" then said something in their language.

"Very well. You bring someone other than our kind to eat food with us. I challenge her right to eat our food!"

"Rhinn! That is no way to be. You know nothing of her." Chrav sounded angry to me.

"We must take her animals back to the Zebron.

He will be angry she rides them."

Some of the others agreed with him.

"Rhinn!" I raised my voice. "These two animals belong to me. Not this Zebron. Most mannish races have horses. We have them for transportation and plowing the fields to grow our food. Horses are our friends. We take care of them. We clean them and feed them. And I accept your challenge," I told him. "No!" Chrav yelled. "She does not know our ways. Let her set the challenge. You would choose the spear, Rhinn. Most mannish do not know the ways."

He lowered his voice to a whisper the others might not be able to hear. "Choose the bow."

"Agreed, she may choose." Rhinn stiffened, unsure of himself.

"I choose archery. Best two out of three shots wins."

"It will not take three shots to kill you!" Rhinn almost laughed with his friends.

"No, not at each other." I almost laughed. "You nor I would not eat again. We would both die. We will use a target. That tree twenty-five paces away. The one between those two huts." I pointed at it. "Closest to the center of the cut branch even with the bottom of the roof. Can you see it from here?"

"As plain as I can see where to put an arrow in your chest from here."

I know he was lying. It was getting to dark to see the cut branch good from this distance. At least for someone without Elven sight. He pulled his bow from off his back and an arrow from his quiver.

"Have you no manners, Rhinn? Let her go first," a female said, while others moved out of the way.

"He can go first. I have to string my bow any- way," I said as I pulled my bow out of the sheath. Pulled a bowstring out and strung my bow.

He shot. His arrow flew straight. Not one sign of wobble. He hit the cut branch at the edge, but the arrow ricocheted off and stuck in the side of the hut.

"Scorch, when I say breathe, take a breath and hold it, until you hear me release the arrow," I asked him.

"I will, but you will need to tell me why, afterward."

I pulled an arrow from my quiver. Put it to the string.

"Breathe."

I could feel him take a breath as I drew the string to my cheek. He must have big lungs. I aimed, released, straight to the cut branch. Up and to the left, maybe a finger width from the center.

"Thank you, that was perfect. I picked a bad time to practice this."

Rhinn's second shot was better, he did stick it in the branch. About two fingers width from the middle. My next shot was down and to the right about two fingers width. His last shot was beside mine. Best two of three, I had won before he even shot his last. But he did try. I'll give him that much. I didn't even ask Scorch to hold his breath. But he did. He either heard the bow creak as I drew or was reading my mind. I am not sure of which. My shoot slid right down in front of Rhinn's that put my last arrow closest to the center. "It looks as if we both eat tonight, Rhinn.

Thank you for the challenge. I have not done that in a long time." I relaxed a little. He did not look happy.

"The challenge has been met! Welcome, Calarel, to our home. Let us eat," Chrav proclaimed. Most gave welcoming words, a few, mostly females cheered for my victory I had won. But there were a few scowls from the small group that were with Rhinn.

It was a nice meal. Even had meat, horses do not eat meat. I learned a lot at this meal. There are five clans, depending on how the feud was going between two other clans. The last clan to try and invade Chrav's clan failed miserably. By the time the evening meal was done and everyone had at least their second mug of wine, at least four people had said that I was welcome to stay in their hut.

"I would be honored to stay in each of your huts. But I normally go to sleep four hours after the sun has set. And I get up one hour before the sun rises in the morning. I am not sure I can just lie in bed the extra hours," I told them. "If you want me to stay with you, I will set up my tent in your village."

I would say half of those that were gathered around stomped a hoof. Some vocalized agreement.

"We would like to learn more of the events that are going on with the world around us. It would please us if you stayed. Tonight you stay in the Prayer Hut," Chrav told me, as everyone listened and seemed to agree.

"I would not want to insult any customs you have. I will stay." I did not want to offend them; they seem like really nice people. At least, they seemed like people. "Good! You need the time to let the Gods heal your soul after the loss of your companion," Chrav said almost in a sympathetic voice. "Thech, Stekia, prepare the Prayer Hut for Calarel!"

Two female Centaurs headed toward a hut that I thought most be Chrav's hut. It had a tall doorway and wide. The only hut with double doors that I have seen. The door frame was made of large timbers cut square and across the top was another large timber that reached past the uprights by three feet. Carved with a face in the middle, at the ends, it looked like hands holding the waves of water from flowing off the ends. It was the biggest hut in the village.

"You must prepare also, Calarel," an older male said to me. "It will not take them long. I am called Kug. I will help you on this journey to find peace in your soul."

I thought my soul was at peace. I had avenged Abon's death.

"This night may be a hard journey for you, I think," he said as he walked away toward another hut. "I must tend to my horses first. Where should I put my things?" I asked.

"You must do so quickly, it is not right to keep the gods waiting once you begin to call them. Where your horses are is a good place. No one will disturb your possessions while you are in the Prayer Hut." Chrav looked at Rhinn and one of his friends. "No one!"

They only walked away after giving a nod.

I quickly unsaddled Scorch and Stormy, removed the hackamores, and brushed them both down. I asked Scorch to let me know if anyone came to take anything. He agreed not to take action and call me first. I went to the Prayer Hut.

As I walked up both females came out, neither had on their shirts. All the females wore a shirt that covered at least their human torsos. Some covered the start of horse hair that was less than a hand below their belly button. Some wore them longer, some shorter. I tried not to stare at them. It is not like I have not seen other women nude before, but they were part horse.

"I am ready," I told them.

"Here, chew on these. Do not swallow the leaves themselves, only the juices," the older one told me, as I put the leaves in my mouth and started to chew the leaves. "This is Stekia. She will begin studying under Kug in another few seasons. And I am Thech. Chrav's mate." She pointed to a younger male. "That is Relt. He is our youngest. Nine summers now. He learns the trades well. Okay. Spit out the leaves."

I did. One was bitter and the other was almost sweet.

"Make sure you get all the leaves out of your mouth. The leaves themselves will make you ill. Not the juice of them."

I made sure I had every last piece of leaf out of mouth. I must have looked funny moving my tongue around my mouth in an attempt to make sure.

"I think you are ready. Remove your clothing and lay them beside the doorway," Stekia said, still chuckling.

"Ooh, no. I cannot do that someone might see."

It sounded as if the words stretched out. I heard them plain enough. But they sounded to last too long. I was undressing in front of the door.

"It's fine. No one looks at the person preparing to enter the Prayer Hut," Thech told me.

I felt better about it and undressed faster. I had to sit on the ground to remove my pants. I could not get my balance.

"Remove everything, Calarel."

"Even my smallclothes?" I thought I was blushing, but maybe not.

"Yes, those too."

I took everything off. "The ground is soft here."
"Yes, it is. Come let us go inside," Thech said. I tried to get up, but only succeeded in scooting a little bit across the ground.

"We can help you," Stekia said.

They both took a hand and pulled me up and led me inside. Thick beams supported the roof. They helped me get on a thick wooden table. Both Thech and Stekia put pails on the table.

"This will help you relax," Thech said. And they started to rub some scented oils. They started on my face. "Close your eyes and relax."

They rubbed oils over my whole body. It felt relaxing after a little bit. I opened my eyes to watch. After they had me covered with the oils that had nice scents of walnuts and something else I could not place, Kug came in.

Standing at the end of the table close to my head, he began chanting, he stopped abruptly.

"Calarel, I must ask you something that can affect the outcome of your prayer night. I do not know if you want it shared."

"Well, I guess that depends on what it is?" I asked them "There seems to be two in your mind," Kug told me softly after he had bent to whisper in my ear. "Oh yes. I have a blood bond with Scorch. Do not tell anyone. It a secret." I laughed, I meant to be serious.

"You must tell this Scorch not to take any action this night," Kug told me. "This scorch must try to not feel your dreams or your emotions. I do not have time to consult with the spirits, it has begun. Your Scorch must not intervene."

"Did you understand what he said? I am not real sure I did. Do what has been said. I feel good. I feel like a weight is no longer on me."

"From what I can tell, you should feel good. I will do my best to remove myself if I can. Good luck, Calarel."

The feeling of Scorch went to the back of my mind. I did not want to let go of the little piece that I could still feel.

Kug started his chanting again. "Your arms feel light as feathers, raise them above the table." My arms floated up to about a forty-five-degree angle. He chanted some more. "As you become tired, your arms will become heavier." More chants. "When your arms reach the table again, you will be in the state that the gods can reach you and ease your pain."

Thech and Stekia were both swaying to their rhythmic chants. They seemed to be in a trance. I could hardly see the rafters when I felt my fingertips touch the table.

There was someone standing in front of me. I could not recognize them, too much glowing light around them. But the voice was booming, it came from everywhere at once.

"Calarel! You are not to be here at this time. You are here to lessen a pain that you most learn from."

Another voice. It was female, but I could see no one, only the first glowing figure.

"I see things ahead of you. I will show you a little. But you will not remember them. Until it is too late. If you remember at all."

The male figure laughed out loud. A laugh that could easily frighten you to death.

Visions, lots of visions, Fire Drakes whirling through the air, lightning bolts zipping across at chest level from hands and swords. Skeletons by the hundreds driven back by great walls of flame. People dying all around in different places. Battles and more battles but never victorious. Weddings at great castles. Banners hung across streets in many towns. Demons worse than in any book in the great libraries. And I am involved in all of it.

I sat up right. I was shaking. Why? Scorch must be in the gray, he felt that distant. Thech, Stekia, and Kug were all asleep on the floor. The torches were all out. They looked to have burnt out rather than being dowsed. There was faint light coming from the door way. As if it were just before dawn. I climbed down from the table, almost slid off with the oils still on the table and me. I went to the door and peeked outside. Two more women stood as guards. They watched as I opened the door a little more.

"Where can I bathe?"

"You rise early. As you said you would. Most sleep well into the day after a prayer night," the taller said. "Come, I will take you to the springs to bathe."

"I need my boots and my clothes."

"If your feet look as tender as…" she paused for a moment as she looked at the two scars on my body, "soft as the rest of your body. Come, I will carry you on my back. You do not want to get the oils on your clothes."

"But someone might see me," I exclaimed softly, so I would not wake the others in the hut.

"Everyone is asleep. No one will see. Besides, we do not wear our tops all the time. It would be nothing new," she replied.

"Well, maybe not for you." I came the rest of the way out the door. I think she tried to keep her eyes on mine. But they drifted and the other woman all but stared.

She looked back to the older woman. "Sorry. I cannot remember the last time a mannish race was in the village."

"Treka, bring her things. She needs to bathe." "I'll bring them. I don't think her body has seen

the sun. She is white as a baby. But she looks strong enough to win at wrestling even you, Beilona."

I grasped Beilona's wrist, and she helped me on to her back. "I've been bare-back riding before. But never in the nude."

"That's okay, I've never had anyone nude on my bare back either." She started for the place she was taking me to.

As we left the village, we passed by a guard. "Up early this morning."

"Yes! We are going to wash in the springs. Let Treka follow, but no one else. Please," Beilona commanded more than asked.

"Okay, Beilona. Just be careful. It's still dark down there."

"We will," she continued on without stopping.

We talked on the way.

At one point, I had to wrap my arms around her or slide off. "Sorry."

"Loosen your grip a little. I do need to breathe.

You can hold on, but not so tight." "Sorry."

"You say that a lot. 'Sorry.' I can see why you do, not knowing your own strength. You are stronger than any woman in our village and maybe half the men. Well, maybe not half, but some." She laughed a little.

So did I, a little.

"My sister says I will never find a man because I will scare them all away. Because I am too strong for them, but I like my strength."

"Why would you want to be so strong?" Beilona almost sounded as if she didn't want an answer. I answered anyway.

"I'm not really sure. But I do know that when I need strength, I like the fact that it is there. I tend to find people that are not good. Thieves mostly, but others that are against the laws and rules. That's who killed Abon and tried to kill me yesterday, just a bunch of dumb thieves."

I could feel the tears are forming in my eyes.

The trail was about ten feet above the water; it looked to be deep enough. The water almost looked smooth. I slid off her back.

"I'll race you to the water."

"How do you intend to run on the ground when you don't have your boots?"

"Race or not?" "Race."

She took off down the trail.

I took two steps and jumped from there. I yelled, "I win."

I don't know if she heard me before I hit the water. I was hoping it wasn't too cold. I was pleasantly surprised, it was warm. I swam underwater toward where I thought she would be at. I was pushed to the surface of the pond by the springs that feed the pool. I swam to the edge.

"Are all the mannish tribes as crazy as you are?" She carefully stepped into the pool.

"One can only hope not." I laughed lightly.

We bathed and talked and laughed as if sisters. We became good friends in the summer month I was there. I helped tend the gardens. I would join the hunting parties.

An Arcane gate opened in the ten foot by ten foot area marked by the gray granite stones protruding from the well-trimmed grass. Aravea stepped through the opening and let it close behind her. It was a rare occasion that she came here. It was always warm, even in the dead of winter. It seemed to be mid-spring here inside these walls. A small palace in the mountains of the Elven Territories. It seems secluded from the rest of the world. Mostly it was. From the inside of the fifteen-foot-tall walls of granite, you could see tops of other mountains and the blue sky with a few wisps of clouds. A smoke house of stone with a wooden roof. And a two-story granite stone house, large enough to house thirty people or more. A man dressed in gray robes came from the side door and walked toward her.

"Pleasant to see you again, Lady Lotithil. Please, this way. I will take you to Lady Ancalime," he said when he was a little more than five steps from the small area she stood in. As she stepped out of the grass on to the stone walkway, he bowed deeply. "May I carry your things for you?" he said as he stood straight again.

"Not this time, Marel. I believe I will carry it. Thank you. I do hope she is not busy?" she said, nod-ding slightly.

"No, my lady, she was expecting you. Right this way."

He turned and walked toward the door. Marel held the door for Aravea. Then after closing it again, he led the way down a few corridors that had stand tables in them. Each table had a different item placed on top of it. Aravea could feel the power of some of those items. He led her to the Greeting Room.

"If you would wait here please?" he asked as he tapped on the door.

From the other side of the door, a hardly audible "Enter" could be heard. He opened the door enough to allow himself in. "Lady Lotithil to see you, my lady."

"Allow her entrance, Marel." The voice was soft and flowing. A young voice if ever one was heard.

Marel opened the door.

"Enter please. I will have fresh wine sent right away."

Aravea walked into the room. He bowed his way out and closed the door.

"Sha'Quessr creoso." Lady Ancalime did not look her age. Almost grandmotherly, but Aravea knew she had to be close to two times her age of four hundred ten years.

"Diola lle. You honor me. I have brought both of the Angelicas with me. I have them shielded from each other. But I am sure they are not why you have summoned me."

"You are correct in your assumption, Aravea. I believe that you have made contact with one of the chosen."

"I may have, but he seems to not want to get involved in what I have to offer."

"I speak of the one you had retrieve the Angelicas. She, I think, is the one we seek most. I think Tulkus may have had play in that choice. I do not know why. I have been told she has lost her companion and is now with the Rah'edan south of Cynar. It is hoped that they can heal her spirit. When the time comes, she will be sent to you."

"From what I saw of her, she is strong of mind and body. But I do hope that by saying her companion was lost, you do not mean her bond with the demon horse has been broken. That I do not think she will survive," Aravea said calmly, but inside, she began to feel a little worried. "If that is the case, from what I understand, she will be lucky to survive a month at most. Even with help from the Rah'edan."

Gilraen sat in thought for a moment. There was a little tap at the door.

"Enter," she said in a normal tone of voice. She continued as a maid in gray garb entered carrying a porcelain bowl and a finely worked pitcher to match. She filled two goblets of high polished silver with wine. Handed one to each woman and left the room. "It must not be so! I have heard nothing of this. What do you mean demon…" she emphasized the word demon. "Horse? And bonded how?"

"Calarel is the girl's name. Her horse told her, I read its mind. It was created by other beings on another plain. There was no link to this creator that I could find, in the short time I had with the horse.

Perhaps those higher could find out more than I. She took a blood bond with the creature. There must have been some small rite performed. I do not know for sure. Or perhaps it has something to do with the creature's nature. I cannot say." Aravea took a drink from her goblet. Much more than just a sip. "Let us hope the death was of her friend Abon, a Halfling. That would mean the other horse will pass from the loneliness of the bond to him, if he was bonded to it." Another sip of wine. "She does hide the fact that the horse and her communicate with each other. It would seem they work well together."

"That is yet to be seen. There has been a request that a certain artifact be found by her. It may be a tricky task for you but I believe that you can tend to it easily."

"You know I will do what I can to help in this." Time was passing as they talked of present needs and things of the future, and it grew late in the afternoon.

"I have taken much of your time, Gilraen, and I must go. Let me know the next time I may be of service to you. Tenna' ento lye omenta."

"Tenna' san, Aravea Tenna san."

Aravea heard the door latch and Marel was there in the hall. She nearly gave a start, but suppressed it. "I'll walk you out, Lady Lotithil," he said as he stood from a bow she had not expected.

"Thank you, Marel" was all she needed to say. And he led her back to the area she had used each time she came here. He always stopped short of the end of the stone walkway and bid her pleasant journeys. She opened the Arcane Gate to the area in her yard she knew no one would be and walked through.

§§§

One evening, the hunting party came back with three horses. The horses looked to be purebred. Very fine looking animals. I found out they were the Zebron horses, whatever that was. By sunrise the next morning, I had everything packed and ready to go. Scorch was ready to leave the Centaurs, Stormy would follow Scorch wherever I took him. She ate little, enough to sustain most of her health, but not much more. I have been here sixty-five days, almost a month. I could think of Abon without getting tears in my eyes or have that feeling in my gut. The one you have that everything inside is getting tight.

It was the bonding that was getting to Stormy. I wish I knew how to cure that for her. She seemed so sad. And nothing I did helped.

I think I hugged over half the tribe. Before we finally headed toward the southwest to this Zebron's place. I learned that Chrav made each trip to the Zebron ranch. He spoke common the best of any in his tribe. It was midafternoon when we abruptly came out of the thick forest. In the far distance stood a large what looked like a two-story house, stables, and a barn to the left. There were two men repairing the fence that was ten paces from the edge of the forest.

"Chrav," called out one of them, as he looked up at the movement. "It has been a long time."

"Yes, it has been almost three seasons. You are keeping watch on your fences."

It almost sounded like a joke. The workers only smiled.

"We have found three this time. And a friend."

Chrav only looked at the gate. He stepped closer to it but never touched it.

The younger of the two workers jogged to the gate and unlatched it. "Please come in, Chrav. All of you may come in. Zebron invites you as always. You are honored guests of Zebron."

A hoof crossed the fence line before Chrav said anything. "I thank you for honoring me to your home," and each said the same as they entered through the gate. A custom, I guess.

As I came through the gate, Chrav introduced me. "I would like you to meet Calarel. A good soul of your kind."

The other worker had mounted his horse to be on the same level as the rest of us.

"Chrav, a friend of yours is a friend of Zebron.

We welcome you, Calarel! With open arms."

He rode over next to Scorch and gave me a small hug. I hugged him back more meaningfully, then he hugged me. He went on to hug the others.

The younger man closed and latched the gate after Stormy came through. "Beautiful horses you have here."

Stormy didn't even flinch as he ran his hand along her side. "Big too." Then he went to retrieve his horse.

"Run ahead and tell Zebron, Chrav has come to visit," the one already on his horse told the other. "My name is Randall. Glad to meet you, ma'am." He looked at Chrav. "Come up to the house, we will have a drink after your long ride."

As we headed to the house, I noticed another building at the far side of the clearing. It looked to have three small smoke stacks sticking out of the roof. There must be three more on the other side of the steeply pitched roof. I could see at least five small wisps of smoke drifting up from that direction. I wondered what was going on there.

When we reached the stables, there were a few men standing around waiting for us. Groomsmen and trainers by the looks of them. And a man who looked as if he were a lord. Dressed in fine clothes. Braiding up the sleeves of his jacket, a circle with a Z in the middle embroidered on the collar.

"Welcome to my home, Chrav." He gave a slight nod. "Welcome all of you. Please join me in a small midday meal."

He opened a gate and walked through. As each Centaur reached the gate, they handed the rope they used as lead for the horse to a groomsmen or trainer.

As I rode through, two groomsmen came to me on the other side of the fence. They both had puzzled looks on their faces. No lead on Stormy must have been why they hesitated reaching for the hackamores on Scorch and Stormy. The reins attached to Stormy's hackamore were tied and looped over the saddle horn. They kept a pace distance from us.

"Hello, young lady, my name is Zebron," he said as I climbed down.

I laid the reins across the saddle. "I am Calarel Nessis. I am glad to finally meet the man that is friends with Chrav and his clan." I only gave him a slight nod, wasn't sure if I was to curtsy or bow, the nod sufficed.

"Two very nice-looking animals you have here. I usually pride myself on my knowledge of horses, but these two have me stumped. I don't believe I have seen that breed before."

He looked to be trying to remember the breed, rubbing his chin.

"They are a warhorse from somewhere across the oceans."

"He will figure out we are not like the others."

"Hold your ground, Scorch. Act important like Hawk's horse does."

"How well trained are they?"

"I have not met better. My father trains war- horses for some of the realm's guardsmen. I have trained a few horses myself."

"You look to be a guard yourself. Not meaning any disrespect of course." Then turned and called out toward the stables. "Bring out the tables and an extra stool."

The stable hands and groomsmen all pitched in to move some rather large tables and platforms out of the barn. They set them up so that the Centaurs could stand easily on one side and mannish races could sit at the other. The servants had a raised walkway in the middle to be able to serve the tables from the middle. Zebron seemed to take good care of his friends.

I took my shield and hung it on the saddle and then my backpack. I pulled the job posting from one of the pockets. The contact's name was Zebron. I took it to him and asked if the position was still open. I didn't really think it would be but it couldn't hurt.

"No. Sorry, but with your knowledge, I sure could have used you. So you were in Cynar for a while."

"Yes, for over a year. It was time to move on to something else."

That was all he needed to know.

"Well, I've heard rumors. There is someone near Rime, I think it's Rime anyway. Someone is looking for someone to travel around and gather antiques of some sort or another," he told me in between talking to Chrav and the others. He must have been some kind of high-ranking diplomat at one time, the way he handled three conversations at once.

With everything set in its place, we all gathered around the tables. And the servants began bringing out plates of food. How they prepared so much so fast, with only half an hour's notice, I have no clue.

After an hour or two around the table, Chrav and Zebron worked out a payment for the return of the horses. A couple of baskets of vegetables and two casks of ale. Chrav and the others collected their ropes and were ready to make the trip back to their camp.

"Chrav, I must thank you for the things your people have taught me. And tell Rhinn I will continue to practice with the spear. Next time, he can pick the challenge," I told him as I stood on the second rung of the fence to give him a hug. It would have been easier to climb up in the saddle.

"You, Calarel, are welcome in our village any- time. Do not be a stranger to us. And we thank you for your teachings," he replied as we hugged.

I hugged each one as they went through the gate to the pasture. We all waved more than needed. And the tears came to my eyes, I had to wipe them away before I turned around to face the others.

Stella, Zebron's wife, said, "They are a nice group of creatures."

I guess she didn't really know them well. "That group of creatures, as you put it, are Centaurs. Yes, they are very nice people, once you get to know them." After I said that, she had a look that could kill,

but it faded fast. As she looked at me in the eyes, my eyes still wet with tears, she smiled.

"I meant no disrespect to them. Come inside and we can get you freshened up." She put her hand around my elbow and started leading the way.

"I need to tend my horses first, and then I will join you."

She looked at Zebron, who only nodded to her. "Oh, of course, tend to your horses. I'll meet you in the parlor when you are done."

She turned and walked toward the house, giving Zebron a small peck on the cheek on the way.

"Would you like some help with them?" Zebron asked as he looked toward Stormy.

"Okay, if you really want to. You can help with Stormy." I changed direction a little to go to her first. As we came to be in front of Stormy, I introduced them, "Stormy, this is Zebron. Zebron, this is Stormy." Zebron reached up and rubbed her nose, then behind the ears and down the neck, before he spoke again.

"This horse is ill. But I detect no fever or any- thing of that nature," he said softly as not to disturb Stormy. "Does she have internal injuries?"

I stood back a little, rubbing Scorch's neck. "I guess in a way, you could say that she has a broken heart." That was the only way I could think of not tell- ing him about the bond she had with Abon. "Her last owner has passed. The Deities watch over his soul."

"I'm sorry to hear about the loss of your friend. The Deities protect him," Zebron said as he bowed his head as if in prayer. "I have never heard of a horse grieving so, over the loss of a rider."

"I do not understand it ether, but as you can see." I did not finish what I was going to say. "I told him I would watch over her."

Zebron started for the stables.

As we entered the stables, one of the other horses frisked a little. Scorch snorted, and the other horse backed up in the stall. Two of the stable hands came toward us to take the horses.

"We will tend to these two, thank you," Zebron announced. "You can use these two stalls here."

We unsaddled both Scorch and Stormy and removed the hackamores. I grabbed my saddlebags and backpack, and we went to the house. I have only seen the inside of one other house this pristine, and that was the house of a lord in Cynar. We entered through the kitchen. It had to be the largest kitchen I had ever seen. Two cookstoves, a fireplace with two sections to it. Each side had a large swinging rod that held a large kettle at the end on a hook. One woman slicing carrots and another slicing potatoes into one of the kettles that was swung out from the fireplace. Two people were washing the dishes from lunch.

"Stew for dinner, I'm guessing?" Zebron asked no one in particular.

A rather large woman answered, "Yes, my lord. Your favorite, venison stew, the way you like it, of course."

"Very good," he replied. "Right this way, Calarel." He gestured toward the door closest to us. There was a pair of swinging doors at the other end of the kitchen as well.

We entered into a dining hall, with a large table and twelve gilded chairs around it, gilded china cabinet full of ornate-looking china. The floor was waxed so much, you could see your reflection. There were doors that slid into the walls to close off the dining area from the hall. We crossed the hall into another very large room with several cushioned couches and chairs.

Stella removed the book from her lap and placed it open pages down on the small table in front of the couch.

"We will continue our lessons in a few minutes. After I show Miss Nessis to her room and help get things ready for her."

"Yes, ma'am," they both replied. "You're a teacher."

"Yes, and their mother. Our third is taking his nap. Come along, I will show you to your room. And have a bath drawn for you."

"Well now that you are in her hands, I will tend to my duties. Please make yourself at home and enjoy your stay with us," Zebron said as he started to head down the hall.

"I do not really want to impose on you and family. I can move on down the road," I replied.

"Nonsense, Calarel, you will stay for the night, and after breakfast, you can start your journey fresh," Stella said as she led me upstairs, to the second door on the right. "You can use this room. It is large and has a small room here." She opened the door. "In here is a tub for bathing. I'll have water up to you shortly."

"Yes, ma'am, thank you."

When she said shortly, she meant it. It was a wonderful bath, with fragrances of rose and some- thing else I couldn't figure out. They asked about dirty clothes, so they could be washed. I gave them my dirty clothes.

We had a grand dinner, more than I could eat. And some very good ale after. Zebron was not only a horse breeder, but also had his own ale brewery on the far side of the pasture to the south. He is an Ambassador to the realm. This meant he was higher in ranking than a Lord. Why they took me in, I have no idea.

He told me to go to Rime and speak with the innkeeper at the Red Feather Inn. And to be sure to tell the innkeeper that he had sent me. We all went to bed. I finally stopped reading and turned out the lamp. I told Scorch good night and asked him to tell Stormy the same. He said he would.

I woke the next morning, got dressed as usual, and went out to practice with my sword and give Scorch and Stormy their apples. I was practicing when I saw Zebron come outside. He watched for a little bit.

"You must practice every day the way you handle that sword."

"I do. My father taught me the way of arms from when I was little."

"Well, if you're done, come get some food."

We had a big first meal. They asked me to stay one more day. I did. I helped in the stables by cleaning out a few of the stalls and helped with some of the training of a horse. Zebron asked why I was helping the paid help. I told him to repay the kindness they had shown me. It was only fair I told him.

"Well, you can come stay anytime you like," he replied laughingly.

I slept well that night. In the morning, I gave Scorch and Stormy their apples and brushed them both. I did my exercises and then packed my things. We had another wonderful first meal. I saddled the horses and thanked them for all they had done for me. Stella gave me some dried beef for the trip. I waved goodbye from down the driveway and was headed toward Rime.

I had two choices. One was to head south to the intersection and go up to Lugard and add close to one hundred miles or go through Cynar. And hope that the troubles were over. I headed south. I'm in no hurry, but this is the long way around.

A day past the intersection where I had to turn east, Scorch stopped.

"What's wrong? Is something coming?" I asked aloud.

"Look up above the trail. A little to the north,"

Scorch told me

Ahead of us a little to the north of the trail was a large reddish brown dragon. It was huge, larger than I ever imagined.

"I am guessing, but that must be about fifty feet long with wings about eighty feet from tip to tip."

"Bigger." Scorch stood looking with ears perked, trying hear a sound from that direction.

We stood there motionless until it was out of sight. It was a magnificent creature. I would not really want to meet one face to face. But it was very graceful in flight, for being so large.

A few hours later, we came to a place that would have been a good place to camp for the night, if not for a pair of freight wagons already there. The horses were picketed. And a cook fire was burning strong, I did not stop, only nodded as I rode by. One man jumped up and came running in my direction.

"Wait, Calarel! Stop!" he yelled.

I stopped and swung Scorch around to face him, as he came running up to us. He slowed to a walk before he was to close.

"I was hoping that it was you. I hate looking like a fool thinking it's someone you know and it turns out to be a stranger." He came to a stop beside Scorch and put his hand on my thigh.

"Yes, it is me, Wil. How are you doing?"

"I'm doing well. Where is your friend, the Halfling?"

"We met up with some thieves. They killed Abon."

"I'm sorry to hear that, Calarel. Come camp with us tonight. It would be well past dark before you get to a good place to camp for the night."

I looked in the direction I was traveling, and he might be right. Dense forest started not more than three hundred paces from where we were. Maybe half an hour before the sun would be touching the horizon. "Okay, but I take first watch. If you keep watch, that is?"

"Well, we do, but there is no need for you to do that, Calarel. We can handle the watch we do every night. You can get some extra rest."

"Wil, I am Half Elf. I do not need but four hours of sleep a night. Two of you could get a little extra sleep tonight."

"It wouldn't be right for you to stand guard while two of us sleep. We get paid to guard the wagons, you don't."

"Okay, then I'll move on." I started to rein Scorch back around to continue down the road.

He started to grab for the hackamore and changed his mind and put his hand to his neck to scratch at the stubble of his beard.

"Okay, but we stand guard with you."

He acted like he was ready to start walking with me if I started down the road.

I reined Scorch back around toward him and headed for the camp. "Okay, I will stay the night with your wagons. But I usually stay up until after the midnight hour and rise about an hour before the sun and do exercises for an hour."

"Yes, I remember you being up early in the morning."

"I hope nobody else has troubles with that." "They won't," he said as we neared the group

of men sitting around the fire that had a large kettle hanging above it. The aroma of stew wafting through the camp made my stomach rumble. "You all remember Calarel."

Most nodded, two stood up. One was an older man with more gray in his hair than brown. He was strong looking and in good physical shape. Old enough to be a grandfather and they called him Grampa. The other was Rand. Tall, looked to be skin and bones, but he moved in a way that said otherwise. Most had leather armor, and all wore daggers.

We sat around the fire and ate rabbit stew. Grampa was a good shot with the bow and a good cook. We all talked for a while. I had to lie about the bandits, I couldn't really tell them how I defeated all four of them by myself. Most everyone went to sleep in their tent or under a wagon. I set up my tent and started watch. I took note of where the next person for watch slept. Wil stayed up for his watch with me. "Why do you not go get some sleep, Wil? I will wake up John when my watch is over."

"No, that's okay. I'll stay up until then," he insisted.

"If he would ever go to sleep, you could go to the gray, Scorch."

"Unfortunately, Stormy has to leave us now. The Creators have asked her to come to them. You need to saddle her and give her one last apple before she goes."

"Oh damn, not tonight. Why tonight?" "What's wrong?"

As I started to get up from the log by the fire, I told him that one of my horses had to go. He looked at me as if I were crazy. I walked over and grabbed Stormy's saddle blanket; he grabbed her saddle and brought it to me. After I had the blanket on her, he put on her saddle and went to buckle the chinch strap, but he backed away as she started to fade a little.

"Grab her saddlebags quick!" I demanded. He ran the three paces, picked them up, and ran back just as fast. I threw them on the saddle, opened the one bag that had the apples in it, and gave her one. I could almost see all the way through her. She took the apple. There was a tear that was slowly sliding down her cheek.

"Stormy, Scorch and I will miss you. I hope you can come back to us."

I wiped the tear away and gave her a hug. Then there was no horse there. I looked at the wet spot on my finger.

For a moment, Wil stood there with his mouth out. "What happened to that horse?"

"I hate to say goodbye. I hope it is not forever." I added a tear of my own to the one that was already on my finger. "Scorch, go ahead and go, take as long as you need," and he disappeared.

"Close your mouth, Wil, you look ridiculous." "Did I just see those horses disappear?"

I sighed rather loudly for a sigh. "Yes. One faded away to another plane of existence, and the other disappeared to a place that they go to every night for about an hour. Scorch will be back when he is ready. Please, Wil, I would appreciate it if you told no one about what you have just seen." I thought about the situation for a moment. "To make things easier on you and myself, I will leave as soon as Scorch gets back. How you explain not waking up John in ten minutes is up to you."

His mouth worked, but nothing came out. Then he finally spoke, "But, but I have to wake up John!"

"No, you cannot wake up John. He will see that both of my horses are gone, then when Scorch comes back, appearing out of nowhere. How will you explain that?" I held my hands out and raised my shoulders. "Oh well, Calarel has these Demon horses, and they just disappear and reappear in the night. And they have these powers that even she does not know what all they come do. Now it is bad enough that you had to learn about them, but the whole camp does not need to know that, do they?" I asked him a little more sarcastic than I wanted to.

He started stammering again. Then took another breath and began again. "No, I guess you're right."

I packed everything up and had it ready for when Scorch came back. John's watch was almost over when

Scorch came back. As I started to saddle Scorch, I asked if he was okay and if he was ready to move on. His answer was a simple yes. I pulled my backpack on, I gave Wil a hug.

"I will not forget you, Wil. You are a true friend." I put my foot in the stirrup and grabbed the saddle horn and pulled myself up into the saddle. "Goodbye for now, Wil. I hope we see each other again."

"Calarel, where can I find you?" He sounded sad when he asked.

"I will be around. We will see each other on the road again, I am sure."

"Let us go five miles down the road if you can, Scorch."

We were in the middle of the road somewhere to the east with no camp in sight.

Chapter 6

It took me almost two weeks to get to Rime. It was a good trip, without problems. I got a room at the Red Feather Inn. I told the Innkeeper, Fred, that Zebron had sent me, and to acquire about a job about antiques.

"Well, how is Zebron doing? Did you meet his wife? And those two kids of his?"

I laughed a little and told him they were fine and that it was three kids now, all boys.

"As far as the job goes, it may be a few days, but I will get a message out to the hiring party. You could stay as long as you need."

"Thank you, Fred."

The next day, I went walking around. To see what was in town. For a small town, it had just about everything you could want. Some of the shops had their wares on tables in front of them. Most had displays in front windows. I stayed at the inn most of the time just in case the employer came by. As I sat eating my lunch, I saw a half elf about my age, come in and talk to Fred. It was a short conversation; she had a package with her, perhaps that might be the reason for the fast visit with Fred. I remember seeing her somewhere before, perhaps in Lugard.

It was a pleasant day, if not boring. Night came, so I went to bed.

In the morning, I woke at my usual time, about an hour before the sun came up, I dressed as usual with my armor and swords. I went out to the stables and brushed Scorch. I gave him an apple from his saddlebags. Then I went out to the yard to exercise and practice with my sword. After I was done, I went back into the inn and had a wonderful breakfast.

Egwene, Fred's wife, braided my hair; she did a braid that started at the front of my head and added more of my hair as she worked her way to the back. When she finished, she tied the leather cord I used to tie my hair; she concealed the leather with a piece of ribbon. Just to make it look a little softer, she told me. I decided to go for a walk. As I was walking to nowhere in particular, a little ahead of me, I saw a man push a woman into an alley. I increased my pace to arrive at the corner of the building sooner. Once there, I peeked around the corner of the building. He had a coin purse in one hand and was standing back up. The woman was lying on her back. I rushed to him, grabbed the back of his collar, and pushed him to the ground close to her. As he rolled over to see who had put him on the ground. I pulled my sword and put the tip to his neck. "He stole my coin pouch."

"Give her pouch back, and maybe I will not call for the Guards."

The cutpurse and the woman could see me taking a big breath to yell for a Guard or Legionnaire.

In a near panic, he laid her pouch at arm's length. "Okay, don't call them, I'm giving it back."

She grabbed it and looked at the knot which had not been untied. The only thing she could think of was to say "Thank you."

I never took my eyes from his. "I hope you have learned a lesson, thief."

"Yes. Yes, I have."

"I wonder what makes you think that you must steal from people?" she asked.

"I ain't got no other skills that are useful." He did not look away from the side of my blade.

"I think that is a lie you tell yourself to justify being a thief. I do hope you can find something else to do besides being a cutpurse. What other work do you do around here?"

"Work? I don't work."

"You must have some other means of getting money?"

The woman on the ground started getting up from the ground.

"Well, of course. I do trades with some of the people around here. I make a little money doing that. But it's not enough. I have to steal sometimes to get some ale." He looked at her.

"I would think that having both hands would be more important than an ale or two. Have you ever been in prison before? I hear it is a rotten place to stay. Stone floors, dark, damp, and cold. Once you get sick, you stay sick until you die."

"Do you want to press charges against him?" "No, I have my money back."

I let him up. He continued down the alley. After he had gone a few building lengths, I sheathed my sword.

"You are very brave. Thank you for helping me." I waited as she continued, "I can't think of a time I have ever been more scared in my life. I don't know who was more afraid, me or him."

"I would like an ale!" I looked in the direction of the inn.

"I can't really afford to buy you an ale and get a room for the night."

"What is your name anyway?"

"My name is Terry Seligon. And yours?" "Calarel Nessis. I still want an ale."

"I can't believe you did that!"

"He was lucky this time. I should have turned him over the authorities."

We went to the inn. We had lunch, and I had just one ale while we talked. Terry told me of her life to this point. How her mother had died several years ago. How her father had raised her and her sister cruelly. She decided it was time for her to get away and find a way to save her sister. That was her purpose in her life. And she thanked me for showing her that she had much to learn. She said she was too weak to fight and win against him. I told her she was not really weak. I think she ignored me for the most part.

She listened while I told her of adventures I have had. How I was a messenger. I sometimes helped to catch thieves. That sometimes, there were rewards for them.

In through the front doors walked a woman, a beautiful High Elf.

"Calarel, I would swear you could see her aura," I looked puzzled, I am sure. "Her what?"

"A faint light glowing around her."

I turned to look at who she was talking about.

It was Miss Lotithil.

She walked to our table and stopped behind me. "I have a job for you, Calarel, if you want one." "Well, I have heard about a job here. That is

why I am here, something to do with antiques," I told her.

"Yes, I know. I had that posting put out. I need someone to deliver an item for me." She looked down at the satchel she was carrying. "It will be a long journey, perhaps as long as three weeks or more."

"That long? Where am I to deliver this item?" I asked.

"You need to go to Lethys and find a shop called Tarsis Wares. It is in the central part of the city. Once there talk to Kedol Tarsis. He is the owner and proprietor of the shop."

She would look toward Terry occasionally while she talked.

"Okay, I can do that," I replied.

Fred came over to our table. "Miss Lotithil." He gave her a deep bow. "What a surprise to see you here so close to the evening meal. Would you not prefer a private dining room? I can have meals brought to you right away if you like."

"No, thank you, Fred. I have other business to attend yet."

"Very well, Miss Lotithil. Perhaps a glass of cool tea then?"

"No, thank you, Fred, I am fine." "Calarel, ma'am, anything to drink?"

"Oh no, thank you. Not yet. But I am getting hungry. But in a little while."

"Very well, I'll check back with you in a little bit." He went to check on a few other customers. "Miss Lotithil, I would like to introduce you to

Terry Seligon, a friend of mine." I looked at Terry. "Pleased to meet you, Terry." She studied Terry for moment. "I believe that we might have a few things to talk about later." Aravea looked back to me. "Inside this satchel, you will find the item, which you are to give to Kedol Tarsis along with the letter that is with it. You will also find a coin purse with enough money to get you there and back. I believe. Please be able to account for the money spent," she said as she handed me the satchel. "Yes, ma'am, I will do the best I can, as before."

"So is there going to be three of you on this trip?" "No, Miss Lotithil, just me, unless, Terry wishes

to join me."

I looked at Terry, hoping she would join me on this little quest.

"It would be better if Abon were with you." "Yes, I would agree with you. But he was killed by thieves shortly after we left Cynar."

I tried to not to show the pain I felt.

"I am sorry to hear that, Calarel, my condolences. It would be best if there were two of you traveling together." She looked at Terry.

Terry looked at me. "I would be glad to have your company, Terry, if you want to come along."

"Well, I am just traveling around to learn more. Sure, I'll go with you, but I don't have a horse. Will that be a problem?"

"No, I do not think so. Between the both of us, we should be able to get a good horse for you."

Cheryl was walking back toward the kitchen; when Aravea gained her attention, Cheryl stopped and faced her.

"Yes, Lady Lotithil, can I get something for you?" "Yes, Cheryl, I would like to speak with Fred if he isn't busy."

"Of course, Lady Lotithil, right away," she responded as she curtsied.

"We will see about getting you a horse to use at the very least."

"Miss Lotithil, how fast do you want this delivered?"

"Calarel, I do not dare to set a date, because you would ride the horses into the ground if I did not give a sufficient amount of time. Master Tarsis is not expecting you for at least half a month. That should give you enough time to make the trip without being in a rush."

She turned to watch Fred hurry over to where we were.

"Sorry I took so long, but we are a little busy. What can I help you with?"

"Would you know where we can get a horse?" "You need a horse?" he asked with puzzlement in his voice. "I have one you can use. Or are you looking to buy one?"

"I believe we need to buy one, it would be about two months before they could return your horse to you, Fred."

"Two months you say." He hummed to indicate hesitation and rolled his eyes in thought. "Well, for you I would lend you a horse, for a couple of months if needed." After another moment's hesitation, he continued, "Perhaps say, at half the price of buying a horse?"

"Master al' Vere, always the businessman, what if your horse becomes lame?"

"That is an easy question and one of concern, I can well imagine." He smiled. "You would pay the other half of the cost of the horse. Simple enough, I would ask no more than that, Lady Lotithil."

"Very well, done. How much would you want for the horse Master al' Vere?"

"Let me see, would thirty-two silver be too much for the lending of a horse? And another thirty-two if the horse is not returned in good shape?"

"That would depend on the horse, Fred. Sixty- four silver is a little high, is it not?"

"He's a good horse, Calarel."

"I would like to see the horse first before we complete the deal."

"Well, of course, I wouldn't buy one without at least seeing it. Junior should be back by now." He gestured toward the hall that leads to the back. "If he is, you can have a look at the horse."

"I hope you are not going to lend us Junior's horse."

We started toward the back door, with the satchel over my shoulder. As we came out the back door of the inn, I saw a portion of the fence open and Junior stepped through. I had never seen the gate before, would never have thought to look for it either. "Hello, Calarel." Junior bowed toward Aravea. "Hello, Lady Lotithil. Ma'am. Do you need your horses or the coach rigged up?"

"Junior, did you unsaddle Whisper? Calarel and Miss Terry would like to borrow him for a while," Fred told his son. I caught the quick little nod and smile Fred gave his son.

"Junior, is Whisper your horse?"

"No." He frowned as he looked to the ground in front of him. Then he looked back up at me. "But he is a really good horse, and if Pa is only going to loan him to you, that means he will be back. And I know you, which means he will be in good hands. So if you want, you can use him."

"Thank you, Junior, I was hoping it was okay. Is Whisper a good horse? Be honest."

"Oh yes, Calarel. Whisper is a real good horse. Maybe not as good as Scorch, but he is good," he exclaimed.

"Well, your word is good enough for me, Junior. Can you have Whisper in the stables right after first meal in the morning, please?"

I pulled my coin pouch from behind my weapons belt and dug out thirty-two silver.

"Here you go, Fred, thirty-two silver for the use of Whisper."

Once we were back inside away from Junior, Fred asked, "Now why did you do that?"

"Do what, Fred? Accept his word that the horse was a good one."

"Yes."

"Fred, you have a good boy, and he knows a lot about horses for his age. I think he is a good judge of horse flesh. Let him learn as much as he wants about them. He may someday be in a position like my father. Who by the way, is a horse trainer and horse trader. He breeds horses for the realm. And besides, if Whisper is the same horse I saw him on the other day, he is a good horse."

"So," he said, drawing out the word, "you're one I will have to watch for."

"Yes, I think you may be right, Fred, she is one we will have to watch out for. Well, since that is taken care of,

I need to be about my own matters. Have a good night and a pleasant trip." Aravea looked from Terry to me.

"Fred, watch her. I believe that if she takes a liking to that horse, she may find a way to get it from you, if you're not careful."

With that said, she headed for the door.

Terry and I sat back down at our table. "Calarel, I hope you're right about the horse.

I'm not much of a rider."

"I do not think you will have much trouble with Whisper. From what I saw yesterday, he will do fine and so will you. Have some confidence in yourself."

Cheryl came over to our table, and we ordered some dinner and had a few drinks while a woman played a harp. She played and sang some songs I knew and some that Terry knew.

Fred cleared two tables away after a few people asked if he would, so they could dance. We both watched the people dancing, one man, tall, slender, and not too bad looking asked Terry to dance. She danced a couple of songs with him. Then she came back to the table alone.

"I need to get a room somewhere. I'm feeling tired after that."

I waved at Fred, and he came over to us straight away.

"Can I help you with something, Calarel?" he asked, sounding cheerful.

"Yes, Terry needs a room if you have any left.

You seem a little busy today."

"Of course I do. I saved a room for her next to yours just in case." He smiled.

"Very thoughtful of you, Fred." Terry smiled in return to him. "Then which room is yours, Calarel?" "She is in the first room on the right at the top of the stairs and you are the next one down the hall.

Oh, here is the key to the door." He pulled out a key from his pocket.

"Thank you, Fred."

"I will go up with you. I want to put this in my room anyway. I am getting tired of carrying this satchel around with me." I stood from my chair.

We both went upstairs and went to our rooms. I went into my room and placed the satchel under the bed, as far as I could reach. I wasn't tired yet, so I went down to the small library downstairs to find a map. When I walked into the library, there was a man sitting on one of the four chairs at the small table and had three books open in front of him.

"Here I think I found…" He looked up from the book that he was reading as I closed the door behind me. "Oh," he said with a surprised look on his face. "You are not Nathan."

"No sir, I am Calarel, I am just looking for a map." He looked to be a merchant by the looks of his clothes; shirt was good quality silk, a jacket of fine dark tan woolen material. I could not see a signet on the collar or the cuffs of the sleeves, indicating the ranking in a merchant guild. Two equally high-quality cloaks hung on the coat stand in the corner. "Perhaps you can help me? I'm looking to find the owners of a parcel of land, which lies along the road from Lugard to Duintolea. All the information I have found so far would indicate that it is owned by a Joseph Wellington. You wouldn't know him, would you?" he asked, sounding a little hopeful.

"Ah no, I am not from around here, but there is a Wellington's Apothecary in Cynar. I remember seeing that just outside the Old Wall Road, on the Duintolea Road," I said as I recalled one incident with a thief. The old woman was chasing a man out if the shop with a broom.

I walked to the wall that had a map framed under a sheet of glass. I found Rime easy enough, but Lethys I have never heard of. I searched north, northeast, and east.

"No, that is Little Rock Hold. Lethys, where are you?" I said to myself, after searching for a few minutes. "Southeast of Loran, across the Bay of Elysea, past Elysea Head." I heard from behind me, the man at the table had been quiet enough to forget. "Not much there, it's one of the two port cities for the Rhakhaan realm. Best to go by ship if you can," he added.

"Why do you say that?"

"They are having troubles with the Garks. They seem to be on the uprise again. Mainly they tend to stay closer to the mountains and foothills, but you just never know when a group of them may stray down to the coastline."

"Garks? What are those?" I turned from the map to wait for an answer.

"Hmm, not as well traveled as I expected. Well anyway, Garks are a gray fur-covered ape-like creature. With long arms that reach to their knees and a long prehensile tail." He stood up. He is High Elf, long silver hair that covered his ears the way he tied it in the back with a braided silken tie. He walked over to the map and pointed to Lethys. "The Garks are normally found in these areas along the mountains here." He pointed out a few places on the map along the mountain range that was the eastern border of the Rhakhaan realm. "And I have seen one family group around here." He pointed to a place on the map closer to the coast, about midway to where I was going, once in the Rhakhaan Realm.

"Thank you, good sir. I do appreciate the information," I replied graciously, while nodding.

The door started to open, and I widened my stance to block the door from swinging into him, giving him a little more time to move away from the door. Nathan walked into the room and looked around to find his friend turning toward him and me behind the door.

"You would not believe the horse that is out in the stables. He is huge, at least four hands taller than a warhorse," he explained excitedly. "And well trained, wouldn't even let me pat his nose."

"Scorch, you okay?" I thought to him. "I hope you did not try too hard, I would hate to have to pay for repairs."

"I am okay, there should be a rather excited man in there somewhere. The way he backed out of the stables, I guess he thought I might come after him."

"Oh no, ma'am, I know better than to corner a trained Warhorse. When he reared up, I figured it was time to go. That is one big horse. Is he yours?"

"Yes, he is mine. I guess I had better go check on him. Sometimes, he gets a little rambunctious." I went out the door, which I closed behind me. I went upstairs to my room and readied myself for bed. It did not take long to get to sleep once I was under the covers.

I woke up at my usual time, about an hour before the sun came up. I washed myself off, dressed, and donned my armor and weapons belt. I took an apple out of the saddlebags and headed down the back stairs. The kitchen was bright with two lanterns, I could hear the sifting of flour, and someone was mixing something in a bowl, as I walked by the door to the backdoor that leads to the stables. It was fairly nice out this morning, a few wispy clouds that hid little of the moonlight and stars. The stable doors were closed; I opened one of them and walked inside. There was no light in the stables, which meant I was the first out there.

"Good morning, Scorch. How was your night? Peaceful, I hope."

"Good morning, Calarel. It was a quiet night. Did you sleep well?"

"Yes, I did, thank you, would you like some- thing green this morning?"

"I like something green every morning, you know that. Why do you bother asking? Besides, it is more need than desire."

"Well, that may be true. But I can still ask just to be nice. Unless you would rather I just gave it to you and did not say anything at all."

"No, I think I like the way you are doing it now rather than silence." Scorch sounded a little worried about my response.

I only laughed. *"I would never treat you that way, my friend,"* I told him as I gave him his apple and then headed back out the door. The gray sky of early morning still showed a few stars as I went to the area that was open enough for me to do my exercises.

I exercised and practiced with my sword until the sun was a sliver above the horizon. Then went back into the inn and up to my room to freshen up for first meal; after I was done, I went down to the common room to find a table.

There were not many people in the common room. The bar stood empty, one of the waitresses stood at a table talking to the only other person there, one of the constables. He was talking to her and watching me as I took a seat that would allow me to watch the entrances to the room. When the waitress looked to see what he was looking at, she saw me seated. She said something to him and patted his shoulder in a friendly way, then headed toward me.

She approached the table I was at, and she asked, "Good morning, Calarel. You're up early this morning. Can I get you something to eat?"

I was about to say I would wait for my friend to come downstairs, when I heard someone coming down the stairs. I looked in the direction of the stairs, it was Terry. She wore a pair of pants and soft sole boots that laced up to just below her knees and a nice-looking shirt that matched her pants.

"Yes, I will have a few hotcakes, some sausage, and a couple of eggs. And a glass of milk too."

Terry sat down across from me. "Good morning. Are you ready to have first meal, I hope?"

"Yes, I'll have some toast with some preserves.

What kind of juice you have here?"

"We have some apple juice that is good. And we might have pear, which might still be good." The waitress tried to hide the look of dislike for the pear juice. "I think I'll have some apple juice." I guess she saw the look as well.

"I'll have it out to you soon," the waitress replied as she went toward the kitchen doors.

She did not lie, she had our meal out to us quickly, and our meal was good as usual. After we finished, we went next door to the merchant store to get some supplies for our journey. We packed every- thing, and I paid Fred for twelve meals, three nights stay, plus the one night for Terry and the stabling for three nights. I almost protested the cost, but the quality of service and the comfort of the bed were worth the three and a half copper he charged. I left the remainder of one and a half copper as a tip.

When we arrived at the stables, I found Junior brushing Scorch.

"Good morning, Junior. You might spoil him if you brush him too much. He may never want to leave." Junior jumped down from the stool he was using to brush Scorch's back and came out of the stall to greet us.

"No, Calarel, I don't think that will be a problem. I think he is ready to go somewhere now.

Whisper is ready too. I have him saddled already. He is in this stall over here, ready to go for you, ma'am."

I started heading toward the tack room. Junior ran past me to open the door.

"I'll carry Scorch's saddle blanket for you, Calarel," he said as I walked through the door.

"Okay, that sounds like a deal to me," I told him as I took hold of my saddle.

I picked it up and carried it out to the stall that Scorch was in. Junior handed me the blanket, and I laid it across Scorch's back. I finished saddling Scorch and tied my bedroll and saddlebags. I tied my bow sheath to the saddle fender and was ready to go. I pulled a couple of copper pieces out of my coin pouch and gave it to Junior.

"A little something extra for taking such good care of Scorch," I told him.

Terry and I both mounted up and started our trip. I let Terry's horse set the pace, although I think Scorch wanted to travel faster, being four hands larger.

After two days' travel toward the east, we arrived in Spurrie in time for the evening meal. Terry and I rode straight to the inn. Martha greeted us as we came through the door. Her clothes were clean, including the white apron she wore around her ample waist. Her hair done up in a bun with two small sticks sticking out both sides of her hair. "Come in, Calarel, come in. So glad you have come back to Spurrie."

"Just passing through, Martha, and this is the best place for a good meal."

I sniffed the air for aromas coming from the kitchen just behind the double doors at the other end of the room.

"I do have the best cook. Sherry has been with me almost since I opened the doors." She paused to take another long breath. "The other inn on the east side of town is not as comfortable as it is here either." "Speaking of comfort, could we get rooms for the night?" Terry set her backpack down.

"Oh, of course, my dear, sorry for ranting on so." Martha smiled at Terry while pointing to the stairs. "On the third floor, you will find four rooms with two beds, and of course, I have the single rooms up there as well."

"Well, first, I think I should tend to our horses. Terry, I will take the horses across the road." We both went out the door. Martha just stood there looking at us for a moment. I helped Terry untie her things from the saddle.

I took Whisper and Scorch into the stables and stopped at the first stalls.

"Hello," I called out.

The stalls were large enough for the horses to turn in. So I led Whisper into a stall. And Scorch just waited patiently for me, as I walked to the office at the other end.

I opened the door and stepped inside. Not a big office, but still had plenty of room. Besides the desk and chair, a few filing cabinets, a bookcase with more ledgers than books. Behind the desk sat a rather large man eating, who only looked up and ignored me and went back to his meal.

"Well, I can see why you dismissed my call earlier. I mean, your cold sandwich might have gotten colder or perhaps the rat in the corner would carry it off!" I said.

He stood up quickly to look in the corner by the file cabinets. Didn't see anything and asked, "Where?" "Well, now that I have your attention, I would like to stable some horses for the night," I told him. "All my hands have gone for dinner," he replied, "they should be back in an hour. We'll take care of them then."

"Oh, well in an hour, I will be taking a bath. So I guess you need to make sure and come get me at your convenience," I retorted. "In the meantime, stay away from my horses. Both of them will be in the first two stalls on the right side, at the other end of the building. I guess you are going to be responsible for damages caused by your own ignorance. Right!" I turned and started to walk out of the office.

"Hey, you can't just walk in here."

When I turned to walk toward the horses, Scorch was backing toward the office wall, preparing to kick it in.

"*Stop, Scorch. You can have fun later, after everyone is gone.*"

"Good sir, where is the good grain, so I can feed my horses."

"Scorch, find the good grain."

As he came out the door. "The grain is right there around the corner, in the feed bin. What makes you think you can come in here and start doing whatever you want?"

"This is a stable for the public. Or is this a privately owned stable of the Northeast Transport Company that only caters to them?"

"No, we are open to the public."

"Good," I said as I opened the feed bin and looked inside at the feed. "Are the rat droppings free or do you charge extra for those?"

Scorch was standing by some grain bags. *"Here, this smells good to me."*

"Ah, there we go, some fresher feed." I walked over to where Scorch was, picked up a bag, and laid the bag over Scorch's saddle.

He started for the bag of grain. "There is nothing wrong with the feed in the bin. You can use that just like everyone else."

Using our bond, I asked Scorch to move forward about ten steps. He complied and moved forward about ten steps. Leaving the stable master looking at me instead of the side of my horse. "I will gladly pay for the good grain and for the stabling. But I will not allow my horses to be fed that garbage in the feed bin. I will tend to my horses, and you can go back to your sandwich. Before that rat eats it."

"Go ahead, but you'll still pay full price." He pointed at me.

I walked over to Scorch, biting the inside of my cheek not to say anything else. When Scorch and I got to the stall where I had Whisper.

"He's not a very nice man."

"No, he is not, is he?"

I pulled the grain bag off the saddle and cut off a corner and used a quarter of the bag of grain to fill each of the feed troughs, unsaddled both horses, and brushed them both down.

"*Have a good night, Scorch. If anyone tries to take the feed from you, let me know. I will be across the road at the inn.*"

I turned to leave and go to the inn.

"*Six horses coming. We'll be okay. Don't worry.*"

"*I know, I am not worried about you. It's the other horses I am worried about. How many get sick from this place. How many are mistreated? Is this a place you want to stay? From what I have seen, this is not a place I would want you to stay.*"

As I was walking across the road, a wagon with two guards went into the Wagon Wright. I continued to the inn.

I went ahead up to the third floor and checked to see if the first two rooms were occupied. They didn't seem to be. Clean and orderly as they were the last time I was here. But still, had no locks on the doors. I put my backpack on the bed along with my saddlebags. I still don't know what is in the satchel that I carried, I was about to push it under the bed, but decided not to. I would carry it with me this evening. Something in the back of my mind said to keep it close.

Terry came through the doorway. "She has no locks on the doors. Anybody could go into any of the rooms and steal stuff."

"Not likely. There is only one way up here, and you could see them going through the common room to get out with what they steal. Besides, I did not have any problems last time I was here."

"Well, if you say so, I guess I'll believe you." We went back downstairs and ordered our meals.

The wagon drivers and guards came in before we ordered our meals. I stopped one and asked, "Do you like the service you get at the Wagon Wright?"

"Not really. What business is it of yours?" "None really, just a concerned citizen. Have you

had problems with your horses getting sick after staying there?"

He thought a minute and finally spoke, "As a matter of fact, I had to put a horse down due to sick- ness the last trip to Duintolea. And it was the day after we left here. What are you saying, lady?"

"I am saying that the feed has rat pellets in it, and he feeds it to your horses."

"Scorch, how is the water?"

"I would say it's a couple of days' old."

"Is anyone there yet?"

"And I doubt the water is changed regularly. We can go over there if you want. I'll show you how good they treat your animals."

He agreed. He and I headed to the stables. I dumped the water in each of the stalls that our horses were in as we passed. They all had larvae and some bugs swimming around in or on the water.

A stable hand came up and asked what I was doing. I told him to get fresh buckets and water for my horses. And the driver and I headed for the feed bin, I opened it and a rat scurried away from the door as I opened it. The driver seemed to be getting a little upset for some reason. And started heading for the office door, as the other stable hand came out ahead of the stable master.

"Lan. I think Master Bashere is going to be upset very soon. Especially after I tell him what I've just seen. I'll be back after I have some dinner to check things over again." The driver swung his hand around pointing at the stalls. "And it had better be to my satisfaction, because you know Master Bashere loves two things, his sword and his horses. And these are his horses, you know."

"I'll take care of it right now. I'll get some new help if that's what it takes. Get busy you two, and change out the feed." Lan motioned for his stable hands to get busy.

"What about the water, Lan? Perhaps you would like some?" I pointed at the trough of water.

"In clean buckets, Lan. You have about an hour, if you're lucky. Let's go, lady. I'm sorry I don't even know your name."

"Calarel. It's nice to know that someone else cares for their horses." I shook his hand. We headed back to the inn.

"My name is Fredrick. I'll tell Master Bashere about this place. Maybe he'll get this money grabber replaced with someone who can do the job."

As we walked back into the inn, I told him thank you.

The men he was with all had big smiles on their faces and whispered among themselves. I went back to our table, and he went to the table with the other men he worked with. They didn't stay up too late.

I finally went up to my room and began get- ting ready for bed. It was a little early when my head touched the pillow, but I slept well.

I awoke at my usual time, an hour before daybreak. I washed the sleep from my eyes and the rest of my face. I dressed, donned my armor, put my weapons belt on, and headed down stairs. I went out to the back and exercised, then did my practice routine with my sword. When I was done, I asked Scorch if he would mind that I didn't bring him his apple until we were ready to leave. He said he didn't mind. I went back up to my room and cleaned up a little and went down for first meal after I knocked on Terry's to wake her up.

When she came downstairs, we had breakfast. I paid Martha for the meals and the rooms, and then we went up to the rooms and brought our things down and headed to the stables. Once there, I gave Scorch his green apple and brushed him while he ate it. Terry brushed her horse before a stable hand came over and saddled her horse for her and I saddled Scorch. By the time we had everything packed up and were walking our horses out of the stalls, Lan came out of his office.

"Good morning, Lan. How much for stabling our two horses?"

"For you, dear lady, I think that four tin pieces would be too much, so perhaps three will do quite well." I pulled four tin out of my pouch, gave him three as he requested, and tossed the other one to the stable hand that helped Terry saddle her horse. "Thank you, Lan. Perhaps we will see you on the return trip."

I mounted up and Terry did the same. "Terry, shall we go the long way or the shorter way?"

"The shorter way would be better, I think."

So once we rode out onto the road, we headed south. Past a bakery, the aroma of fresh bread coming from it. A few houses, each having a small garden behind or beside them, depending on the lay of the land.

The road was in good shape for what used it most. It was not very wide, only one wagon at a time in most places. There were places where a wagon would stop to wait for the other to pass. You could see the next passing point from the one above. It was a curving road that leads down one slope of a hill and up another, for miles. The hills started to become flatter. The wayward pines were giving way to the junipers that grow in small thickets with knee- high grass in between. We traveled until the sun was half its height above the horizon and made camp at a place that looked to be used once before.

The grass was shorter and looked to be a little better for Terry's horse and Scorch. We unsaddled the horses and brushed them down. We hobbled Whisper and then went to find some firewood. I found a piece we could use as a stake which we drove into the ground and tied a lead from it to Whisper.

"You're not going to tie Scorch, just let him run free?"

I looked at Scorch who was eating some grass. "He will not go far."

I started to unroll my tarp. I set up the tarp as a shelter. We made a fire and cooked some dinner. After dinner, we sat by the fire and talked for a while. I told her I would take first watch and would wake her up about four hours before daybreak. She agreed and crawled between her blankets.

It was a quiet night; the moon was shining brightly, bright enough for me to read by with the fire still burning. I walked around with Scorch talking to him, trying to discover what all of his abilities were. He went to the gray a little early so that Terry would not discover him missing during her watch. His abilities seemed to be limited to the high rate of speed far beyond any other horse. Him being able to be in one place one moment, then another place the next, what Aravea called teleporting. And those hard gusts of wind that he could only do twice a day seemed to be all he could do.

After Scorch came back from the gray, I woke Terry up for her watch. It took a little bit for her to be awake enough to stay awake but she did, while I slept.

I woke at daybreak, got dressed in my armor and weapons belt, ready for the day ahead. I exercised and practiced with my weapons. I gave Scorch his apple and brushed him from head to tail. We made first meal and packed up after we ate.

We traveled all day again eating lunch in the saddle. Why, I have no idea, we are in no hurry. We let Whisper set the pace; he seemed happy walking along at a good ground covering pace for his size. We were about to stop for the night when a buggy with a man and woman came up the road. We asked if there was a town near and they told us the next town was about a mile and a half further. We thanked them and moved on toward the town.

As we rode into the town, I noticed that most everybody was half elf and a few mannish races mixed in. In the middle of the town square was a statue, more like a marker really, standing about twelve feet tall in the middle of a pond. When we were close enough to read the statue, it read "Creoso a' I'-Eldalie Ndor." "What does that say, Calarel? I don't know that language," Terry asked as we rode by it.

"It says Welcome to the Elven Territories. Well, close enough anyway," I told her. "We could travel for another two hours or spend the night in an inn. Your choice."

"Let's stay at the inn," she replied as she pointed at the inn across the road just past the town square.

"That sounds good to me. Have you ever had Elven Mead Wine?" I questioned, and then continued without letting her answer. "I could use a bath myself and a good meal sounds real good too."

"Elven Mead Wine?" she questioned. "What's the difference from Mead Wine?"

"Elven Mead is aged a little longer, it has a smoother flavor," I told her.

We rode between the inn and a clothier shop toward the stables. The two large stable doors were open. A tall, tanned, broad-shouldered blacksmith was working at the side of the stables under an open walled shop. A young man worked the billows as the blacksmith drove a piece of metal in the hot coals. The younger man, barely a man, maybe in his twentieth year if that, pointed at us and said something softly to the blacksmith. He looked in our direction and yelled out that he would be with us in a few minutes. If he was anything like my father, that few minutes could be up to half an hour or more, not wanting the metal he was working with to get cold, he would finish his work. The fact that it was almost dinner made that metal all the more important than two women on horseback. I just waved a greeting to him; Terry and I went ahead and rode into the stables and dismounted. We unsaddled our horses and brushed them down.

About the time we were picking up our gear that we were taking into the inn with us, the blacksmith came into the stables. "I'm sorry, ladies, I would have been in here sooner but…"

I tried to be courteous about cutting off what he was going to say, but I already knew what it was. "That all right, Master Blacksmith. I know the work must be done in a manner that puts it as a necessity above others sometimes. The only thing I would ask of you at this time would be for fresh feed and water for the horses, please."

"Very good, my lady," he said as he raised an eyebrow and nodded. "Thank you for your understanding. I will see to the feed and water immediately."

We went into the inn through the back door. We walked past a staircase that leads up to the rooms and down to a cellar, across the hall was the kitchen. The aromas gave a promise of well-cooked food, which was about ready to be served.

We continued toward the common room. The common room was much like any other I have been in, the bar along one wall with no windows in it. On the opposite wall, there was a room that was maybe fifteen feet wide and ten feet long, most likely a library or large private dining room. A small stage with the floor raised about one foot above the rest. And another staircase that leads upstairs to the rooms. Several tables had people seated at them, one table had some guards, another some merchants by the looks of their clothes, and some families out for a meal.

A waitress stopped at the table we sat down at just long enough to tell us she would be with us shortly, then continued to the table where the guards were sitting. She placed the plates that had an abundant amount of food on them.

She took our orders for drinks and food. It didn't take long for her to bring the drinks. And it was not much longer before she brought out our meals as well. We asked about rooms for the night; she brought us some keys to the rooms we would use. Told us that baths would be available soon, which we were both glad to hear.

It was a pleasant evening, the musicians were good. Some people danced to some of the songs. Some I have heard before, but the words or the titles were different.

It was around the middle of the night when most everyone went to their rooms or home. I had one last ale while Terry went up to her room. The waitresses cleaned around me, until I finished my ale and I went upstairs and to bed.

I woke about an hour before daybreak as usual, got dressed in my regular way of dressing. Donned my armor and weapons belt, one apple from Scorch's saddlebags and headed down the back stairs and out the back to the stables. I gave Scorch his apple and went out to the back to exercise and practice with my sword and axe, mainly the sword.

The shadows were beginning to be more defined by the time I was done this morning. So I went back inside the inn and the kitchen was a flurry of activity. I got to the door of my room and Terry came out of hers.

"You ready for breakfast?"

"Almost, let me freshen up a little. Come on in, and we can go down together."

As I opened the door, a man tried to run out. I slammed my knee into his thigh, causing him to hit his hip into the door frame. And much to my surprise as well as his, Terry punched him in the neck. I think that was an accident the way she reacted.

I grabbed his collar and pulled him back into the room as I rushed in. He was off balance to start with, so he was easy to throw to the floor, which he hit rather hard. He tried to grab his belt knife but was a little too slow. I kicked him in the shoulder, driving his hand away from his still sheathed dagger.

Terry ran down the stairs calling for the constable. I unsheathed my sword and put the tip on the hollow of his neck.

"Don't even think about it. I have no problem killing a thief," I told him as a bead of blood started to form where the tip of my blade was touching him.

After a minute had passed, I heard more than one set of footsteps getting closer to the door of the room I was in. I was wishing the thief on the floor would try to get away from me, but he hardly even breathed. His eyes locked on the shining silver metal of my blade. And my white knuckles on the hilt of my sword.

I heard a voice from behind me. "You can let him up now. He will be going to the cell he deserves and has deserved for some time now."

I heard someone else say, "About time too. Guess you didn't case this one good enough, did you?"

"Terry?"

"They are constables, they were in the common room eating breakfast," she replied quickly.

As I let the tension ease from my muscles in my arm, I stepped around to end up above the thief's head and took a non-offensive stance, but was ready for attack if needed.

He still had the satchel on his back under him. "This woman attacked me for no reason at all. She could have killed me with that damn sword of hers." "Really now? Let me guess you walked into the wrong room."

The constable paused just for a moment. He was half common man and wood elf. Tall, wiry, most likely a good shot with a bow, by the looks of the quiver that hung at his belt, but no bow.

"But wait, don't you live on the north side of town? About three blocks from here, if I'm correct."

"Well, I stayed here last night, I drank too much. So I just stayed here."

Thief still lying on the floor, rubbing his shoulder where I kicked him.

"Now I know you're lying, Rayhan. You left a little after ten last night. I was in this inn last night and followed you most of the way to your home. You were trying to take this lady's satchel, weren't you?"

"I would never."

"Sit up! And give me the satchel, without opening it. Now!" The constable reached out for the satchel. Rayhan did as the constable asked. The constable took hold of the satchel and started to open it. "Now, Rayhan, tell me what's in here."

"Ah…some papers and ink and a pen, with a feather on it." He watched the constable for any sign that might give away that he missed something. The constable only raised one eye brow. "And a few coins."

I let the tip of my sword slightly pierce the floorboard in front of me. Just enough to make some noise.

"And you, ma'am, can you tell me what is in here?" the constable asked.

"Yes, I can. There is one medallion, one sealed message to Kedol Tarsis. And a small coin purse, nothing else, unless he dropped something inside."

The constable pulled out the message, looked at the seal and the name.

"Rayhan," he said, moving his head from side to side while carefully replacing the message into the satchel. "I'm afraid I have to place you under arrest for thievery. I have no choice. You have gone too far with this."

"We are sorry, my lady. This will be dealt with justly and swiftly. Please have a pleasant day," he said as he handed the satchel to me and grabbed Rayhan by the collar and pulled him to his feet physically and hurried him out the door.

Terry came in after they were gone. "That was weird."

"Yes, it was. I thought he was going to take that thief's side at first. It makes me wonder who this Kedol Tarsis is." I pulled the message out of the satchel and looked at the red wax seal, which was undisturbed. "Or should I be wondering who Aravea is?" I handed the message to Terry to look at.

"She has a very interesting sigil on her seal. Can you read it?" she asked

"Yes, it says House of Lotithil."

"Nothing special about that," she replied.

"Agreed, let's get something to eat," I said as I put the message back in the satchel and put the strap over my head so that it hung on my back. I washed my face.

We went downstairs and ordered first meal. We ate our meal, went back upstairs to get our things, paid the innkeeper, and went to the stables.

We saddled our horses and rode south again for a day and half. We turned off the road and went east. After another day and a half, we came to another road and headed south. After a day's travel, we came to Arthanus.

Arthanus was a small village, maybe fifty people lived there. They had a two-story inn. There was a small grassy area across from the inn, where small children played, their mothers keeping watch over them talked among themselves. Next to the inn were stables with the doors open. Next to that was a blacksmith's open shelter by the sound of the hammering. We stayed in Arthanus for two days. It was nice and peaceful. The place kind of reminded me of Valeria.

§§§

"Miss Lotithil, a pleasure to see you again," Marel said, greeting her from the walkway. He never touches the grass that was always green no matter what the season. "If you will follow me, I will lead you to my Lady Ancalime." He announced as she stepped onto the granite walkway.

"Yes, Marel, please lead the way. I hope I am not late." Hoping to have not spent too much time in her studies.

"No, my Lady Lotithil, you are not late, the evening meal has not been served. We await another guest's arrival yet."

Marel opened the door to allow Aravea in. Then after closing it again, he led the way down a few corridors to the Greeting Room.

"If you would wait here please?" he asked as he tapped on the door.

From the other side of the door, a hardly audible "Enter" could be heard. He opened the door enough to allow himself in. "Lady Lotithil to see you, my lady."

"Allow her entrance, Marel." The voice was soft and flowing.

Marel opened the door. "Enter, please. I will have fresh wine sent right away," as Aravea walked into the room. He bowed his way out and closed the door.

"Sha'Quessr creoso Aravea." "Diola lle."

"Aravea, you have sent our champion on a journey that could prove to be deadly to her. I would think that she needs the item we spoke of at our last meeting. And perhaps, some training with it." Gilraen Ancalime never seemed angry, but she did sound a little worried.

All the years Aravea knew her, she could never think of a time that she was this way. There seemed to be something more than just what was said. "Gilraen, is there something wrong? Something I should know about that has not been told to me?"

"Yes, there is. I believe that we may be too late in starting this."

"Nonsense. You know as well as I do that bad news travels fastest and good news tries to hide in the crooks and crannies. You cannot say you do not." Aravea smiled.

"But when bad comes, it seems to overwhelm. You know what we face at this point, and it has started with the less intelligent beings, and it will spread," Gilraen said with too much certainty in her voice.

There was a light tap at the door. Gilraen took a deep relaxing breath.

"Enter," she said in a normal tone of voice.

A maid entered the room with a finely worked silver tray, on the tray were three gilded silver gob- lets. The ornate porcelain pitcher sat in a bowl of the same design, both had condensation on them.

"My lady," she paused in what she was going to say until Gilraen nodded. "Your other guest has arrived. Should I wait to pour until he enters?"

"Yes. Thank you, Liluth, that would be best."

Liluth set the three goblets toward the front of the tray, and waited to pour the wine. By that time, there was a knock at the door. The maid looked to Gilraen, and with a small nod, the maid went to open the door. As she opened the door, Marel looked nervous for the first time that Aravea ever noticed.

Marel looked at Gilraen and awkwardly announced the new arrival. "My lady, a Master Curatuk, I believe. He came as a drake."

"Excuse me, Marel, a drake?" Gilraen looked surprised.

"Yes, my lady." He lowered his voice to a whisper. "He is blue, my lady."

"Perhaps you should allow him in, Marel. It might be considered impolite to keep him in the hall for such a long period." Aravea looked at Gilraen.

"Ah, yes, my Lady Lotithil," Marel replied as he stepped from the door, opening it wide while doing so. The man standing on the other side of the door stood statuesquely over six feet tall, broad shoulders, muscular arms and legs. He wore a dark blue with white braiding down the outside seam of his pants. With a shirt that matched in color and the braiding was just as white from the collar down, sky-blue but- tons that looked to be some kind of gem. His belt woven of what looked to be gold and silver interlaced with a light blue. His hair, pulled back, was white, almost matching the braiding on his clothes. On his head a gold band with a blue gem that seemed to have a white star in the middle. When he stepped forward to stand in the door frame, Aravea's breath caught in her throat, his skin had a light blue hue, as if he were half frostbitten.

"I speak to you in the common mannish tongue, because you would not understand my native language." Aravea did not hear the words, only his voice; to her, the words had no meaning, but only for a moment. "I come bidding you peace and health." He bowed toward the two ladies.

"Peace and health in return to you, kind sir."

He waited until Gilraen replied before standing again. Then stepped through the door.

"By your leave, my lady." Marel backed out the door, closing it behind him. She did not even have time to nod before he was gone.

The maid, just now realizing that she held the pitcher of wine, tapped the edge of the porcine bowl, trying to put it back in the chilled water, and nearly knocked one of the goblets over with her hand trying to silence the bowl. She handed each a goblet and bowed her way out the door.

"I am here at the behest of our Great Seer. I was told by her that this time and place are where I need to make myself known. She has told me of events that would not be believed at this time." He look at the wine, but did not drink. "She has told me that you would know of the change in balance between the light and the dark of life's creatures. That you would be preparing to defend the light." He looked at the glass of wine once more, but still didn't drink of it.

"If I understand you correctly, then perhaps introductions would be a required step. I am the Lady Gilraen Ancalime, please call me Gilraen." Gilraen, with a motion of introduction, said, "This is the Lady Aravea Lotithil."

"You may call me Aravea if you like."

"I am the," he spoke slowly as if trying to translate the words, "High Arcane Mage Drake Curatuk Nezreil. Leader of the Council of Life of Ulm. If it pleases, name me Curatuk."

"I like the way your name sounds, Curatuk," Aravea replied. "Would you like something other than wine to drink?"

"Yes please, if that would not offend, my lady. I do not drink distilled beverages. They can cloud the mind and the body. At this time, I feel the need for my mind to be clear, and I know I need a clear mind for my mode of travel."

Gilraen reached back and pulled a cord that hung between two windows. "If it is not an intrusion on your privacy, what is your mode of travel?"

"I am an Arcane Mage drake, this is my common form, the form that most people know and see me in. My magical form is that of an Arcane Frost drake." He was looking at Gilraen and then looked at Aravea.

Aravea looked into his eyes as he looked into hers, his eyes changed, the dark round iris became cat-like irises, only rotated ninety degrees from that of a cat. Then just as quick were round again. "So you are saying you are a frost dragon."

"Yes, perhaps ten feet shorter than a mature Frost drake by birth. But other than that identical. And that I use Arcane magic instead of Frost. There is not much difference. The tint of my skin like all Ulmerains is from the extreme cold that we live in."

"You said that your Great Seer sent you. What is it that your Seer deems it necessary that you come to us?" Gilraen leaned forward a little more.

"Our Great Seer has foretold of future possibilities and ways that might change what she sees now. I have come to you, because you both are part of the possible changes. She has seen an evil that could scour the world. Change it to something we the fol- lowers of righteous Deities and believers of mankind would not desire, unless something is done to change the present foretelling."

"You must be talking of the growing evil that has been perceived by us and others."

Gilraen sat up straight.

"Yes, it could be known by others." Curatuk nodded.

There was a tapping at the door. Curatuk stepped further into the room and turned himself to still be facing both Gilraen and Aravea, but could also see the door with little effort.

Gilraen sat back in her chair. "Enter."

The door opened slowly, and Liluth entered and curtsied. "You have need of something, my lady?"

"Yes, would you bring us some tea? Chilled please."

"Yes, my lady, as you request."

Liluth walked to the serving table and retrieved the porcelain pitcher and tray and left the room after a bow.

As soon as the door closed behind her, Curatuk continued, "I cannot tell you how to slow or stop this evil. But I would suggest that you find a Campaign, more than one I would think. For the man at arms, a friend of mine has an ancient artifact that he is willing to give toward this cause."

Aravea was starting to sit in the chair beside her, but continued to stand. "What kind of artifact are you speaking of?"

"A hand and a half sword, it is a Holy weapon. It will aid in defending the righteous." He stood rigid like a statue the whole time; his voice was level, but not monotone. "This weapon will be in a cave that is in the only tree less hill two and a half days travel due south of Spurrie. It will be protected by a defender. A great beast."

"What kind of great beast are you talking about?" Aravea began to look worried. She laced her fingers together and move her thumbs in circles. "I don't know if Calarel is ready for that yet."

"Aravea, this would be a good time to test this savior of yours." Gilraen sat forward with her elbows on her desk.

"If she is, then we will know it. If she is not, then we will know and need to find another. I do not know how much time we have. But I do not think it is long. It has already begun."

Curatuk looked at Aravea.

"We do know it has started. We have taken certain items out of play already. Hopefully, the lack of these articles will slow them enough to get her trained better than what she is." Aravea started to pace back and forth a little. "I know Calarel must be the one.

There are other forces that are trying to help us with this battle it seems. She is now a companion of a, by most definitions of the word, demon. I have met this demon that looks like a horse, a rather large horse at that. It is very intelligent, and it has powers of teleportation or shifting to another plane of existence. I am not sure which. I was not able to spend enough time with it to find out."

"Aravea, you are starting to pace again," Gilraen said to her.

"Sorry, I will try to reframe from doing that." Aravea started again. "But—"

A light tap at the door stopped her from saying what she was going to say.

"Enter," Gilraen responded to the tap at the door.

Liluth entered through the door, went straight to the serving table, and poured three tall glasses full of the tea. Handed one glass to each of them in the room. She then went to the door, turned around, and asked if there would be anything else.

"No, that will be all, thank you," Gilraen replied, and Liluth bowed her way out of the room.

"What makes you think that this Calarel is the one?" Curatuk asked, then watched Aravea over the rim of the glass of cold tea.

Aravea turned toward him and finished her swallow of tea before speaking. "She has been in my dreams several times. As she has grown up to what and who she is today. I have seen battles that she may be part of. Call it a foretelling, if you will. She was where the dreams told me she would be. She has her companion. And with her now, she has a friend that she just met. Who I have seen in some dreams that I can only call the future. We shall find out on this journey if she really is the one or one lucky enough to be in the right place at the right time. I do know that she is a very honest person. On this journey, I hope to find out if she is able to protect herself and others." "And how are you planning on doing that?" Gilraen nervously got up from her seat. "You have not put her and others in too much danger, I hope." "No more danger than anyone else traveling at this time," Aravea replied.

"How long are we going to stay here, Calarel?" Terry asked. "We still have a long way to go if we are to get that medallion delivered."

"True, I guess we should get moving. But it is so peaceful here." Watching the last few children run for home after being called for the evening meal.

"Are you homesick?" Terry stood, looking out at the Green in front of the inn.

"Yeah, a little, I guess, I have not been home in a while now." I started to get up from the bench that was on the porch of the inn.

"Well, is it on your way? We could make a detour if we don't stay in one place to long," Terry suggested while laughing a little.

"Well, it would be about two weeks' travel, maybe more from here. Perhaps if we could, if we take a ship to Duintolea and travel hard, we might be able to see my home town."

There was a scream in the distance from the south end of town. Then the sound of a door slamming shut, then something hitting wood hard. Terry and I turned to look at the commotion. Down the road were four creatures we had never seen before. Almost five feet tall, gray to dark gray fur covered their bodies. They all had long muscular tails they used for extra balance and strength. As the one at the door tried to kick it in.

I started toward the middle of the street.

"Hey! You ugly beast. Come try that with me!" I yelled toward the creatures. "Terry, go grab my shield for me, would you?"

"First, let me see your sword, quickly, I have no time to explain."

I pulled my sword and handed it to Terry, then I pulled my axe.

"Well, are you going to come get me? Or do I have to come get you?" I yelled in the direction of the beasts. "Hurry up, Terry."

Terry started muttering something again. After a few seconds, Terry handed my sword back.

Most only looked to see what the commotion was and closed and locked their doors. Two men came out in to the street. One with a short sword and the other had a broadsword. Neither had any armor to speak of. I was the best equipped for this fight.

Terry was running for the inn to get my shield. I switched my weapons so I held the sword in my right hand and could use the axe as a shield. I had practiced using two weapons a few times. But was not very confident doing that.

The creature that kicked in the door of the house down the street came stumbling back out into the street. It looked wet as if it had hot liquid thrown on it. It was trying to wipe it off. I could see steam for a moment.

The other three were headed straight for me and the two men.

"Watch out for their tails. They could use them as weapons, I would think."

The Gark approached fast at a run. I took a defensive stance that would allow me to drop to one knee. I flipped my sword around, so it was pointing down, right before the Gark I faced reached me. Then dropped forward to one knee. Using the force of my movement and putting all my upper body strength into the swing of my sword. Slicing through the light leather armor the Gark was wearing and into its mid- section. The Gark spun, trying to get away from the sword that was slicing it a third of the way through and tripped the Gark to its left, making it an easy target to the man to my right.

The man on my left tried to block the swing of the third Gark's club, but took a hard blow to the head and fell to the ground. I hit that Gark's tail with my axe as it went by.

I stood up and spun around to attack the Gark that I had hit, but it was on the ground trying to hold its intestines in, without much luck. The man that was on my right was taking another swing at the Gark that was tripped by the one I hit. The third Gark was getting ready to hit the man on the ground.

I stamped on its tail where I hit it with my axe as I stabbed it in the back at the same time. It spun around, ripping its insides apart where my sword went into it, I lost my grip on the sword as it spun. I used my axe as a shield and blocked most of the Gark's swing. The man on the ground had rolled away and was starting to get up. I switched the axe to my right hand and stepped sideways to avoid the Gark on the ground. The third Gark tried to keep facing me, but his tail hit the Gark on the ground; it howled in pain from being hit in the midsection again. The third Gark, trying to face me, spun to attack what- ever had caused it more pain in its tail and swing its club down hard on the one that was howling in pain. The howling stopped. I dropped my axe and grabbed my sword, still sticking out of the Gark's back, and yanked it out. The Gark lunged forward and fell over the one it just hit and did not move again.

The man that was on my right was wiping his brow with the sleeve of his shirt. He held his sword weakly, as if drained of strength. He used his wrist to rub his other arm as he looked up the road toward where the last Gark would have been. A man and his son stood over that dead Gark.

The man that was on my left fell down again.

Someone called out for the healer.

I wiped my blade clean on the Gark that was lying closest to me and sheathed my sword. Then picked up my axe and cleaned it as well before hanging it back in the sheath.

Terry came out of the inn with my shield. "Well, it looks like you didn't need your shield after all," she said when she was close enough to be heard without yelling.

"No, not now, but it would have been nice to have. I guess I should carry it all the time."

"You're very good with the sword, young lady. I haven't seen anyone that good since the war. At least not that I can remember. My name is Eldar, your arm is bleeding a little."

"Glad to meet you, Eldar. You fought well yourself."

Terry, still holding the shield, put her hand on my shoulder. "Let's go inside and see how your arm looks." "My arm is okay, let the healer take care of this man first."

An older woman was headed toward us. She knelt down by the injured man and placed her hand on his head.

"I think she knows magic," Terry whispered to me.

"How can you tell?" I asked

"See how she is concentrating. She is preparing to cast or is casting a spell to heal him."

The man on the ground moaned a little and quivered for just a moment, then opened his eyes and smiled at the woman. "Thank you, Merissa."

"Aaah, don't thank me yet. Your head is most likely going to hurt real good for a day maybe. I'll bring some herbs to ease the pain after you're in the bed. Maybe next time you might try not to get hit in the head, I hope."

"Yes, ma'am, I will watch a little better." He looked around and saw me standing a pace away. "Thank you for saving my life. I would be dead if not for you."

Merissa checked Eldar's arm and declared it only a bruise

"It is nothing. I try to save anyone I can. Sorry you got hurt."

Merissa turned toward me. "You are a brave young woman to face those creatures alone. I watched from my window. If Franklin and Eldar had not come out to help, I would have with my frying pan." And she patted my left arm right on the spot I was hit. I flinched away from her hand. "You did get hit. Let's go inside and see about fixing up your arm." We went inside and up to my room, where we removed my armor and shirt. She looked at my arm that was already starting to turn black and blue under the little amount of blood that was oozing from where

I was hit. "I can heal this if you would like me to." Other people were standing in the doorway, mostly women.

"Yes, ma'am. Please do, I can pay you for your skills."

She placed a hand on either side of my head; she began murmuring something I could not under- stand. I felt a warmth flow from her hands in to my head. I felt it flow throughout my body. Then I felt cold as if dropped into a freezing pond and heard laughter in my head; it wasn't Scorch. But a laughter that sounded terrifying. I jerked away from her hands and almost stumbled over the bed. Merissa dropped to her knees and began to verbally pray to her Deity. As people started moving toward either me or Marissa, I noticed that my clothing seemed to be tighter; it seemed that all my clothes had shrunk at least one size.

"Calarel, are you okay? I felt the magic that was starting to remove the pain in your arm, but then there was another magic, a stronger magic. I don't think it was meant to harm you, but I want to make sure I am correct." "Yes, Scorch, I am fine. By another magic, do you mean that someone other than Merissa cast a magic spell on me?"

"It came from her. But it felt stronger than what she was doing. It was as if her power increased two or threefold. I know of no other way to explain it." He sounded worried, as if something was yet to happen from the spell.

"Okay, thank you, Scorch. I will let you know if anything starts to happen."

People were asking if I was okay. I told them I was. And others were asking Merissa if she was okay. But she paid them no attention. She was still praying I knelt down in front of her. No one had touched me that I know of.

One woman was getting ready to try and help get Merissa up. She looked at me, and I shook my head no, and she stood up straight again.

I reached out to take Merissa's hands in mine. When my hands were within a finger's width of her hands, a blue spark of power shot between our hands. She flinched, as if there was a small amount of pain. That is what I felt.

Her head came up from her chest; she opened her eyes, and more tears ran down her cheeks.

"You're alive."

"Yes, I am. You did not kill me, Merissa. I am fine. Are you all right?"

"Yes, I think so. I don't know what happened. I felt a surge of power. I tried to stop before it hurt you. Then I heard someone laugh." She visibly trembled for just a moment.

"I heard laughter too. I thought I must have gone insane. Can someone else use you to cast a spell through?" I hold her hands gently.

"No. I have never heard of such a thing happening before. I am able to channel the power of my Deity through me to heal others. I always feel the warmth of my Deity when I heal in that way. But this time, there was more than the warmth, there was a cold feeling all of a sudden. I could not break the connection fast enough to stop it from touching you."

Another tear ran down her cheek and dripped onto her dress.

"Are you willing to check my arm to make sure it is healed correctly for me?" I was still holding her hands gently. She almost tried to pull away. But I held on to her hands.

"After what just happened, you are willing to let me use my powers on you again?"

"Yes, Merissa. Please check my arm again." I hoped whatever happened would not happen again. But I could not let her know that.

She placed her hands on my head as before. She hesitated a moment and murmured something; again, I could not understand what she said. After just a few moments, she pulled my head toward her, and she leaned forward and kissed me on the forehead. Then gave me a hug and whispered in my ear so that no one else could hear. "I don't know what happened, but my ability seems to be stronger then it was. And I have never sensed anything like this before. But it would seem as if your body is stronger than before."

I sat up straight, not fast.

"Thank you, Merissa. How much do I owe you for your services?" I asked in what I hoped was a normal voice. She confirmed my thoughts of my tight-fitting clothes.

"Oh. I don't think you owe me anything for what has happened. Your wounds are healed and you helped save the people of this town. No one died tonight. I think we are the ones that should pay you." Merissa stood up.

I get up to stand in front of her.

From the conversations of other people, they seemed to agree that I owed nothing.

I pulled a clean shirt from my backpack and put it on. Then took a few silver pieces from my coin purse and pressed it into her hand.

"This is the least I can do for what you have given me. No arguments."

Most likely, she did not make that much in three months or more.

She said nothing and did not look in her hand before putting it in her pocket. Then she gave me a hug. "Thank you. I don't know what has happened, but I know that you are a blessed person and you will do well in your life. It must be something that you are to do."

"Well, after all this excitement, I seem to be hungry," I said as I started to herd everyone out of my room.

We all went down to the common room and had dinner. I think everyone wanted to buy us a drink. Some people were asking Terry to teach them how to use a sword. But most were asking me where I learned to use the sword. By the time most people started heading for home to sleep, it was almost my bedtime. Terry and I finally had to tell the few that remained that we had to go to bed to get some sleep. I slept well, and when morning came, I was up before the sun as usual. I got dressed, belted on my weapons belt, and grabbed an apple for Scorch. And then went out to the stables.

"Good morning, Scorch. How was your night?" I asked him aloud.

"*I had a fair night. How do you feel this morning? Any effect from last night's mishap with the magic? I cannot sense anything different about you.*"

"It is strange, but my clothes seem to be a little tight after last night's mishap. Other than that, I feel fine. I am going to practice for a little bit. Then I will come and brush you."

I headed back out of the stables to the place behind the inn that I have practiced mornings.

I started my exercises and the seam of my shirt sleeve at the shoulder tore loose, before I was finished with my exercises. I went ahead and started my weapon practice; before I was done, the other shoulder tore loose as well. I went to the stable to brush Scorch. The stable hand was there when I walked in. As I walked by him on my way to Scorch, he asked if I needed anything. I told him I didn't and continued toward Scorch. It was like I had grown a little taller, maybe a finger and a half width taller, I thought as I started brushing Scorch.

After I finished brushing Scorch, I went in to freshen up a little and have first meal. As I sat down, Terry came down the stairs and joined me. We had a good meal, and I tipped the waitress.

I told Terry that we needed to get some supplies and I needed some shirts; for some reason, the ones I had were too small. So we went and found some shirts and some supplies for the rest of the trip. After we went back to the inn, we packed our things and went to the stables to saddle the horses, then headed east down the road.

It was an easy day's travel to Southern Hold. I think Southern Hold might be bigger than Duintolea.

It is hard to tell, I haven't been to Duintolea in a long time.

We found an inn on the road that leads toward Lethys. The Stag's Head was the name of the inn. I was expecting the place to be full of rugged men, all smoking pipes, and drinking too much ale. But I was wrong, it was a nice inn. The tables all shone with wax and were all clean. Most of the people inside were upper-class merchants and their wives or lords and their ladies. The food was very good and the room was large with two beds.

When I woke in the morning, I took my armor and weapons out into the hallway to put them on so I would not wake up Terry. The yard was small, but being the only one out this time of the morning, it was not a problem. When I finished my exercises and practice, I brushed Scorch and went inside. Terry was at a table already. We agreed not to share a room again, because I stay up to late and rise too early. And she said I snored. I do not snore.

We left Southern Hold behind shortly after first meal. We traveled for three and a half days. We came to Lethys during the midday meal. So we stopped at a place that had tables and chairs set out in front. There was a lattice work cover above the tables for shade from the midday sun. All the waitresses were dressed the same. The smells coming from inside made my stomach rumble.

We found out where Tarsis Wares is or at least the general area. We spent most of the afternoon looking for the place. But never found it. We did find a nice inn to stay at while we were here. While we were at the inn, I did find out that we missed finding the shop by only a block. We had a good meal and a few drinks before Terry went up to bed. I went to bed at my usual time, about five hours after nightfall. I awoke at my usual time. Cleaned my face and dressed as usual and put on my armor and weapons. I went downstairs and out to the back to practice after I gave Scorch his apple. I practiced and exercised for about an hour. Then I went back up to my room to clean up for first meal and went back downstairs to wait for Terry. She came down shortly after I had taken a seat.

After we had first meal, we walked toward where we were told Tarsis Wares was located and found the sign hanging by three links of chain on each side. It had a saucer and cup and fancy bottle painted on it. On the top of the sign was painted Tarsis Wares on top and Antiquities at the bottom. We went to the door and went inside.

There was a man behind the counter at the other end of the shop. It was only about ten paces from the door to the counter and maybe as wide. All of the walls had shelves and display cases standing six feet tall. Every shelf was full, most had dishes and kitchen wares. And other shelves were full of old items, like bottles and jugs. Some things I have never seen before. A round piece of metal with holes in it and a handle that stood up perpendicular to the round piece of metal.

"Good morning, ladies. What can I help you find?" he said as he was walking around the end of the counter.

"We are here to see Master Kedol Tarsis," I said cheerfully, I hoped.

"I'm sorry, madam, but he has not arrived yet today. Perhaps I can help you," he replied, still walking toward us.

"I think we could use a little larger pot for cooking besides the one we have." Terry broke in on what I was about to say. I closed my mouth and nodded that I agreed.

"Right this way, ladies, I'll show you to the pots that might be what you're looking for."

We followed him around to the third case left of the door.

"Here we go, ladies. I hope one of these are what you are looking for," he said as he swept his arm down the case that had a large assortment of pots and pan.

"Okay, thank you," I said. "We will look at all these and let you know what we decide."

As I reached for one pot and Terry picked up another.

"If you need any help, my name is Jarid. I'll be glad to assist you with anything I can."

I think we looked at over half the items, half of which seemed like junk to me, but I am sure that it was someone's treasure. We were the only people in the shop. Until a short stocky man dressed in a fine red silk shirt with a white collar, a brown jacket that had black cording down the sleeves, fine wool trousers were tucked into high laced boots. He walked straight to the back of the shop. He and Jarid talked for just a minute or two. Then Jarid went behind some curtains into the back, the other gentleman came toward us.

"Hello, ladies. If I understand correctly, you are waiting for me," he said. "My name is Kedol Tarsis." "Pleased to meet you, Master Tarsis." I nodded slightly. "This is Terry, and I am Calarel. We were sent here by the Lady Lotithil, to deliver an item to you." "Excellent," he replied, looking almost surprised. I guess we were a little early. "Let us go back to my office. And we shall see if what she thinks she has is the real thing or not."

"I am sure it is the real thing," Terry said confidently, but a little too low for him to hear as he led the way toward the back.

We went through the beaded curtain, turned right, and up some stairs. The upstairs looked like a storeroom, just as full as the main floor if not more so. Weapons, armor, and what looked like armor for a horse. Lances lay on the floor along one of the show cases. More things like were downstairs: pots, pans, bookends, and plenty books lined the shelves. We came to another door. Behind that door was an office, just as cluttered as the rest of the upstairs.

"Let me move these things and you can sit down," he said as he grabbed a stack of books from a small narrow couch. It was nicely gilded, but the cushion was thin and the back leaned too far back to suit me. I sat on the front edge. "Okay, let me see what she has sent me."

"It is a medallion," I replied as I pulled the satchel off my shoulder. I pulled the medallion out and handed it to him. "And she also sent this letter with it," I told him as I laid it on the desk.

"This is good. It is what she said it was," he said as he examined the medallion. "So what does the letter say?" he asked no one in particular.

"I have no idea," both Terry and I said almost in unison. Terry started to laugh.

"It is addressed to you, we have no interest in what is for your eyes," I told him.

"I didn't mean that you would open it, I was just hoping that perhaps she told you something about what it says," he said quickly, as he reached for the letter, and then looked at the wax seal, untouched until he broke it. He read the letter frowning, and then smiling. "We can do this, I think." He folded the letter back to the way it was and placed it in a drawer in the desk.

He stood up from his chair and walked around to where we were sitting and handed me the medal- lion. "We need to go to the bank and get you a certificate. You will need to take it to Duintolea and deposit into Lady Lotithil's account at the Duintolea Bank. And on your way, I would like you to take this medallion to Katherine Staley in Southern Hold, which is to the north of here."

"Okay. We can do that."

We went to the bank with him to get the certificate. He told us where to find Katherine Staley. He paid for our rooms and meals. We stayed the night at the inn to get a good night's sleep and left in the morning.

www.ingramcontent.com/pod-product-compliance
Lightning Source LLC
Chambersburg PA
CBHW020622110726
47899CB00002B/616